P9-DCO-200

THE CRIMS

THE CRIMS

KATE DAVIES

HARPER
An Imprint of HarperCollins*Publishers*

The Crims

Copyright © 2017 by Working Partners Limited
All rights reserved. Printed in the United States of America.
No part of this book may be used or reproduced in any manner whatsoever without written permission except in the case of brief quotations embodied in critical articles and reviews.
For information address HarperCollins Children's Books, a division of HarperCollins Publishers, 195 Broadway, New York, NY 10007.
www.harpercollinschildrens.com

Library of Congress Control Number: 2017943432
ISBN 978-0-06-249409-2

Typography by Sarah Nichole Kaufman
17 18 19 20 21 CG/LSCH 10 9 8 7 6 5 4 3 2 1
❖
First Edition

For my family, who are nothing like the Crims,
except on really bad days

THE CRIMS

IF IMOGEN CRIM had learned one thing in her two years at Lilyworth Ladies' College, it was that controlling a school full of posh young women was much easier than controlling a family full of criminals. After years of studying these chirpy overachievers, learning their habits and secret languages, Imogen had become a pro at imitating them—until she'd done one better and had simply become one of them. In just two weeks, her control over the school would become official: After two failed campaigns where she'd lost to older girls, she would beat her competition, Bridget Sweetwine, to finally be elected head girl of Lilyworth.

Today were the speeches where the candidates announced their intentions, and Imogen was determined to be perfect in every way. She smoothed her hands over her glossy ponytail one more time, smiled a perfectly straight smile into the mirror, and adjusted her collar. Then she picked up her speech, stepped out of her dorm room, and walked with purpose down the corridor. Her grandmother had taught her to do everything with purpose—walk, talk, use her potty (Imogen had only been two at the time for this particular lesson, but it had stayed with her all the same).

"Im-o-gen!" Ava, her dorm mother, was singing her name. Literally singing it—Ava was an opera singer who had missed her big break but who never missed an opportunity to hit a high C. She'd broken more windows than the beginners pole vault team, but no one really minded—her singing acted as a deterrent to mice, foxes, and burglars with eardrums.

"Your father called," said Ava. "Again."

"I'll call him tomorrow," said Imogen, brushing off the tiniest flicker of guilt. Her father had called three times in the last week, which was unusual, but Imogen couldn't worry about that now. If there was one thing she'd learned about the Future World Leaders Lilyworth created, it was this: They had laser-like focus.

And today, Imogen was focused on proving that she'd

rocked Lilyworth harder than any of her heir-to-the-crown, yes-*that*-Heinz-family classmates.

This is my day, she reminded herself.

She had an election to win.

The school hall was packed with girls, chattering to one another in their black-and-yellow uniforms like a hive of gossipy bees. At twelve, Imogen was finally one of the oldest girls in the school, and she liked the way the younger girls looked up to her. She walked (with purpose) to the front row, where the clique she'd carefully crafted was waiting for her, as usual.

"You'll be amazing, Imogen!" Lucy said as Imogen sat down beside her. She was the optimist.

"You're totally going to kill it," Alice agreed as Imogen looked over her speech. Alice was the realist.

"Who are you going to kill?" asked Catherine. Catherine was the dim one. Every successful clique had one, Imogen had learned—she made the others feel more confident in their standing.

Before Imogen could answer, she glanced up and noticed a familiar blond ball of syrupy-niceness bouncing toward them.

Bridget Sweetwine.

Imogen's eyes narrowed. Bridget Sweetwine was her nemesis. The trouble was, Bridget Sweetwine didn't seem to know it—she insisted on acting suspiciously *nice* all the time. But Imogen knew that no one was actually as nice as Bridget Sweetwine pretended to be. ("Never trust anyone without an obvious ulterior motive. Unless they're a garbage collector. Don't hesitate to trust a garbage collector"—that's what Big Nana, Imogen's grandmother, had always said.)

Now Bridget Sweetwine pranced up to Imogen, her curls bouncing unnecessarily. It made Imogen sick. Mentally, she drafted an email to her clique: *Keep conditioner use to a minimum. All strands of hair should obey the law of gravity.* "I just wanted to wish you all the luck in the world for the assembly!" Sweetwine simpered, wringing her hands. "I'm soooo nervous! Are you?"

She smiled at Imogen like some nauseating Victorian cherub.

Imogen glared back.

Just then, Imogen's math teacher, Mrs. Pythagoras, stepped onto the stage and tapped the microphone. Imogen turned from Sweetwine, fists unclenching. "Good morning, girls!" Mrs. Pythagoras said. "It was on a lovely morning, just like this, that the ancient Persians discovered the triangle. And aren't we glad they did?"

Imogen glanced around. She couldn't help but note that most of the girls—aside from Sweetwine, of course—didn't seem that glad.

"But enough from me! Now for the moment you've

all been waiting for: It's time to hear from the two exceptional students who are seeking your vote for head girl of Lilyworth! Please give a warm welcome to your first candidate: Imogen Collins!"

Imogen smiled at her classmates as she stood up and made her way to the stage, running a hand over her pearls and going over the opening lines of the speech in her head. But just as she was about to climb the steps, the school secretary scuttled onto the stage in front of her and whispered something into Mrs. Pythagoras's ear.

Mrs. Pythagoras gasped. She rushed over to meet Imogen at the side of the stage.

"I'm so sorry, my dear," she said, "but the headmistress has asked to see you in her office right away."

Imogen stared at her, uncomprehending. "Why? What's wrong?"

"I'm afraid I don't know," said Mrs. Pythagoras.

Imogen glanced back at her classmates, trying to look head girlishly unbothered. "Will I get to do my speech later?" she asked from the corner of her mouth.

"I don't know that, either," Mrs. Pythagoras said gently. "But I'm sure that, like a particularly tricky quadratic equation, we'll find the answer eventually."

That wasn't very comforting. Imogen felt her lips drop into a frown and then recovered, waved breezily at the audience, and stepped down from the stage. *This is all very strange.* She had never been to Ms. Gruner's office before. No one went to Ms. Gruner's office unless they were in deep trouble, and Imogen was never in deep trouble—not even shallow trouble. She made sure of that.

Imogen walked back through the audience to the hallway, trying to ignore her friends' curious eyes. She kept her smile pasted on, but as soon as she escaped to the hallway, it collapsed into a scowl. She felt sick with nerves. Taking a deep breath, Imogen walked the short distance to the main office, walked past the secretary's desk, and knocked on Ms. Gruner's door.

"Come in," called the headmistress.

Imogen pushed the door open.

Ms. Gruner pushed her glasses onto her nose and looked up from her desk. She was frowning, as usual, and her dark hair pulled back into a bun so tight that it gave Imogen a headache just looking at it. She was wearing an itchy-looking cardigan in an alarming shade of green.

"Sit down," Ms. Gruner said.

Imogen stepped inside, closed the door behind her, and sat down.

"I am sorry to have to tell you this," said Ms. Gruner, "but you have been expelled from Lilyworth Ladies' College."

Imogen blinked. *I must be hallucinating.* She should have known better than to eat spicy food on the night before the big speech. It never agreed with her. Imogen shook her head. "Excuse me," she said, "could you repeat that? For a moment I thought you said I'd been expelled."

"You have," said Ms. Gruner. "Effective immediately."

This was feeling all too real. "But— You can't expel me!" cried Imogen, panic rising up inside her.

"I think you'll find I can," said Ms. Gruner, pitiless, just as she would be if this were actually happening.

"I'm the best student in the whole school!" Imogen insisted.

"That's a matter of opinion," said Ms. Gruner.

"Oh, really?" said Imogen. Imogen was far too careful to let her superiority be a "matter of opinion." She crunched the data herself each and every night—grateful for the statistics lessons her father had given her as a child. Now she pointed to a graph behind Ms. Gruner's head, which showed that Imogen was miles ahead of her fellow students in every single subject. Everything except needlework—but that was the sort of silly, useless subject that only a true evil genius like Bridget Sweetwine would bother to be good at.

"Yes, your grades are impeccable—but that doesn't matter now. Because it has come to my attention that your place at Lilyworth was awarded based on . . . *fraudulent information*."

"'Fraudulent information'?" she repeated.

"Yes. Fraudulent information." Ms. Gruner opened her desk drawer and pulled out a letter, then handed it to Imogen.

Imogen took it with hands she could not keep steady. *Who would . . . ?* The envelope, addressed to Ms. Gruner, was written in green ink, which made it look rather poisonous. She opened the flap and pulled out the letter. The words were made up of letters cut out from magazines, like a ransom note. *This can't be happening,* thought Imogen. She felt her face grow hot with horror as she began to read:

dEAR hEADMISTRESS,

tHERE'S A PUPIL AT YOUR SCHOOL WHO CALLS HERSELF iMOGEN cOLLINS . . . BUT THAT'S NOT HER REAL NAME. nOT at all.

hER REAL NAME IS . . . iMOGEN cRIM!!!!

hER WHOLE FAMILY ARE CRIMINALS! hER FATHER IS A CRIMINAL! hER MOTHER IS A CRIMINAL! hER UNCLE IS A CRIMINAL! hER OTHER UNCLE IS A CRIMINAL! hER AUNT IS A CRIMINAL! hER GRANDMOTHER WAS A massive CRIMINAL! bUT SHE'S DEAD.

yOU GET THE IDEA!!!

tHEY'RE ALL REALLY, REALLY CRIMINAL!!!!

hER WHOLE APPLICATION IS ONE BIG LIE!!!!!

jUST THOUGHT i'D LET YOU KNOW.

lOVE AND KISSES,

a FRIEND

XXXXXXXXXXXXXXXXXX

Imogen put down the letter. She felt like she'd been punched in the stomach. She tried to control her breathing. *Sweetwine,* she thought, in a sudden, satisfying rush of murderous rage. *She's finally shown her true, evil colors.* No one but Sweetwine could have written that letter. Only she was that cunning, that manipulative, that fond of exclamation marks. Imogen shook her head. She'd known Sweetwine was her nemesis, but clearly, she was even more ruthless than Imogen had realized. That bouncy-haired, daisy chain–loving evil mastermind knew she had no shot at being elected head girl fairly, so she was prepared to get Imogen kicked out. *But how did she learn my secret?* wondered Imogen. *I've been so careful. . . .*

Imogen could feel Ms. Gruner looking at her. She couldn't let the headmistress see how she felt (horrified, humiliated, and a little homicidal). So she took a deep breath and pasted her most amused, electable smile on her face.

Imogen held up the letter. "Surely you don't believe a

word of this, Ms. Gruner."

"As a matter of fact, I do," said Ms. Gruner, folding her arms over her unbelievably green cardigan.

"Do I really seem like a criminal to you?" Imogen asked lightly, fighting to ignore her rising blood pressure. "Would a criminal study that hard for her trigonometry exam? Would a criminal read with the younger girls during her lunch break? Would a criminal write such a brilliant essay about the use of symbolic chickens in *Great Expectations*?"

"That was a brilliant essay. Almost moving."

Imogen smiled graciously. "Thank you. I thought so too."

"But I'm afraid the evidence is overwhelming."

Evidence? She can't mean one measly, poorly punctuated letter . . . ?

As if in answer to Imogen's thoughts, Ms. Gruner reached into her desk drawer again. She pulled out a huge stack of papers and pushed it across her desk to Imogen.

Imogen felt her stomach flip.

Staring up at Imogen from the top sheet was her own face in black-and-white. She was looking at a copy of her passport. Not the fake one—the *real* one. The passport belonging to Imogen Crim.

Imogen Crim—the person Imogen had been two years ago. Before Lilyworth. Before she'd learned the meaning of the words “ambition,” “power,” and “twinset.”

Imogen stared at her foolish, young self with something that felt close to pity.

She was, indeed, overwhelmed by the evidence.

But I can’t leave Lilyworth. I belong here!

Maybe this *was* all a vision; an incredibly realistic, effective bad dream—that would explain the color of Ms. Gruner’s implausible cardigan. She closed her eyes and pinched herself, like people do in books. She opened her eyes again.

She was still in Ms. Gruner’s office.

The cardigan was as green as ever.

Sweetwine’s note was still lying there on the desk.

She was still expelled from school.

Imogen sucked in a breath. There was only one person smart enough to get her out of this: herself.

It was do-or-die time.

She looked Ms. Gruner in the eye. (“When all else fails, tell the truth. Unless a corpse is involved”—Big Nana.) “Okay, Ms. Gruner,” she said, “I admit it. I lied about my family. But that’s because I have nothing to do with them. I’ve worked really hard to make an honest life for myself—”

“Honest? Ha!” said Ms. Gruner, tipping back in her chair. “You have done nothing but lie since you got here!”

Imogen winced. “I just told a few little white lies, so

you'd give me a chance—"

"I'm afraid this school does not believe in giving chances to master criminals."

"I'm not a master criminal!" yelled Imogen, suddenly angry. "Look how rubbish my fake name was—I didn't even bother changing the Imogen bit! A master criminal would have chosen a *much* better one—Marigold Underwhelm or something like that!"

"I beg to differ," said Ms. Gruner. "A name like Marigold Underwhelm would have drawn attention to itself. A master criminal would have called themselves something really boring and ordinary. Something like Imogen Collins, say."

Imogen stared at her headmistress with an expression that would make clear that she was not about to back down. Unfortunately, it seemed that Ms. Gruner wasn't backing down either. "Look," she said, "it doesn't affect my performance here. Since I arrived at Lilyworth, I haven't been involved in any criminal activity. I haven't so much as stolen a cabbage roll from another girl's plate."

"Why would you?" asked Ms. Gruner. "Cabbage rolls are revolting."

Imogen pressed on. "Bad example. The point I'm trying to make is, I've turned my back on crime. And yes, fine, my family likes to *think* they're criminals, but believe me, they're hopeless. My uncle once tried to steal a *carnival.* My mother held a stray dog for ransom—nobody even noticed. My aunt Drusilla actually died slipping on a banana peel. That's the sort of thing we're dealing with here."

Ms. Gruner raised her eyebrows. "Oh, *really*?" she said. "The Crims are hopeless, you say? Then how do you explain . . . this?"

Ms. Gruner reached into her (surprisingly spacious) desk drawer again and pulled out a newspaper. She spread it out on the desk in front of Imogen.

The headline read: "Criminal Family Jailed for Breaking and Entering Wooster Mansion." And the photo on the front page made it clear that the criminal family in question was, indeed, Imogen's criminal family.

Imogen felt like a balloon with a sizable, leaking, rude noise-making hole. She shrank embarrassingly as she stared at the photo, slack-jawed. She couldn't believe what she was seeing. But indeed, there were all the Crims, grinning up at her from behind bars. All the grown-ups, anyway—like Uncle Clyde, with his shock of black hair, giving two thumbs-up; her mother, Josephine, preening for the cameras in a fox-fur coat; Uncle Knuckles, fiddling with his false teeth; and Aunt Bets, who somehow managed to look completely at home in the cell and completely like a member of the royal family at the same time, in a shift dress and pearls. The only person who seemed remotely unhappy to be in prison was Imogen's father, Al. Imogen felt a twist in her gut, remembering the unanswered phone calls. He seemed to be looking directly at her, pleading for her help with his eyes.

Imogen coughed and dragged her eyes away, staring at her hands in her lap.

She knew exactly why her family would have wanted to break into Wooster Mansion—they'd been planning to do it since before she was born—but there was no way they could have actually pulled it off. She hadn't been lying to Ms. Gruner: her family had always been very, very bad at crime. All except Big Nana. But Big Nana was dead.

Imogen looked up at Ms. Gruner, pleading with her eyes. "They're innocent, I swear," she said.

"We'll have to agree to disagree about that," said Ms. Gruner.

Imogen sat up straighter. "But they— Look." *Focus,* she told herself. "Even if they're not, *I* had nothing to do with this."

Ms. Gruner shrugged. "Be that as it may," she said, "we can't have your kind at Lilyworth. The other parents would be horrified to know that their children were being educated alongside a criminal."

"But . . ." Imogen suddenly felt weary enough to lay her head down on the desk.

"No more buts. I'm sorry, Miss Crim. A cab will be here in twenty minutes to take you to the train station."

This can't be. Do something!! Imogen sat up with a start. "Please! *Please* don't expel me!" she begged.

Ms. Gruner took off her glasses and began to polish them. "I'm sorry," she said. "Your progress over these last two years has been exceptional, Imogen. I believed you had a real future ahead of you." She wiped one last speck from the right lens and then placed the glasses squarely back onto her nose, perfectly balanced. "But I've made my decision."

Imogen's mind was racing. These were the types of against-all-odds situations where Future World Leaders like her came up with inspirational speeches, but she couldn't think of anything. Then suddenly, something else came to her. "What if I can *prove* my family is innocent?" she blurted out.

She knew that was a long shot. Even though she was sure her family couldn't have pulled off this crime, their smiling faces in the newspaper made it clear that they were happy to take the credit for it.

"Do you really think that's likely?" said Ms. Gruner.

Imogen decided not to reply to that. Ms. Gruner wasn't saying "no." This was her chance. "If I can prove my family didn't do this, will you let me come back to school?" she pressed.

Ms. Gruner sighed, leaning back in her chair. "If you can prove their innocence, I'll consider it. Assuming I'll be able to see you, what with all the pigs that will be flying around. Until then . . ." She narrowed her eyes at Imogen, then pointed to the door.

Somewhat unsteadily, Imogen stood up from her chair, stuffed the poisonous letter into her pocket, and shuffled to the doorway.

She caught one last glance of malevolent green before the door slammed behind her.

Imogen stumbled down the corridor. She was still clutching her speech, now crumpled and torn like her stupid, stupid dreams. Was it really just an hour ago that she'd thought she had a chance of becoming head girl? Of graduating Lilyworth and—who knew—running the country or something, before she figured out a truly challenging goal? *Of course* her family would somehow find a way to ruin this for her. They managed to ruin everything they touched without Big Nana to guide them. Wasn't that why Imogen had left? She felt a tear welling at the corner of her eye, and angrily swiped it away. *No tears.* Imogen *Collins* did not cry. She merely did what she had to do to make things right again.

So, she *had* to prove that her family was innocent. Then she could return to Lilyworth, take her place as head girl, and move gloriously into her hallowed future. Another boarding school before college, perhaps a tiny scandal to humanize her, early admission to one of the Seven Sisters—maybe an Ivy, if the Sisters were passé—and then, well, who knew? The world would be her oyster. If she weren't busy running it, she'd certainly be piling up a sizable, legal fortune. *Summers at Lake Como with the Clooneys and winters in Aspen, without any chance whatsoever of a crime-related death or life jail sentence. . . .* Imogen shook her head to clear it. *Focus on the now.* Getting back to Lilyworth had to be step one.

Which meant she was headed home, to convince her family to confess that they *hadn't* committed a crime.

SEVERAL HOURS LATER, Imogen stood on the pavement outside Blandington train station, waiting for her cousin Freddie to pick her up. She looked around at the village where she had grown up, and yawned. Blandington wasn't the most boring village in the country—that would have been too interesting—but it was very, very dull, indeed. All the houses were the same aggressively bland shade of beige. The neat flower beds were full of neat white roses that looked like they'd rather be red. The birds were halfheartedly singing the same boring tune, in the key of G, which everyone knows is the most boring key of all.

Imogen felt hopeless and heavy. When she'd left for Lilyworth, Imogen had sworn she would never come back to Blandington. Everything here reminded her of Big Nana, and it hurt too much to remember Big Nana. Blandington was also full of reminders of the person Imogen used to be, and it hurt to remember that, too.

Which led her to check her phone. The sooner she was picked up, the sooner she could prove her family was innocent and get back on the next train. Where *was* Freddie? He was forty-five minutes late to pick her up, and she'd called him three times, but he hadn't answered. He was probably asleep, or accidentally setting fire to his hair, or something—he was the most forgetful, clumsy, and generally useless of all the Crims. He'd been taking bookkeeping exams for four years, but he still hadn't managed to pass them—he never remembered to turn up on the scheduled day. He was even more useless than Great-Uncle Bernard, who had once held himself hostage by accident.

Imogen sighed. Until Big Nana's death, Imogen hadn't been ashamed of her family. She had been one of them—just as enthusiastic and creative about crime as her relatives. Like all her cousins, Imogen had kept a "crime journal" of her best criminal plans—from stealing the carousel at the local park to making all the math textbooks at her primary school explode. Big Nana had called Imogen the most promising criminal in the Crim family in generations, and it had filled Imogen with pride. But then Big Nana had tried to pull off the Underwater Submarine Heist in the treacherous waters of the North Sea.

And she had never come back.

What if she had taken Imogen with her? Could Imogen have saved her? Or would Imogen be gone now too? These were the types of questions Imogen liked to avoid asking. She focused on a particularly boring streetlight and took a deep, cleansing breath. *I can't get out of here fast enough.*

Imogen tried Freddie's number one last time. Nothing. Maybe it was time to call one of the Horrible Children. Her younger cousins were reliable, in a way—they would reliably do the exact opposite of what you'd asked them to do. They could be lots of fun, though, and Imogen had adored them when she was younger—Delia had been Imogen's closest friend before she'd left for Lilyworth. She'd been the coolest girl Imogen had ever seen, with blue streaks in her hair and perfect black-kohl cat eyes—even when she was eleven. Another cousin, Henry, had been thoughtful enough to give her a skeleton key as a good-bye present. Imogen smiled. As much as she didn't relish being back in Blandington, she was looking forward to seeing them again.

Just then, an ice cream van screeched to a stop in front of her. The back door flew open, and one of her twin cousins, Nate or Nick—she couldn't tell which—stuck his chocolate-covered face out and screamed, "GET IN!"

This wouldn't have been a tempting offer at the best of times. Imogen had a tendency to get carsick, particularly when there was food involved, or when the Horrible Children were being especially horrible, or when she was involved in a high-speed joyride.

She had a feeling she was about to get very, very carsick indeed.

"NOW!" yelled Nick (or Nate), grabbing Imogen's arm and hauling her into the van.

She landed in a heap on the floor of the van, on top of five-sixths of the Horrible Children: Nick and Nate, the seven-year-old twins; Isabella, the most dangerous toddler in the country; Henry, the twelve-year-old; and Sam, who, at thirteen, was a year older than Imogen but certainly didn't act it. It was the most uncomfortable family reunion she had ever been to, and that was saying something—the Crims had once held a get-together in an unused public toilet.

"Imojim!" said Isabella, punching Imogen really hard in the face with her tiny fist.

"Great right hook!" said one of the twins, stroking Isabella's twisty blond hair. The other Horrible Children nodded fondly.

"Just like Big Nana," said Henry. "She'd have been so proud."

Imogen was still recovering from the tiny but powerful punch when the van lurched off again. "My bags!" yelled Imogen. "Wait! Please can we turn back and get my things?"

"Sorry! No time!" came a female voice from the driver's seat.

A female voice that sounded very much like her cousin Delia.

Which wasn't possible, because Delia was only fourteen years old and definitely did not have a driver's license.

Though that would explain why they were now driving on the wrong side of the road . . . and why the driver was wearing Delia's favorite purple-sequined jacket.

"What did it say on that big red sign? I haven't got my glasses on," said Delia.

Had Imogen really been looking forward to seeing her cousins? That seemed like a distant memory now. *"Stop!"* she shouted. "It said STOP!"

"No need to shout!" shouted Delia.

Which is when Imogen heard the police sirens.

"Don't look at me, look at the road! And please tell me you didn't steal this van," Imogen begged pointlessly.

"Okay," said Delia, smirking.

Nick and/or Nate cackled. Delia reached behind her to give them both a high five, which meant—

"PUT YOUR HANDS BACK ON THE WHEEL!"

yelled Imogen. She grabbed on to the nearest thing to steady herself, which happened to be Henry, who happened to be spray-painting "Henry Crim Woz Ere" onto the inside of the van. Henry hadn't changed, Imogen noted. From the look of him, he was still "tattooing" himself with ballpoint pens. And from the smell of him, he still wasn't washing very often.

"Oi!" said Henry. "You ruined my tag."

"Good," said Imogen. "Don't you remember what Big Nana used to say? 'Never graffiti your surname on stolen goods.'"

"Hey! We didn't steal the van. We *borrowed* it," said Delia, sounding hurt. She careened onto a cobbled side street, with the police following closely behind. "We wanted to get you an ice cream, with a flake and everything. We were trying to do something nice for you to welcome you home." She swerved around a corner so fast that the entire van tilted to the left.

"You didn't need to *steal an ice cream van* to get me an ice cream cone," said Imogen, who at this point was feeling quite sick and didn't really feel like ice cream, anyway.

"I told you. We didn't steal the van. We *borrowed it*. We were just going to take some ice cream, but Henry must have knocked off the brake or something because the stupid thing started rolling downhill! Toward a playground full of children! I mean, what choice did I have, really?"

Delia's voice was pleading.

"Oh," said Imogen, bored. "The old rolling-down-the-hill-toward-a-playground-full-of-children excuse."

"It's *true*!" Sam said a bit defensively. He was sitting with Isabella at the back of the van. His voice came out as a squeak, and he slapped his hand over his mouth in horror. He'd been unusually quiet so far, and now Imogen knew why—his voice must be breaking. Either that, or he'd stopped impersonating people (his specialty) and started impersonating donkeys. At least he wouldn't be able to prank call her pretending to be her mother anymore.

"Wait," said Henry, who was peering out of the back window. "Where have the police gone?"

"We've lost them," said Delia, smiling triumphantly. She steered the van into a back alley—which, unfortunately, turned out to be a dead end. "No big deal," said Delia, starting to reverse. But then the police car swerved up behind them, blue lights flashing, blocking them in.

Delia's smile disappeared and was replaced by a look of absolute dread. She groaned and dropped her head to the steering wheel. "Oh no! What are we going to do?" she said.

"Just tell them you borrowed the van," Imogen said a bit snarkily. "I'm sure they'll understand."

But then the door of the police car opened. Two

officers stepped out. They didn't look happy. Imogen felt sicker than ever.

Delia turned as white as a very scared sheet. "Imogen, please, you have to think of something to say to them," she said. "You were always the smooth talker."

Imogen wondered why Delia was so worried. The first time Delia had been arrested, when she was eight, she'd been so proud that she'd insisted on calling her parents *herself.* But there was no time to point that out. Imogen racked her brains. "What if . . . ," she said. And then, "What about . . ." But it was no good. Her mind was blank. She was out of practice. Also, really—what possible reason could they have for driving an ice cream van at nearly a hundred miles an hour on the wrong side of the road? "What if we say we have a relative with a deadly waffle cone deficiency? No, they'll never buy that. . . ."

"Please," said Delia. "Just tell them *you* were driving."

"No way!" said Imogen, bristling. "I've had a clean record for two years now!"

The policemen were walking toward the van.

"You have to," begged Delia. "Please! I'm on my third strike with the police! One more time, I'll go to juvenile detention! Remember how we always used to bail each other out?"

Imogen felt a pang of sympathy, but she shook her head. "I'm sorry. *You* chose to steal the van—"

"Borrow!" Delia interrupted angrily.

"Borrow," said Imogen. "Right. Either way, I'm certainly not going to be an accomplice to a crime."

Delia looked whiter still. Imogen frowned. She couldn't work out why Delia was quite so afraid of juvenile detention. Aunt Bets had spent almost her entire adolescence there, and she'd told them, "It's just like summer camp. Except you can never leave, and you get beaten up quite a lot, and everyone calls you 'bird face,' and no one wants to snog you." Exactly like summer camp, then, in Imogen's experience.

The policemen knocked on the van door. "Come on out," said one of the officers.

Imogen and Delia looked at each other. Imogen could see the fear in Delia's eyes. And Delia wasn't scared of anything, not even Aunt Bets's piranha pool.

"Come on, Delia," said Imogen. "Just tell them the truth."

"Please!" said Delia, gripping Imogen's arm. "Just say it was you! There's a Kitty Penguin concert next week that I've got tickets for."

Imogen curled her lip in disgust. Kitty Penguin was a truly terrible singer who dressed up as a flightless bird for her shows. Bridget Sweetwine was her biggest fan.

Imogen rolled her eyes at Delia.

"What?" Delia said defensively. "My friend Janie

wanted to go. Plus, I bought a black-and-white dress especially for the concert. And a diamante beak."

"You are ridiculous," Imogen told her.

"I know, I know," said Delia. "But you won't let me go to juvie—will you?"

Imogen took a deep breath. No. She wouldn't let Delia go to juvie. Now that Imogen was back, she was once again the leader, Big Nana's protégé, and it was up to her to save the day. Just like always.

Imogen climbed out of the van and walked up to the policemen, trying to look as meek and innocent as possible. There were two officers, one short and one tall, standing there with their arms crossed. The shorter man had his legs crossed, too. He was obviously trying to look really authoritative, but he actually resembled a constipated goat. He reminded her of someone. . . .

"Well, well, well! Imogen Crim. Didn't expect to see you back here anytime soon," he said.

Imogen felt a wave of relief wash over her as she realized who he reminded her of: himself.

She let out the breath she'd been holding. She couldn't believe her luck—the policeman's name was Donnelly, and he was a police constable—and a Crim.

Donavon Donnelly was actually Imogen's second cousin. When she was younger, he'd given her shoplifting lessons by taking her to the supermarket to steal

Skittles and radishes (Imogen had always believed in a balanced diet). But he'd decided on a career in policing, so he'd taken his mother's maiden name, which everyone agreed was a wise move. None of the Crims blamed him for becoming a cop—it was useful to have a man on the inside, after all. But it was always hard to tell when he'd take pity on them.

"So," said PC Donnelly. "You want to tell me and PC Phillips here what you were doing breaking the speed limit without a driving license in a stolen ice cream van? I mean—that's a lot of laws you've broken right there. I'm almost impressed."

"Thank you," said Imogen, smiling and hoping that meant he was feeling generous.

"I said 'almost.'"

"Right." *I'm going to have to talk my way out of this.* Imogen stood up straighter, scrambling to look properly apologetic. "Look, I'm *so* sorry," she said in the voice she used at Lilyworth whenever she was trying to get out of lacrosse practice. "It all happened so fast. We were just looking after the van while the driver went to the bathroom, and suddenly, the emergency brake slipped off—somehow—and we were about to run over some children, so I grabbed the wheel. . . ."

"Oh, of course," said PC Phillips with a scowl. "The old

rolling-down-a-hill-toward-a-playground-full-of-children defense."

"We really were, though!" said Imogen, feeling her cheeks flush.

PC Phillips rolled his eyes. "Let's put that aside for a moment. There's another problem with your story," he said. "You're too young to drive."

"But those children were too young to die!" said Imogen, opening her eyes wide like innocent people do.

"Nice try," said PC Phillips. He unclipped the handcuffs from his belt.

Imogen felt as though she might cry. All that hard work to turn her life around, and she was about to be punished for a crime she hadn't committed. What about her record—spotless for two years? Surely they'd let her off this once? She shot a glance at PC Donnelly, silently begging him to do something.

He sighed and shook his head. Imogen felt her heart sink.

But then, just like that, he came to her rescue.

"Whoa," he said, "let's slow down for a minute. You didn't mean to steal the van. Did you, Imogen?"

"No," said Imogen, trying to squeeze as much earnestness as possible into the word.

"Okay. Well, I'm the senior officer here, and I believe

you. We'll let you off with a warning this time—"

"Will we?" said PC Phillips, opening and closing the handcuffs with a mournful sigh. He'd clearly been looking forward to using them.

"We will. But you, Miss Crim, are getting an official warning."

He pulled out a notebook and wrote "Official Warning" on the first blank page. He then ripped out the page and handed it to Imogen. It didn't look very official, but she thought it probably wasn't the time to point that out.

"If you're back in town, you'd better stay on the straight and narrow," PC Donnelly said, giving her his sternest look, which only made him look like a terrified puppy. "And, young lady, if I ever catch you driving again, or thinking of driving—or doing anything that *rhymes* with 'drive'—you'll be going straight to jail. Do you hear what I'm saying?"

Imogen did hear what he was saying. She had very good hearing.

"Thank you, officer," she said. "I'm going to take my cousins home now and put them all straight to bed. And I promise I won't dive or jive or speak to anyone called Clive. . . ."

"Or disturb a beehive," PC Donnelly said helpfully.

Imogen smiled. "I *definitely* won't do that."

"That's what I like to hear," he said. "PC Phillips—

would you be so kind as to take this van back to Mr. Martelli? He's probably finished his bathroom break by now."

PC Phillips grunted and, with a final glare at Imogen, walked to the ice cream van, reluctantly clipping the handcuffs back onto his belt. He opened the back door, and the Horrible Children filed out. "There sure are a lot of 'em, aren't there?" muttered PC Phillips.

"Too many, you might say," said PC Donnelly, getting into the police car.

Imogen watched the two officers drive away. She let out a breath she didn't know she'd been holding. Now that Headmistress Gruner knew her real name, a new crime on her record could stop her from being let back into Lilyworth. She walked over to the Horrible Children. Their eyes lit up as she approached them. "You're welcome," she said.

But they hadn't been smiling at her. They all ran (or crawled, in Isabella's case) right past her. Imogen turned and saw them all hurtling toward a man who was staggering out of the grocery store across the street. She couldn't see his face behind all the bags, but she recognized him from his mismatched shoes and messy brown hair with crumbs in it: Freddie. The Horrible Children overtook him and hurled themselves into the back of a tiny car. Freddie didn't seem to notice. He opened the car's trunk, filled it with shopping bags, and climbed into the driver's seat.

Imogen crossed the road and got into the passenger seat of the car, but Freddie didn't notice her, either. He turned on the engine and smiled at the Horrible Children in the rearview mirror as he pulled away. "Sorry the shopping took so long," he said. "I forgot we needed milk, and then I forgot to get bread, and then I thought I'd forgotten my wallet, but it turned out I was holding it the whole time. Still . . . I'm sure you found some way to entertain yourselves."

Delia elbowed the twins, who had started sniggering.

Imogen cleared her throat, and Freddie turned to her, startled. "Imogen!" he cried. "You're not supposed to be here till two!"

"It's four," said Imogen.

Freddie looked at his watch. "It's only half past ten!" he said.

"You've got that on upside down," Imogen pointed out.

"So I do!" said Freddie, turning his watch around. "Anyway—how did you get here?"

"Funny you should ask that," said Imogen. "The kids picked me up in a stolen ice cream van." Her cousins gasped, and too late, Imogen realized what she had done. She had broken Big Nana's golden rule: "Never tell on a fellow Crim. Unless you're bribed with something really nice, like a solid-gold wardrobe."

"Wow," said Delia. "So you're a tattletale now as well as a goody-goody?"

Imogen could hear the hurt in her cousin's voice. Delia had never quite forgiven Imogen for leaving. And Imogen hadn't exactly reached out to her cousin over the past two years, even though they'd once been as close as sisters. "Sorry," she whispered, and she meant it, but Delia was already staring sullenly out the window.

"What have I told you about stealing cars, children?" asked Freddie, turning to scold the cousins and driving straight through a red light.

"We should always ask an adult to help us," said Henry. "But this wasn't a car. It was a van."

"All the same, I'm stopping your allowance for another week."

"But that's 347 weeks we haven't had an allowance now!" squeaked Sam.

The rest of the Horrible Children didn't seem that bothered, though. The twins were playing cards (both of them were cheating), and Henry was busy teaching Isabella how to use a lighter. Delia, meanwhile, had taken matters into her own hands. Imogen watched as she reached over and pulled Freddie's wallet from his pocket, took out a twenty-pound note, and slipped it back. Imogen didn't tell on her cousin this time, but Delia scowled at her, anyway. Imogen sighed. She had only been back in Blandington a few hours and she'd already made an enemy. Somehow this wasn't as satisfying as the mutual hatred she shared with Bridget Sweetwine.

Imogen closed her eyes and tried to imagine what was happening at Lilyworth now. It was just before dinner, and normally, Lucy and Alice and Catherine would be gathered in a circle around her in the common room, laughing hysterically at her jokes.

What would happen without her there? Would Alice try to make the jokes? God, would *Catherine*?

As if Freddie knew what she was thinking, he turned to Imogen and asked, "How come you got kicked out of Lilyworth? I thought you were going to be headmistress."

Imogen grunted. "Head *girl*," she corrected. "I was. But then someone wrote an anonymous letter to the headmistress telling her that I'm a Crim and that I lied on my application."

Delia raised her eyebrows. Before Imogen had left home, she'd never gotten on the wrong side of anyone, except for one time when she stood up in front of Uncle Clyde just before Aunt Bets hit him with a saucepan. "Don't like it so much when someone tells on *you*, do you, Imogen?" Delia said.

"This was different. This was an evil, lying goody-goody who was out to destroy my life," said Imogen.

"Sounds familiar," said Delia.

Imogen decided to ignore her. She felt completely and utterly alone. She didn't fit in with her family anymore, and just being around them made her miss Big Nana in a way she'd never wanted to feel again. She told herself she just had to hold on till they got to the Crim house. Then she could lock herself in her parents' quiet, tidy apartment in the east wing and never see her cousins again, except for birthdays, Christmases, and parole hearings, like nature intended. In the meantime, she'd talk to Freddie. He might be terrible at everything—especially driving, Imogen thought, as he went the wrong way around a roundabout—but at least he was pleased to see her.

"So be honest," she said. "Uncle Clyde didn't really pull off The Heist, did he?"

Uncle Clyde had spent the last twenty years planning The Heist—a carefully crafted, amazingly idiotic scheme to steal his long-lost Captain Crook lunch box back from Jack Wooster, his former friend and current enemy. Jack Wooster hadn't *stolen* the lunch box exactly, but when they were both eight years old, he'd persuaded Uncle Clyde to swap it for a pair of X-ray specs. These X-ray specs *did not work.* Uncle Clyde had realized that immediately. But when he pointed this out to Jack, he had refused to swap back.

Reclaiming the lunch box had become a matter of principle for Uncle Clyde. The fact that it was now worth a small fortune might have had something to do with it, too—Captain Crook had become something of a cult figure since the character had been discontinued for sparking a crime wave among the under-fives.

The plans for The Heist took up a whole wall in Uncle Clyde's room; it was a complicated assortment of drawings, charts, maps, and rubber bands. They involved every member of the Crim family (he updated the plans each time a new baby was born), along with several innocent animals and an unsuspecting bouncy castle.

Everyone in the Crim family knew about The Heist. Everyone knew it was a terrible idea. Everyone had always refused to go along with it.

Until now, apparently.

Freddie's eyes widened so much, Imogen wondered if he'd lost a contact lens. "No, he really did!" he insisted. "It was amazing, really—the whole thing went exactly according to plan."

"That really *is* amazing," said Imogen, still skeptical.

"Well . . . except for the bit I was supposed to do," said Freddie. "I think I overslept or something. I can't quite remember."

"You missed the whole thing?"

Freddie nodded. "But that's good, in a way. I didn't

end up in jail, so I'm around to look after the kids!"

And it's clear Freddie's doing a wonderful job, Imogen thought, glancing behind her. *Look, Isabella's wearing a towel as a nappy.*

"So was everyone being arrested part of the plan, too?" she asked.

"Well . . . no," said Freddie. "But at least all the kids got away!"

"Yes," said Imogen, watching as Henry "tattooed" his name on Isabella's arm in pen. "That really is a blessing."

"I've got to tell you—they can be a bit of a handful at times!"

"You don't say," said Imogen.

"But it'll be so much easier when you're living with us."

Imogen stared at him. She felt a creeping sense of dread. "Living with you? Er, I just assumed I'd live in my parents' apartment." *Away from all of you,* she thought, *and the chaos you cause.*

"Oh, no," said Freddie, shaking his head. "You have to stay with me till your parents get out, because you're a minor. And who knows how long that'll be, eh? You'll be sharing a room with Delia."

Considering recent events, "You'll be sharing a room with Delia" was the most horrifying sentence Imogen had ever heard. Except maybe "I'm afraid the evidence is overwhelming" and "You have been expelled from Lilyworth Ladies' College." Imogen cast a quick glance at her cousin and could see from her expression that the feeling was mutual.

"I hate to disappoint you, Freddie," said Imogen, turning back to him and smiling sweetly to hide her panic, "but there is no way I'm living with you. I'll stay in my parents' flat."

"No you won't," said Freddie. "You're twelve. That's too young to live alone. Them's the rules!"

"But you don't care about rules!" said Imogen, not bothering to hide her panic anymore.

"I'm sorry," said Freddie. "I'm putting my foot down." And he did—onto the accelerator.

"Brake! *Brake!*" Imogen cried as Isabella sailed through the air and landed on her lap, still slurping happily at her sippy cup.

"Imojim!" said Isabella, and she jabbed Imogen in the stomach with her tiny but powerful foot.

"Great roundhouse kick!" said one of the twins.

"Why isn't she in a car seat?" Imogen asked Freddie.

Freddie shrugged. "I've lost it," he said. "I think it was absorbed back into the car. See? You *have* to come and live with us. I need your help."

"Wait." Imogen sniffed the air. "Is that smoke?"

She turned to look. It *was* smoke. The backseat was on

fire, and the Horrible Children were roasting marshmallows over the (rapidly spreading) flames.

Imogen grabbed Isabella's sippy cup, took off the lid, and emptied the contents on the fire. The flames fizzled and died.

"You're such a killjoy," Henry moaned as Imogen snatched the lighter from him and pocketed it.

Imogen looked at Freddie and shook her head. It was a miracle that the Horrible Children were still alive, with him looking after them. She didn't seem to have much choice. It wasn't as though things could get much worse, anyway. "Fine," she said. "I will come and live with you."

They were nearly home now. Imogen looked out the window at the streets of Blandington: There was the toy shop where the twins had stolen their My First Prison. . . . There was the tree Henry had torched in his very first arson attack. . . . There was Aunt Bets's money laundry. And there was the hedge Imogen and Delia had used as their hideaway, where they'd made each other crimeship bracelets and sworn never, ever to tell on each other, no matter what. Imogen felt another stab of guilt.

And suddenly, there it was in front of her: Crim House. As Freddie pulled into the driveway, the sheer ridiculousness of the building struck her for the first time.

Once, a long time ago—before the Crims moved in—the house had been as dull as every other house in

Blandington. It'd had the same gray front door and the same gravel driveway. But it certainly wasn't boring anymore. The gravel in the driveway had been replaced with marbles stolen from local children. The front door was now painted in multicolored stripes—all the Crims had an opinion about what color it should be, and none of them were good at compromise.

The house itself was a little wonky; before her death, Big Nana had stolen two floors from a nearby mansion and grafted them onto the roof. And to celebrate Isabella's first birthday, Aunt Bets had stolen a Boeing 747 and glued it to the conservatory. The house now had an east wing, a west wing, and two airplane wings.

Imogen climbed out of the car and picked her way through the strange objects littering the front garden: a fake dinosaur skeleton, the bottom half of a horse costume, an empty box labeled "SNAKES! DEFOREMED BUT DEADLY. DO NOT OPEN!"

She looked up at the house and sighed. She thought she'd left all this behind, but now here she was . . . back where she had started.

She couldn't bear to call it "home" without Big Nana there.

OF COURSE, FREDDIE had forgotten his keys. Crim House was the most regularly burgled house in Blandington—mostly by Crim children practicing their breaking-and-entering skills—so there were twelve separate locks on the door.

"We'll just have to break in again," Delia said. "Who wants to pick the first lock?"

All the Horrible Children put up their hands. Imogen did not.

"Aren't you going to do one, Imogen?" Nick (or Nate) asked, wiggling the first lock open with a broken TV antenna he'd picked off the yard.

"No," said Imogen, her arms crossed. Although in her mind, she was already going through the steps. . . .

"Don't you miss crime at all?" asked Nate (or Nick).

"No," Imogen said again quickly.

"Liar," Delia said as she pushed one of her bobby pins into the second lock. "You always said there was nothing like the thrill of breaking the law."

Imogen flushed. It was strange to hear her own words quoted back to her. Had she really said that? "Yes, well. I've changed," she said.

"We can see that," said Delia. She didn't make it sound like a compliment.

When the door was open at last, the Horrible Children ran inside and headed straight for their rooms.

"We've put an extra bed for you in Delia's room," Freddie said as he and Imogen followed the others inside.

"Shame," Delia called from upstairs. "If I'd known you'd turned into a rat, I'd have gotten you a cage instead."

Imogen put her hands on her hips. "Yeah, well," she said, "if I'd known you'd turned into a brat, I'd have . . ." She tried to think of a comeback. She couldn't. Freddie gave Imogen a sympathetic look. "My insult skills are rusty," she explained. "At Lilyworth, I was very nice to people."

That wasn't *entirely* true. At Lilyworth, Imogen would have cut a girl like Delia down to size in no time—she would have given her one of the terrifying stares she used on first years, new teachers, and anyone who described themselves as "kooky"—but Delia had a strange power over her. Although Delia was annoying and selfish and a liar and childish and spiteful and vain and mean and quite possibly psychopathic, she was also the best friend Imogen had ever had.

Imogen walked into the living room and picked up an old family photograph from the mantelpiece. There was Big Nana in the middle, smiling her crooked smile, her red hair blazing. The other Crims stood around her like eccentric planets orbiting a very criminal sun.

"Not the same without her, is it?" Freddie said, coming up behind Imogen.

Imogen shook her head, putting the photograph down. She shouldn't have been surprised by how much she missed her grandmother, but Big Nana had always told her "Missing people is stupid. Especially if you have a catapult," and as a rule, Imogen tried to follow her advice.

"Big Nana would be so pleased to think of you and Delia sharing a room," Freddie said, smiling.

Imogen looked at Freddie. "Yeah, right," she said. "Big Nana always said you should never share a room with a relative unless they're an interior designer."

"She also said, 'Keep your friends close, your enemies close, and your family even closer,'" said Freddie. "Or was it 'Keep your enemies close, your family closer, and your friends in a dungeon'? Either way . . ."

Imogen sighed. She wasn't going to win this one. "Fine," she said. "I'll share with Delia."

Freddie smiled and patted her head, as if she were a dog. "Good boy, Imogen."

"I'm a girl."

"That's what I meant. Want me to carry your bags upstairs for you?"

"Actually, they got left behind at the station, when the kids picked me up," said Imogen.

"I'll get them," said Freddie, pressing some buttons on his phone.

"Thanks," said Imogen. "Who are you texting?"

"Oh . . . no one. I'm setting an alarm to remind me why I'm leaving the house," he explained as he walked back toward the front door. "The other day I went out for a pint of milk and I ended up joining a mariachi band. I got quite good at playing the maracas, but everyone had dry cereal for breakfast."

As soon as Freddie had left, Imogen climbed the creaking stairs to the second floor. On the wall between the twins' bedroom and the bathroom was an old tapestry showing some medieval criminals stealing things from some monks. And behind the tapestry was the door to her family's apartment. She pushed it open and shut it behind her, leaning against it as she looked around.

Compared to the rest of Crim House, Imogen's parents' apartment was very ordinary. The main part of the house was cluttered and chaotic—the floors were covered in ugly stolen carpets; the walls were covered in bad stolen art; and every time you opened a cupboard, things like blunt axes and child-sized straitjackets and bottles marked "Poison?" tumbled out. But Imogen's parents' apartment was clean and tidy and calm, with white walls, and furniture that didn't fall apart when you sat on it. That was her dad's influence—he liked everything to be well organized and functional. In fact, his prized possession was a shiny filing cabinet that he polished every day. Her mum's influence could be seen in the feather boas strewn across the sofa and the huge DVD collection of classic Hollywood films (arranged in alphabetical order by her father).

Imogen looked up at the huge photograph of Josephine, dressed in her favorite fur coat, that hung above the fireplace. Her mother was her own biggest fan—she had autographed it: "To Josephine Crim. You're a star! Love from Josephine Crim." All Josephine had ever wanted was to become famous (and for Imogen to make a bit more of an effort with her appearance—she was always sneaking lipsticks into her pocket). Judging by the newspaper headline Imogen had seen at Lilyworth, it looked like her dream was finally coming true.

But Imogen remembered her dad's pleading look in the same photo. Glancing over at her father's carefully organized collection of *Accounting Today!* magazines, she had a hard time imagining her father playing any part in Uncle Clyde's heist plan—even to please her mother, which was generally how he got himself into trouble. *So why would he do it? He wouldn't, would he?* That was why Imogen was here—to look for clues that her parents had taken part in The Heist.

Or *hadn't.*

As she looked around, she felt like she was ten again, about to leave for boarding school. Everything reminded her of how her life used to be—the smell of her mum's perfume (Stolen Diamonds: For Her); her dad's collection of mugs, pinched from accountancy firms around the country; the cushions embroidered with heart-warming messages: "Villainy Begins at Home"; "Home Is Where the Stolen Art Is"; "World's Best Carjacker!" But she found nothing at all to do with The Heist.

The last room Imogen checked was her dad's office. She'd always loved coming here as a child and reading *Zen and the Art of Small Business Accounts* while he worked. (She'd picked up a lot of tips, actually, and she had been the head of both the Capitalist and Buddhist Societies at Lilyworth). She looked at the framed certificates on the wall—her dad's bookkeeping degree, her mum's safe-breaking diploma, a swimming certificate from when she was eight—and noticed a new addition, in a golden frame: her most recent report card from Lilyworth. All As (except for the B in needlework). Imogen ran her fingers over the glass, feeling a tug of love for her father. He had always been really proud of her, even after Imogen wanted to leave. It had been him who'd suggested that she might like to "get away for a while" after Big Nana died. When he'd suggested boarding school, she'd found Lilyworth. She suspected he hadn't expected her to go quite so far for quite so long. But he'd never asked her to come home.

Imogen walked over to her dad's precious filing cabinet. A thin layer of dust had gathered on the surface. She pulled a hankie from her pocket and wiped it down, ready for when her dad came home. She opened the drawers and looked through her father's papers—maybe there would be a clue in here—but there was nothing to suggest he'd been involved in The Heist.

Of course there wasn't.

She sighed. Searching the apartment hadn't thrown up any clues. She'd just have to go to the police station where her family was being held and hear it from the horse's mouth. And if the police horse wouldn't spill the beans, she supposed she'd have to visit her parents.

Imogen slipped out of the house and walked through Blandington till she reached the gray, pebble-dashed police station. She hadn't been there since being questioned for the last crime she had committed, just before Big Nana had died: shaving the fur of her headmistress's white poodle, Snowy, and selling it on the black market as designer wool. As Imogen walked into the police station, the four officers on duty looked up from their computers (Imogen could see their screens—they were all playing solitaire). Imogen knew all of them. She'd seen PC Donnelly and PC Phillips just that morning, obviously. Then there was Inspector Jones, who had broken up Isabella's christening when it had gotten a bit rowdy, and Detective Sergeant White, who had tried and failed to prove that Nick and Nate were responsible for the so-called "Twin Break-Ins," in which two of every item was stolen from local shops one December (actually it had been Uncle Clyde, trying to save money on the twins' Christmas presents).

"Well, well, well. If it isn't little Imogen Crim," said Inspector Jones, standing up. "Long time no see. You're the spitting image of your mother. Except without the handcuffs. Ha! Ha! Ha!"

Imogen glared at Inspector Jones. Even now, with her criminal days behind her, there was no sound she hated more than the laughter of a police officer.

"Actually, PC Donnelly and I saw Imogen earlier

today. Didn't we?" said PC Phillips, clipping and unclipping his handcuffs.

"Indeed we did," said PC Donnelly, wagging his fingers at Imogen. "Now, what can we do for you? Have you brought us any doughnuts?"

Imogen decided to ignore him. "I'd like to see my family, please," she said.

"They're your family *now*, are they?" said Detective Sergeant White, scratching his nasty little beard. "Not what *I* heard. I heard you tried to disown them. Made up a fake name and everything! Thought you were better than them, didn't you? But look at you . . ."

"Hard to turn your back on a life of crime, isn't it, Imogen?" said PC Phillips. "That's why you stole that ice cream van this morning."

"That's a waffly serious offense!" said Inspector Jones, laughing his horrible laugh.

"Did she have a flake driving license?" asked Detective Sergeant White, laughing even more horribly.

"It wasn't long before I scooped her up and took her into custard-y!" said PC Phillips, laughing so hard that he handcuffed himself by mistake.

"That's a rubbish joke. You don't get custard from an ice cream van," Imogen said, watching coldly as Inspector Jones helped PC Phillips unlock himself. "Anyway, don't any of you have anything better to do than arrest a whole family for stealing a tatty old lunch box?"

"You really are out of touch, aren't you?" said PC Phillips, beckoning her over to his computer. She caught a glimpse of his screensaver: a picture of him stroking a really tiny pony. He quickly opened a browser window to hide the picture. "Now, then—let me show you something. . . ." He typed "weirdlunchboxes.com" into his browser. "Just wait till you see how much that lunch box is worth," he said, sitting back in his chair.

"Oh, I know," said Imogen. "It was valued at over a thousand pounds, wasn't it?"

"Not even close," said PC Phillips, grinning at his screen, waiting for the website to load. But a message popped up: "Page not found."

"That's weird," he said, frowning. "It was working earlier on. Doesn't matter, anyway. . . . I have a printout I can show you, somewhere around here. . . ." He pulled a file from his desk and leafed through it. "Here!" he said, pushing a piece of paper toward Imogen.

"This is another photograph of you with a small horse," said Imogen, studying it. PC Phillips had his arms around the pony's neck in this one. The pony didn't seem to be enjoying the hug.

PC Phillips snatched the photo back and slid it carefully into the folder. "Don't know what that's doing in there," he muttered. He pulled out another piece of paper. "This, I mean."

Imogen looked down at the printout he passed to her. There was a photo of the Captain Crook lunch box, and below it, the estimated value: over *one million pounds.*

Imogen was so shocked that she dropped the piece of paper. *"What?"* she said. "No way! That's insane!" Then she bent down automatically to pick the paper up, because there is no excuse for littering as Ms. Gruner liked to say.

"I know. Crazy, the things people are into, isn't it?" said PC Phillips.

"Yes," said Imogen, glancing back at the screensaver of him and the tiny pony.

"The valuation tripled just a couple of weeks ago. We don't know why," said Inspector Jones.

Typical, thought Imogen. *Uncle Clyde timed The Heist perfectly so that everyone would get the maximum jail sentence. It's almost like they all* want *to spend the rest of their lives in jail.* And then she realized—most of them probably did.

PC Phillips led Imogen down a damp corridor, lit by a single, flickering lightbulb, to the cells. He stopped outside the biggest one. Through the bars, Imogen could see her family, sitting side by side on benches around the edges of the room, looking very much at home. Her mother,

Josephine, was doing the crossword in the newspaper, as if it were an ordinary Sunday morning; Uncle Clyde was doodling something that looked like a penguin—he was probably working on a plan to steal one from Blandington Zoo; Aunt Bets was knitting a toy machine gun for Isabella; Uncle Knuckles was managing to look terrifying while pouring tea from a flowery pot into delicate china cups; and Imogen's father, Al, was sitting slightly apart from the others, staring at his hands, as if he was wondering how he'd gotten there.

Imogen suddenly felt shy. She hadn't seen her family for a very long time.

Josephine was the first to look up and see Imogen. She jumped up and ran over to her, trying to embrace her through the bars the way people did in the soap operas she watched on TV. "Darling!" she cried. "It is simply *delightful* to see you! You look so glamorous—like a wealthy tax evader! Though I *do* wish you'd start wearing lipstick."

Imogen hugged her mother back as best she could. Despite the circumstances, it was good to see her again.

"Hello, dear," her dad said, walking over and trying to kiss her on the head but banging his head on the bars. He gave a halfhearted chuckle, rubbing his temple. "Ha, er, not a lot of room in here." Imogen squeezed his hand through the bars.

"Hi, Dad."

"Look, darling, have you seen?" said Josephine, thrusting her newspaper at Imogen. "We're the main story in the *Blandington Times.* Can you believe it? Front-page criminals at last!"

Imogen looked down at the paper. The other front-page stories were "Old Man's Hair Turns Gray" and "Lonely Cat Meets Other Cat and Decides It Prefers Being Alone," so yes, she could believe it. She studied the picture of her family. Someone had drawn a mustache on Uncle Clyde's face. "Who did that?" she asked, looking up.

Uncle Clyde looked up and waved his pen at her. "Just wanted to see what I'd look like with facial hair. That style's called the Imperial. I thought I might rock a nice, thick handlebar mustache, too. What do you think? Solid criminal style, that."

Imogen raised one eyebrow. "Bit boring being in jail, is it?" she asked.

"A little bit," Uncle Clyde admitted. "But it's good to have a bit of me time to try out some new looks. We'll be on TV a lot over the next few weeks, so we have to make a good impression." He suddenly peered past Imogen, down the hall. "Did Freddie come with you?"

"No," Imogen replied, turning behind her and wondering if she *should* have brought Freddie.

When she turned back, Uncle Clyde was shaking his head. "He keeps saying he's too busy to come visit," he complained. "Do you suppose that means he's up to something?"

"Something?" Imogen asked incredulously. "Freddie?" Unless "something" was driving in endless circles around the roundabout, she couldn't imagine he was.

PC Phillips rolled his eyes at Imogen. "If you're all right here for a bit, I'd better be getting back to the front office," he said.

But as he turned to leave, Uncle Knuckles jumped up from his seat and banged the teapot against the bars to the cell. "OI! YOU!" he shouted. "WOULD YOU MIND BRINGING US ANOTHER CUP OF TEA? DECAF WOULD BE LOVELY IF THAT'S ALL RIGHT. THE CAFFEINE IS DOING TERRIBLE THINGS TO MY BOWELS." PC Phillips backed away, his hands over his ears. Uncle Knuckles—with his enormous muscles, shaved head, and scarred face—looked and sounded like a cross between a serial killer and a chainsaw, but he was actually the gentlest of the Crims. He was a very talented flower arranger and was devoted to his wife, Bets, even though she was almost certainly a psychopath and had tried to murder him on several occasions.

"If I make you another pot of tea, will you promise never to use that word again?" asked PC Phillips.

"WHICH? 'BOWELS'?" said Uncle Knuckles.

"Yes, I think he meant 'bowels,'" said Josephine.

"One of my favorite words, 'bowels,'" said Uncle Clyde.

"What was that?" asked Aunt Bets, with a worrying gleam in her eye. "Need me to rip out someone's bowels? I have a nice sharp knitting needle—"

"That won't be necessary," Imogen said quickly.

"Just give me the teapot," said PC Phillips, reaching through the bars and taking it from Uncle Knuckles. "But I must remind you, this isn't a restaurant. Have you forgotten you're in jail?"

"ARE YOU CALLING ME . . . FORGETFUL?" asked Uncle Knuckles, grabbing the bars with his meaty hands.

"No, of course not," said PC Phillips, smiling nervously.

"BECAUSE I HAVE ACTUALLY BEEN HAVING A BIT OF TROUBLE REMEMBERING WORDS RECENTLY. WHAT'S THAT LOVELY DRIED FLOWER STUFF PEOPLE USE TO MAKE THEIR ROOMS SMELL NICE?"

"Potpourri?" said PC Phillips.

"THAT'S THE ONE!" said Uncle Knuckles, smiling the way a lion smiles at a baby elephant before it eats it. "THAT'S THE ANSWER TO TWELVE DOWN, JOSEPHINE!"

"Of course!" said Josephine, writing it down in her crossword.

PC Phillips blinked. "Right, then," he said. "I'll be back with the tea in a bit. I'm warning you, you won't get this kind of service in maximum security. They buy cheap tea bags and they always run out of Earl Grey."

"You mean we're going to maximum security?" asked Josephine, clapping her hands with delight. "Did you hear that Al? I can hold my head up high! We're a danger to society. At last!"

"Yes, dear," said Al, smiling weakly at Imogen. "Just what we've always wanted."

As PC Phillips's footsteps faded into the distance, the Crims went back to knitting, doodling, and planning unpleasant murders. Imogen stood there, watching them and shaking her head in disbelief. They all seemed to have forgotten she was there. The more she watched them, the angrier she felt. No one had asked her why she wasn't at school; no one had thanked her for coming to see them; no one had even offered her one of the crookies they were passing around. (Crookies are cookies made with stolen ingredients. The flavors are a bit hit-or-miss.)

Her family's lack of interest in her stung, though she supposed it shouldn't have surprised her. Big Nana was the only one of them who had ever paid her much attention. And when Big Nana had gone, they'd grieved for a bit and then each gone back to their bizarre and foolish criminal obsessions.

No one had been as devastated as Imogen.

And that, along with the very real desire to turn over a new leaf, was why she'd left them behind.

Now, Imogen rattled the bars of the cell to let everyone know she was still there.

No one seemed to notice.

She gave an angry cough.

"OI! YOU!" shouted Uncle Knuckles. "DO YOU HAVE A COLD? I HAVE A LAVENDER-SCENTED HANKIE SOMEWHERE IF YOU NEED IT."

"I don't need a hankie," said Imogen. "I need you all to explain something to me. What the hell are you thinking?"

"Right now?" asked Aunt Bets. "I'm wondering what PC Phillips would taste like on toast."

"No," said Imogen, trying to keep her voice steady. "Why are you all pretending you carried out Uncle Clyde's ridiculous heist?"

"Are you kids using 'ridiculous' as a compliment these days?" Uncle Clyde asked hopefully.

"No we are *not*," said Imogen. "Come on. Mum? Dad? Admit it. There's no way you did this. I *know* you didn't think The Heist was a good idea."

The Crims looked at one another.

"Well?" said Imogen, crossing her arms.

Josephine laid down her paper. "You really have been

away too long, darling," she said. "Have you forgotten the Code of the Crims?"

Imogen blushed. The truth was, she *had* forgotten the Code of the Crims—tried to, anyway. The code was "Nothing is more important than family. Except dinosaurs." No one really knew where that last bit of the code came from, or what it meant, so they ignored it and concentrated on sticking by their fellow Crims, no matter what. For example, no one was quite sure how many murders Aunt Bets had committed over the years, but that was just one of her little quirks; she was family. And most of the Crims would have preferred it if Josephine stopped pickpocketing people at family dinners, but what could they do? She was family too. And everyone had been really hurt when Imogen had decided to change her name and go to boarding school and try to forget she was a Crim altogether—but they didn't hold it against her (except maybe Delia). She was still family, even if she didn't want to be.

Imogen couldn't bring herself to look her mother in the eye. Pulling off The Heist had been Uncle Clyde's dream since he was a boy. It made sense that his family had tried to help him make his dream come true. A slow, horrible dread crept through her. Maybe she'd underestimated them—and overestimated them at the same time. Maybe they *were* guilty.

But that didn't matter, she reminded herself—she still

had to get back to Lilyworth. If they truly *had* done it, she'd just have to find the lunch box and persuade her family to give it back to Jack Wooster and show some remorse. Then, if she really begged Ms. Gruner . . .

It was a long shot. The longest shot she'd ever taken, including the time Big Nana had given her a crossbow and a pair of binoculars and told her to shoot down Uncle Clyde's kite. But failure was not an option. She couldn't stay in Blandington. Her future was at Lilyworth now—and in whatever high-powered, universe-running position Lilyworth led her to. Big Nana had always told her, "If you want something badly enough, you'll find a way to get it, unless it's my secret stash of toffee—you'll pry that out of my cold, dead hands." And Imogen wanted to get back to Lilyworth very, very badly indeed.

She decided to try a different tactic. "Look, Mum," she said. "I'm trying to be a good daughter. I'm following the Code of the Crims—I'm trying to get you out of here. Don't you realize how much trouble you're in?"

The other Crims just stared at her.

"But that's the brilliant thing!" said Josephine. "We were *on the news*. On the television, sweetie!"

Imogen sighed. Being a celebrity criminal was the ultimate goal of all the Crims, though only Big Nana had achieved it. Imogen remembered the time her grandmother had been arrested for dressing up as Prince Charles and stealing 578 silver spoons from a Buckingham Palace garden party. The family had thrown a big party to watch her arrest on television. There had been balloons and cupcakes with Big Nana's face on them, and everyone had danced to "Jailhouse Rock."

And just two weeks later, during the Underwater Submarine Heist—a terrible idea, in retrospect—Big Nana had died, and Imogen's whole world had fallen apart. The person she aspired to be exactly like when she grew up (only with more teeth) had been killed. She had never even considered that Big Nana *could* die—she'd assumed Big Nana was pretty much immortal, like a god or a cockroach. And she'd never really considered that committing crimes was wrong or dangerous—it was just what her family did. But Big Nana's death put everything in perspective.

Big Nana was the best criminal Imogen had ever known, and crime had still killed her.

That realization had ended Imogen's criminal career. She'd headed off to Lilyworth, vowing to use her cleverness to secure a future for herself.

It seemed, however, that none of the other Crims had learned similar lessons about crime paying (or not).

Imogen sucked in a breath and turned back to her mother's delighted face. She thought of the two years she'd spent at Lilyworth, not even coming home during school vacations. Then, she'd only been able to imagine the very stupid ideas her family was involved in. Now here it was, smacking her in the face. And suddenly, it made her *furious.*

"Why are you all so STUPID?" she yelled, looking from her mother to the others. She caught the eye of her father, biting his lip in the background, but quickly looked away. "How can you still think it's glamorous to break the law? You're going to be in prison for the rest of your lives—and you got me kicked out of school, too, the school I *love* and have been doing *very well at.* NOT THAT ANY OF YOU EVEN NOTICED!"

Shaking, she turned away and stomped up the corridor.

"Darling! Wait!" called Josephine.

"Imogen, dear!" her father called after her. But Imogen was already back at the front office. The police officers were playing Scrabble now. They looked up, seemed to notice her beet-red face, and laughed at her. All except PC Donnelly.

"Reunion going well, is it?" asked Detective Sergeant White. "Ha! Ha! Ha!"

Imogen swallowed. She wanted to knock his block off, to explode in a hail of expletives—and Imogen Crim *would* have. But Imogen Collins was Teflon. She would not let them get to her. She took a few deep breaths, then smiled her most Bridget Sweetwine–like smile, and said in her most head girlish voice: "I have a proposition for you: If my family can show you how sorry they are—and if they return the stolen lunch box to its rightful owner—will you let them go?"

The police officers looked at one another. "That's an interesting proposition," said Detective Sergeant White.

"Is it?" said PC Donnelly.

"Maybe if they were really, *really* sorry . . . ," said Inspector Jones.

"Maybe if they sang us a song about how sorry they were?" suggested PC Phillips, scratching his head.

Imogen's heart lifted. Her plan might work after all. "I'm sure that could be arranged!" she said. Uncle Knuckles could be *quite* musical.

The police officers looked at one another again and started to laugh.

"As *if*!" said Detective Sergeant White. "The Crims have been the scourge of Blandington for two whole generations now! We finally have the evidence we need to put them away for good! Did you really think we'd let them go?"

Imogen's heart crashed back down. She turned before they could see how disappointed she was and pushed the door to the police station open, the horrible sound of police laughter ringing in her ears.

"Wait!"

Imogen looked around. PC Donnelly was hurrying down the corridor after her, like an uncoordinated elk.

"Listen," he said quietly, "if you can persuade your family to give the lunch box back, they'd definitely get a reduced sentence."

"Really?" Imogen didn't want to get her hopes up again.

"Really. It's still worth trying to convince them."

Imogen smiled at him sadly. "Not sure how easy that's going to be," she said, "seeing as going to prison is the culmination of their lives' ambitions."

PC Donnelly put his hand on her shoulder. "If anyone can persuade them, it's you," he said. "You're a smart girl. You know what 'culmination' means."

"I'll try," said Imogen, feeling slightly better. "Thanks, Donovan."

Imogen dragged her feet as she walked back to Crim House. The sky was as gray as the streets of Blandington. It seemed as though the sun had realized what a terrible day it was and retreated behind the clouds. *Maybe I'll just give up, too,* thought Imogen. *Why should I bother trying to help my family? If the Code of the Crims meant anything to* them, *they'd be trying to help* me*—they'd be doing everything they could to get out of prison so that I could go back to Lilyworth.*

Imogen stopped walking, staring up at the unexciting trees and reminding herself of something her English teacher at Lilyworth had once said: "Imogen, your essay about the use of symbolic chickens in *Great Expectations* brought tears to my eyes. It made me ponder the meaning of my own existence. It's not every eleven-year-old who realizes that chickens are the perfect symbol for hope." Imogen breathed in, remembering her teacher's hand on her shoulder, and mouthed the words along with her memory. "Imogen, you have such a bright future ahead of you. You could run a company or a charity or an entire country. I hope that you'll stay at Lilyworth and try your very best. You can't let anyone or anything prevent you from realizing your full potential."

My full potential. Imogen opened her eyes. It occurred to her then that this wasn't about helping her family. This was about helping *herself.* She just had to get her family out of jail and prove them innocent—somehow—and then she could go back to Lilyworth and become head girl and destroy Bridget Sweetwine and then go on to run the *actual* world, as God intended.

And then she realized—it was Friday. Which meant the head girl election was only three weeks away. Which meant Imogen had less than fourteen days to find the lunch box and get her family to give it back to Jack Wooster and persuade the police to let them go and beg her head-mistress to let her come back to school, and deliver her incredible campaign speech to get all her fellow pupils to vote for her. . . . She felt dizzy. Her heart began to race.

Don't panic, Imogen, she told herself. *You can do this.* But she was panicking. Because she wanted to get out of Blandington more than she'd ever wanted anything, and she had absolutely no time to lose.

COMING BACK TO Crim House was the exact opposite of relaxing. Imogen walked into the living room, hoping to jump right on the computer and Google sightings of the missing lunch box and techniques for getting hardened criminals to repent their ways, but the living room was very much occupied. The Horrible Children were all there, sitting in a circle playing poker and smoking. Even Isabella was puffing on a cigarette, as if she'd been smoking since birth. Which she probably had, Imogen realized.

There were piles of unmarked banknotes on the table—at least £10,000, Imogen calculated. She was good at mental arithmetic, particularly when it involved stolen goods. She'd once had to calculate exactly how many croissants they'd need to steal to keep them going on the way home from a particularly difficult snail-smuggling trip to the south of France. Scattered among the banknotes were gold necklaces, silver bracelets, and some half-melted chocolate buttons.

Delia saw Imogen looking at the chocolate buttons. "That's Isabella's first haul!" she said, smiling at their little cousin fondly. "She stole them from a baby in the park all by herself!" She shifted over on the sofa and patted the space next to her. "You can play poker with us if you like," she said. "We've only just started. Isabella's a natural, but she might need a bit of help with her hand."

Imogen looked at Isabella. She was sitting on Henry's lap, chewing her cards and spitting them all over the floor.

Henry looked at the half-digested cards. "I think that would have been a royal flush," he said proudly.

"Thanks for the offer, but I don't fancy playing," said Imogen, though watching them did give her a pang of nostalgia. By the time she had left for Lilyworth, she'd been the family Texas Hold'em champion three years in a row. Her poker face had been so good that she'd had to learn how to smile all over again when she went to Lilyworth. But she'd given that all up. Future World Leaders don't gamble.

"Suit yourself," said Delia, pulling another cigarette out of the packet.

"Delia," said Imogen. "Seriously. When did you start smoking? And you're letting Isabella smoke? Haven't you heard of cancer?"

Delia laughed. "God, Imogen—you're so boring these days. Have one." She picked up the cigarette packet and held it out to Imogen.

Imogen took the packet. Now that she was looking at it closely, she could see that the cigarettes were made of candy. She took one and smiled despite herself. "I remember these!" she said. "Weren't they discontinued years ago?"

"Yes," said Delia, trying to sneak a look at Henry's hand. "But Uncle Clyde got a whole case of them in the Crunchybits Heist!"

Ah, the Crunchybits Heist. Imogen remembered it well. About five years previously, the Crims had broken into a sweets factory and stolen a truckload of candy cigarettes and licorice cigars and chocolate machetes. (Crunchybits specialized in making sweets that grandparents disapproved of. Grandparents who weren't Big Nana, that is—the toffee semiautomatic rifles were her favorite.) The Horrible Children had had a lot of dental work that year.

"Are you sure these are still safe to eat?" Imogen asked.

Delia scowled and snatched the packet back from Imogen. "What happened to you?" she said. "Don't you take *any* risks now?"

"Yes, actually," said Imogen, folding her arms. "On the way back from the police station this morning, I crossed the road without looking both ways."

Delia shook her head. "You're really not a Crim anymore, are you?" she said. "Why did you bother coming back here at all? Oh yeah, I forgot—because you're a massive tattletale who loves spoiling everyone else's fun."

"I am *not* a tattletale. . . ," started Imogen, her face flushing, but then Nate (or Nick) put down his cards and shouted "Four of a kind!" and Sam screeched "Cheater!" and Henry set fire to his cards and threw them on the floor, and Imogen got a bit distracted.

"Fire! Fire!" shouted Isabella, clapping her hands as Imogen and Delia stamped on the flames to put them out.

Imogen took a deep breath. She should be in her warm, safe room at Lilyworth, practicing her head girl acceptance speech. Instead, she was putting out a literal fire for the second time in twenty-four hours.

Then a thought came to her, cool and refreshing as a summer breeze: *This is not my problem.* Her cousins might be a mess, but they were Freddie's mess, not hers. She just had to focus on getting her family out of jail and winning back her place at school. She wasn't getting sucked back into any Crim drama. She wasn't going to let anyone or anything prevent her from reaching her full potential.

Not even arson.

Imogen left the Horrible Children in the living room fighting and shouting and giving themselves food poisoning. "Freddie?" she called. It was time for her to begin searching for the lunch box. And she knew just the place to start.

"In here!" shouted Freddie. She followed his voice down the hallway into the laundry room. He seemed to be climbing into the washing machine.

"It might be easier to have a shower," said Imogen.

Freddie emerged from the washing machine, hair rumpled, a pile of pale-pink clothes in his arms.

"Doing Delia's washing for her now, are you?" Imogen asked.

"This isn't Delia's," Freddie said miserably, holding up a single red sock. "What can I do for you, anyway?"

Very little, probably, Imogen thought, looking at Freddie's pink clothes and his wonky glasses and the sweater he'd managed to put on backward. "You might want to go to the living room," she said, turning to leave. And then she paused. *Maybe Delia is right,* she thought. *Maybe I* have *turned into a tattletale—although I prefer to think of myself as a whistle-blower.* She shook off her worry and turned back to Freddie. "You have to go and sort our cousins out before they kill us all," she said.

"I knew I shouldn't have left Delia in charge," Freddie said morosely as he slumped off down the hallway, knocking over a box of laundry powder on his way.

"By the way," Imogen called after him, "is the code to the Loot Cellar still the same as it used to be?"

Freddie stopped and turned to look at her. "Yes," he said. "Why?"

"No particular reason," Imogen said, cursing herself—the last thing she needed was Freddie interfering in her lunch box–finding mission.

And then a scream came from the direction of the living room, followed by a crash, followed by Isabella saying, "KNIFE! So shiny!," and Freddie dashed off.

Imogen hurried down the corridor, past the kitchen and the dungeon and the coin-counterfeiting room, until she reached the door to the cellar. If the Crims really *had* stolen the lunch box, this is where it would be. For as long as she could remember, the Crims had stored their stolen booty in the Loot Cellar. Each of them took the spoils of their crimes straight to the cellar after every heist or burglary or trip to the aquarium. And each of them had taken an oath to protect the location of the Loot Cellar *with their life*! Although unfortunately, Imogen considered for the first time, the name "Loot Cellar" was a bit of a giveaway, and pretty much anyone could have worked out it was in the basement of Crim House.

Big Nana had stolen the door to the Loot Cellar from a local circus school. It had a clown's face painted on the front and was completely terrifying. In the middle of the door, on the clown's red nose, was a complicated combination lock featuring numbers, letters, the Chinese alphabet, and pictures of the Smurfs (Big Nana had been a huge fan). Imogen took a deep breath and typed the code into the lock: "Papa Smurf," "Lazy Smurf," and the word "RECIDIVISM." The door popped open. Imogen's heart beat loudly in her ears as she stepped inside the cellar, shutting the door behind her.

She shivered. The Loot Cellar was freezing, partly because it had been carved out from beneath the house and partly because Freddie had a thing for stealing industrial-sized fridges and a terrible habit of leaving doors open. The cellar was far fuller now than it had been when Imogen had last visited it over two years before. She gazed up at the rows and rows of mostly useless items that had been stolen over the years—shelves and shelves of VHS tapes packaged in boxes that read "Blockbuster," a painted life-sized cow, countless sets of encyclopedias from the year 1994, a badly stuffed otter . . . She felt her stomach twist as she caught sight of the first thing she had ever stolen—a packet of balloons that she'd taken from another child's treat bag back at Delia's fifth birthday party. She took them down from the shelf and looked at them fondly. She bet Isabella would get a kick out of blowing them up and then bursting them. Then she shook off the thought. *I'm not getting sucked back in.*

And then, in the gloom, Imogen saw something else—a painting. She stepped toward it, and gasped—it was Rembrandt's *The Storm on the Sea of Galilee,* famously stolen from the Isabella Stewart Gardner Museum in Boston by thieves dressed as police officers. Big Nana had taught all the Crim children about art history, so they'd be able to appreciate beautiful works of art before they slashed the canvasses and sold them to the highest bidder. Imogen had never really believed her hopeless relatives could pull off a sophisticated art theft . . . but here was the evidence, right in front of her. *Is it possible? Maybe I really* have *been underestimating them. . . .*

Imogen walked gingerly over to the painting. She leaned down to pick it up—but it fell over. And that's when she realized that it wasn't a painting at all—it was just a poster of *The Storm on the Sea of Galilee* that someone had stuck over a picture of a crying clown on black velvet.

Imogen sighed. She felt a rush of relief. *Of course* there wasn't anything really valuable in the Loot Cellar. Except the lunch box, supposedly. But even if that *was* here, how was she going to find it among the eight track players and Bart Simpson T-shirts and disturbing amateur taxidermy?

Which is when someone cleared his throat behind her.

Imogen spun around guiltily to find Freddie standing there, framed in the doorway. "Can I help you?" he asked.

Imogen paused. There was a steeliness to Freddie's voice that she hadn't heard before. "How are the Horrible Children?" she asked, filling time while she figured out how much she was going to tell him.

"Slightly less horrible," said Freddie. "I told them off and settled them down in front of a Postman Pat DVD."

Imogen tried to imagine her criminally minded cousins sitting quietly in front of a show for preschoolers, but she couldn't—that seemed about as likely as Big Nana coming back from the dead or Aunt Bets being voted president of the local Womens' Institute.

"So . . . *is* there something I can help you with?" Freddie said again. "Sorry if you've already told me. Memory's not been the same since I forgot how tall I was and hit my head on the ceiling this morning. Mind you, I suppose it wasn't all that great before that. . . ."

"Yes, actually," said Imogen, deciding that honesty was the best policy. "I'm looking for the stolen lunch box. Do you have any idea where it might be?"

"Of course I don't!" said Freddie. "I'm me! Why do

you need to find it, anyway?"

"If we give it back to Jack Wooster, maybe we can get the adults out of jail. And we won't have to look after the Horrible Children anymore."

"I like your thinking," said Freddie, nodding. "I'll help look. You take the back half of the cellar, and I'll search in the front."

Imogen nodded and walked to the darkest, dampest, most disturbing corner at the back of the cellar, where the very first stolen goods were stored. She felt a prickle of awe as she looked around at the reminders of her family's criminal legacy—there was so much history here in this room. She picked up what looked like a Tudor ruff and called to Freddie excitedly. "Do you think one of our ancestors stole this?"

Freddie turned to look at it and hit his forehead with the palm of his hand. "That's where it is! I was supposed to wear that to play the Ghost of Christmas Past in last year's Crim Family Pantomime, but I couldn't find it anywhere, so I was recast as a 'Kicking Boy.'"

"What's a 'Kicking Boy'?" asked Imogen, handing him the ruff.

"It's a boy who everyone kicks."

"That's not a real thing, is it?"

"I don't think so," Freddie said sadly, shoving the ruff into his pocket and failing to notice when it fell out of the hole in the bottom. "I think Nick and Nate made it up so they could get back at me for getting them mixed up all the time. My bottom was quite sore by the end of the show."

Imogen made a mental note to try to work out which twin was which once and for all. "The Crim Family Pantomime won't be much good this year if everyone is in jail, will it?" she said. But Freddie had already walked back to the front of the cellar and was busily sorting through a shelf of broken saucers.

It took a very long time for Imogen to finish searching her half of the cellar. Her arms had started to ache from reaching up to take things from shelves, and her eyes had started to hurt from looking at so many hideous, pointless, worthless objects. She stood up and brushed the dust from her hands. "Haven't found anything," she called to Freddie. "You?"

"*I've* found something!" he said.

Imogen felt her heart leap in anticipation as her cousin appeared from behind a broken cuckoo clock, carrying some sort of scroll. *Not the lunch box, then. Maybe some sort of paperwork that says where it was stored?* He came closer, passing it to Imogen, being careful not to tear it.

She opened it slowly. And then she looked at Freddie, as disappointed as she had been when she'd realized that

Father Crimemas wasn't real.

"What?" said Freddie, still smiling. "It's a Magic Eye poster!"

"What does it have to do with the lunch box?" Imogen asked.

"Nothing!" Freddie said cheerfully. "But it's so cool. Look at it again and relax your eyes. Can you see the tiger?"

Imogen reached out to smack him, but he dodged away, surprisingly quickly for someone so uncoordinated.

Imogen put her head in her hands and sank to the floor, leaning against a full-size cardboard cutout of the cast of *Home Alone 7: Slightly Disoriented in Milwaukee.* She motioned for Freddie to sit down next to her. "Look," she said. "I just don't get it. If Uncle Clyde and the others *did* steal the lunch box, it should be in here. Right?"

"Right," said Freddie.

"But I've checked my entire section."

"And I've checked mine!" Freddie said proudly.

"Unless they've hidden the lunch box inside something else?" said Imogen.

"Ooh," said Freddie. "You *are* good at thinking, aren't you?"

"Come on," said Imogen, turning to him. "Try to help me out here. What *do* you remember about the day of The Heist?"

Freddie shrugged. "Obviously I completely forgot that

The Heist was happening at all," he said, "seeing as I didn't turn up at Wooster Mansion and do what I was meant to do." He pulled his phone out of his pocket (the one without the hole in it) and sighed. "I really don't know how I forgot that, though. I usually set a phone alarm for important things." He passed his phone to Imogen. Four alarms were going off at the same time: "Get mole checked out," "Pick Imogen up from the station," "Brush teeth," and "Take the roast out of the oven."

"You've turned the sound off," said Imogen, passing his phone back to him. "That might be why you haven't noticed the alarms."

"Good point," said Freddie, fiddling with the phone.

"By the way, I can actually smell smoke," said Imogen, sniffing.

Freddie glanced at the ceiling, as though he might see through it into the kitchen. "I think I put the roast in the oven yesterday," he said. "Yesterday was Tuesday, right?"

"Yesterday was Thursday," Imogen said.

"Ah," said Freddie, standing up. "Excuse me just a moment!" He put the phone back into his pocket—the one with the hole in it this time—and it fell to the floor as he ran out of the room. Imogen started to say something, then thought better of it. Instead, she scooted over, picked it up, and slipped Freddie's phone into her pocket.

While Freddie was gone, Imogen began to search his half of the cellar, just in case he'd missed something, which wasn't exactly beyond the realm of possibility. After about half an hour, she came across something interesting. Not the lunch box—she was becoming more and more convinced that it wasn't in the cellar at all—but the criminal plans journal Big Nana had made her keep when she was a kid. Big Nana gave each Crim a blank notebook for their fifth birthdays to record their ideas for future crimes. She encouraged them to "use their crimaginations" to decorate the front of their notebooks, too. Henry had defaced his with graffiti and burns, Delia's was covered in signed photos of her favorite master criminals, but Big Nana had been most proud of the way Imogen had decorated her journal—she had written "Photographs of My Favorite Verrucae" on the front. "That way no one will ever want to look inside," she'd told Big Nana. Big Nana had kissed her on the forehead and said, "You're the pomegranate of my eye." (Big Nana didn't like apples.)

Imogen opened her criminal plans journal and flicked through the pages, smiling as she read through some of her old ideas: a plan to steal Uncle Knuckles's false teeth and use them as hair clips, a scheme to replace Freddie's cologne with bathroom cleaner so he smelled a bit like a toilet all day, and a plot to hack into the police's walkie-talkies, pretending to be their chief constable, so she could shout at them and get them to call her "ma'am." She still quite fancied giving that plan a go, actually . . . but she was getting distracted. She had to focus on finding evidence of The Heist.

She slapped the journal shut and took out Freddie's phone. It was protected by a password. *If I were Freddie, what would my password be?* she asked herself. *Maybe it's "FREDDIE"? No . . . no one would use their own name as a password. . . .* Except Freddie, it turned out—the phone unlocked as soon as she tapped it in. Imogen went to the calendar and looked back through the days, searching for the alarm Freddie would have set to remind himself to take part in The Heist. Her family had only just been arrested, so The Heist must have taken place some time in the last couple of months. But she went back through the whole of the previous year, and she didn't find a single reminder about The Heist. Maybe Freddie hadn't set one at all? But that was unlikely, she thought, as she flicked past reminders saying "Go to the toilet," "Eat breakfast before it gets dark," and the one he'd set that day: "Collect Imogen's bags from station." Could that mean— No. Her family was crazy, but surely they weren't crazy enough to serve time for a crime that someone else had committed? They had seemed so *proud* earlier. And she wanted to believe that they could pull off The Heist. But—

"Sorry! That took a bit longer than I expected," said Freddie, stumbling back into the cellar, his hands and face covered in bandages.

"Are you okay?" Imogen asked, slipping his phone back into her pocket. "Was the roast on fire?"

Freddie looked confused for a moment, and then he said, "Oh—the roast! No. It looks like I forgot to put the roast *into* the oven, too. But the cousins set the back porch on fire. Again. But it's fine! Totally fine. I caught it before the fire consumed the steps. It's just a bit smolder-y now."

"Right."

"Anyway, the kids are all cozied up together on the sofa, watching the *Madagascar* DVD. That's their favorite."

Imogen couldn't help being suspicious. "Have you definitely taken the lighter away from them this time?"

"Yes."

"And the matches?"

"Of course."

"And the blowtorch?"

Freddie put his hands on his hips. "Imogen," he said. "We can't *completely* stifle their freedom of expression!"

Imogen put her hands on her hips, too. "Freddie," she said, "you are hopeless!"

"That's not true," said Freddie. "I have a lot of hopes. I hope that the cousins will behave themselves. . . . I hope the grown-ups will be coming home soon. . . . I hope there'll be spaghetti Bolognese for dinner—you don't happen to know how to make that, do you?"

Imogen decided not to respond to that. "You have to hire a babysitter," she said in her best head girl voice. "Preferably with some experience in the youth justice system."

Freddie looked at her for a moment. "That is actually not a bad idea," he said, nodding slowly.

"Of course it isn't," Imogen said, offended. "I never have bad ideas."

"Except that time you tried to steal Uncle Knuckles's teeth and use them as hair clips."

"Come on . . . That was ingenious," she said, a little put out. "Anyway, look at this." Imogen pulled Freddie's phone out of her pocket and showed him the calendar screen. "What do you see?"

"Numbers and dates."

"Okay. What *don't* you see?"

"I don't see lots of things. I don't see a penguin, or a no-smoking sign, or a Turkish carpet, or—"

"Or any notes about The Heist?"

"Or that."

Imogen sighed. "When did The Heist actually happen, anyway? Was it last week? Last month?"

Freddie pulled his thinking face. It looked uncomfortable, like he didn't think very often. "I'm not sure," he said. "There is a date that sticks out to me for some reason—December 25. No, wait, that was Crimenas. . . ."

"Do you even remember being asked to take part in The Heist?"

Freddie thought again. "I don't think I do," he said.

"Do you remember the other Crims coming home very excited one day? Maybe as though they had just pulled off the heist that Uncle Clyde had been dreaming about for twenty years?"

Freddie frowned. "There was one night a few weeks ago when everyone was very happy about something. . . . We had some balloons and cake and presents."

"Presents?"

"No, wait! That was Isabella's birthday. You should have seen her—she was adorable. She took the cake and threw it—"

"FREDDIE!" yelled Imogen. A horrible certainty was coming over her.

"YES?" Freddie yelled back. "WHY ARE WE SHOUTING?"

"BECAUSE I'M GETTING ANNOYED WITH YOU!" yelled Imogen.

"YOU ARE?" yelled Freddie.

"Yes," Imogen said more quietly; her throat was getting a bit sore. "Listen: We can't find the lunch box. There's no evidence of The Heist on your phone. You have no memory of anything strange or unusual or exciting happening.

Do you know what this means?"

Freddie looked confused for a moment. And then his eyes lit up, like cheap fairy lights. "It means I have narcolepsy!" he said.

"NO!" yelled Imogen, shaking her head in frustration. "It means . . ."

"THERE WAS NO HEIST!" yelled Imogen.

"THERE WASN'T?" Freddie yelled back.

"No!"

"So I'm not a narcoleptic?"

"Probably not!"

"But you're still annoyed with me?"

"A little bit!" shouted Imogen. "But I'm more annoyed with the others. I can't believe they've confessed to a crime they haven't committed."

"*I* can believe it," said Freddie, looking thoughtful. "Do you remember when Uncle Knuckles learned Italian and went around eating ice cream all the time so people would think he was a mafia boss?"

"Sadly, yes," said Imogen, her mind still buzzing. So her family really *was* innocent. She hadn't underestimated them—or *over*estimated them—or, well, she wasn't sure anymore. Once again, she was surprised to find herself feeling disappointed that her family hadn't actually pulled off the crime. But she shook that thought away—this was a good thing. Her family was every bit as useless as she'd assumed, which meant she didn't have to get them off for a crime they'd actually committed—she just had to prove that they hadn't pulled off The Heist. She'd be back at Lilyworth in no time.

Except, she realized . . . she had no real plan for *how* to prove that. Where would she even start? If her family didn't know where the lunch box was—and if they kept insisting on taking credit for a crime they hadn't committed—how was she ever going to get out of this mess?

Imogen went to bed early that night. As she lay there, listening to Delia and the twins chatting in the living room below, she thought about her dorm room at Lilyworth. Lucy and Alice were probably eating chocolate and reading ghost stories by flashlight, laughing at Catherine's snoring. They would probably stay up far too late without Imogen to tell them when it was time for lights-out.

No matter, though. This time next week she'd be back there with them.

She *had* to be.

The alternative was too awful to even think about.

The next morning, Imogen put on her best twinset and her most serious facial expression and walked back to the police station. She ignored the jeers of the police officers and marched to the cells to see her family.

They were all asleep. They actually looked quite sweet when they were asleep—even Aunt Bets. Her head was resting on Uncle Knuckles's shoulder, like she was an ordinary old lady rather than someone who had once stolen the playground from the local park because she "hated the sound of happy children."

Imogen rattled on the bars to wake them up.

"Darling!" said Josephine, rubbing her eyes. "What are you doing here?"

"You know what I'm doing here," Imogen replied in her best Future World Leader voice.

The Crims looked at one another, their faces blank—except her father, who looked at the floor.

"I know," said Josephine. "Have you come to bring us some of those lovely chocolate croissants from the bakery down the road?"

"No," said Imogen, getting impatient.

"You want to tell us how brilliant we are for pulling off such an impressive crime?" said Uncle Clyde, raising his extremely large eyebrows.

"Pretty much the opposite, actually," said Imogen. She crossed her arms. "Come on. Admit it—PC Phillips won't hear you. There wasn't really a heist, was there?"

Josephine gasped. "Darling! How *could* you? Of *course* there was a heist!" She picked up a newspaper and held it up so Imogen could see the front page. Her family was there, grinning out at the camera. The angle was a little unfortunate—Imogen could see right up her mother's nostrils. "See?" said Josephine. "We're on the front page again today! Not the most flattering of photos, but that's the paparazzi for you! The point is, would the *Blandington Times* really pay so much attention to a crime that didn't happen? I think not!"

"So maybe there *was* a heist," Imogen said slowly.

"*Thank* you," said Josephine.

"The lunch box was clearly stolen."

"Precisely!" said Josephine, sitting down and crossing her legs.

"But you weren't the ones to steal it."

There was a silence.

Imogen watched her family intently to see how they'd react.

Josephine was staring at her nails. Al looked relieved, Imogen thought, and seemed to smile at her with a hint of pride. But Uncle Clyde seemed very, very angry indeed. He marched up to the bars and rattled them.

"*Excuse me*, young lady!" he said. "How *dare* you suggest we didn't pull off The Heist? I was only working on it, refining it, thinking of ways to involve pigs in it, for twenty *years*. Or isn't that enough time for us to get it right?"

Imogen maintained a dignified silence.

"Oh, I get it," said Uncle Clyde, with a nasty laugh. "You think we couldn't have pulled it off because you weren't around to help. Is that it? You don't think we're clever enough to do it without you."

Pretty much, thought Imogen, but she didn't say that, because she could see Aunt Bets sharpening a knitting needle behind him.

"You think we're nothing without Big Nana, don't you? You don't think we could pull off a crime of this scale without her."

Right again, thought Imogen, but she didn't say that either, because Aunt Bets had pulled a hairpin out of her wiry gray hair, and she was sharpening that, too.

"Well, let me tell you something, Little Miss Perfect. I'm a CRIM! Crime runs *through my veins*, just like it runs through yours—even though you've spent the last two years trying to *deny* it! And getting that Captain Crook lunch box back has always been . . . MY DESTI-NYYYYYYYYYYYYYYYYYYY!"

Imogen jumped back from the bars instinctively as Uncle Clyde knelt on the floor and screamed, shaking his fists at the ceiling.

She didn't quite know how to respond. Imogen had never seen her uncle this upset before. Maybe she *had* underestimated Uncle Clyde, after all? He'd certainly put enough work into planning The Heist, ridiculous as it was. She sighed to herself. She'd changed her mind so many times in the past few days that she really didn't know *what* to think anymore. "I'm sorry," she said carefully. "You're right—I should never have doubted my own family."

"Well. Good," Uncle Clyde said gruffly, still on his knees.

"You can get up now," Imogen said.

"I know," said Uncle Clyde.

"You need someone to help you up, don't you?" asked Imogen.

Uncle Clyde nodded. "Just wait till you turn forty," he said. "It's all downhill from there."

Al and Uncle Knuckles pulled Uncle Clyde up from the floor and helped him back to the bench.

"As I was saying," said Imogen, "I'm really sorry for doubting you. It's just that I looked in the Loot Cellar and the lunch box wasn't there." She watched her family. If they really had stolen the lunch box, this news would be a blow. But they didn't look that concerned.

"It wasn't?" asked Uncle Clyde.

Imogen shook her head.

"Huh. Well, it is quite a small object," Uncle Clyde said thoughtfully.

"I suppose so," said Imogen.

"Also." Uncle Clyde looked down and brushed some dust off the knees of his pants. "You were right: We didn't steal it." He picked up his notebook and started to doodle.

Imogen grasped the bars with both hands, her jaw dropping. *"Yes!"* she shouted, pumping her fist. "I *knew* it! Okay, then . . . why are you telling everyone that you *did* steal it?"

"Well, it's merely a minor technicality," said Uncle Clyde, putting down his notebook. "I still *planned* The Heist. It's just that someone else pulled it off! That means we're still responsible for the crime, right? The plan worked. We're still famous criminals!"

"No you're not! You're *stupid* criminals!" said Imogen, exasperated. "If you didn't pull off The Heist, you're innocent—but someone wants you to take the blame. Didn't you read the papers? Whoever did it followed your plan *to the letter.* They even left the Crims' signature inside the front door so everyone would think it was you."

When her family still looked at her blankly, Imogen shook her head. “Don’t you get it?” she asked.

“OI! GET WHAT?” demanded Uncle Knuckles.

Imogen sighed and shook her head. “This wasn’t a coincidence. *The Crims were framed!*”

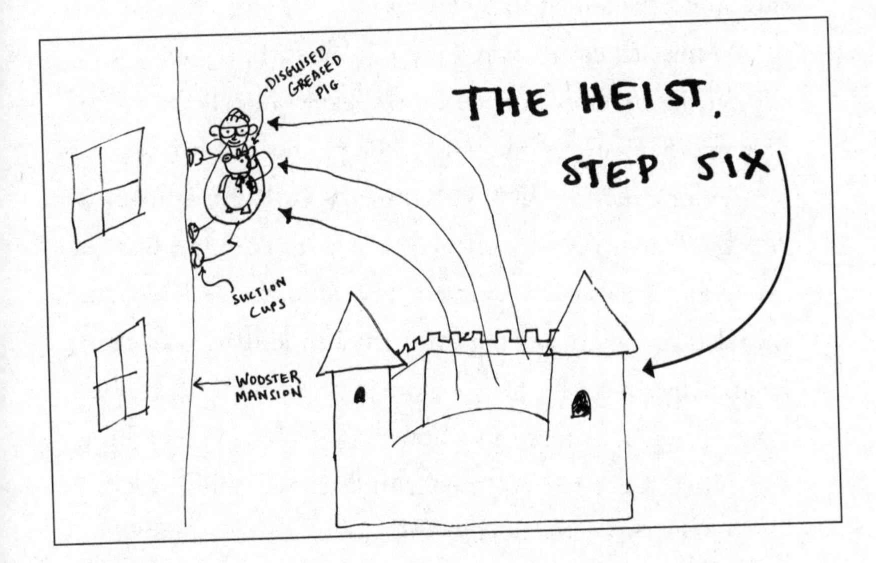

THE AFTERNOON IMOGEN spent at the police station trying to persuade her family to confess their innocence was one of the longest of her life, and she had once taken part in an interpretive dance workshop involving puppets. She tried bribing her relatives and flattering them and attempting to convince them that they'd still have to serve time even if they *hadn't* stolen the lunch box, but Josephine insisted that "wasting police time" wasn't a glamorous enough crime and refused to back down while Al tried to soothe her with a neck rub, mouthing "sorry" at Imogen. Eventually, Imogen gave up and walked back home to Crim House starving, completely exhausted, and thoroughly ashamed to be a Crim.

As she picked her way up the front path, trying not to slip on the marbles or slide on the banana peels the twins planted there every morning, her phone buzzed with a text from Freddie: **Are you nearly home? Dinner's ready!** Her stomach clenched. Freddie's cooking was, as one could imagine, very, very bad indeed. He had once mistaken Isabella's toy pig for a chicken and tried to roast it, and that was one of his more successful attempts. But when Imogen entered the house, she smelled something she didn't associate with the Crim kitchen—edible food.

Before she could walk into the living room, Freddie poked his head around the door. "Chinese!" he said, holding up some takeaway bags. "A man just turned up and handed it to me. Amazing! I didn't even have to pay for it!"

"Do you think he might have delivered it to the wrong house by mistake?" Imogen asked, taking the bags from him and carrying them to the table.

"Possibly," said Freddie, frowning. "He did keep calling me Mr. Murphy, but I assumed that was a term of endearment."

Ten minutes later, Imogen was sitting on the sofa, eating hot, spicy noodles and duck with sweet plum sauce, feeling almost happy for the first time in days. Good food had that effect on Imogen—even when everything else was awful, a mouthful of truly delicious food could make everything okay for a few moments—until she remembered that she'd stained her favorite cardigan or fallen out with her best friend or been kicked out of school for being a master criminal. When the pleasure of the first few bites had worn off, she realized something: She couldn't see or hear or smell the Horrible Children. "Where are the cousins?" she asked Freddie.

"They wanted to get to bed nice and early tonight," said Freddie, spooning some more duck onto his plate. "Said they were exhausted. Anyway, don't worry about them—tell me more about what happened at the jail."

"There isn't that much more to tell," she said, ignoring the very loud alarm bells going off in her head about her cousins. "Uncle Clyde admitted they didn't do it. Someone else pulled off The Heist."

"I can't believe it!" Freddie said, shaking his head. "I mean, I suppose it makes sense—I have no memory of it whatsoever—but then I can't remember putting my underpants on this morning, and there they are!" He looked down his trousers and frowned.

"You're not wearing any, are you?" said Imogen.

Freddie shook his head. Then he shrugged and helped himself to more noodles. "I suppose The Heist being a fake is good news for you, at least?"

"Yep," said Imogen. "I'm going to write to my headmistress tonight and tell her. But she won't believe me till I've proved it. She practically thinks I'm Al Capone."

"It must be wonderful to have someone think so highly of you," said Freddie.

Just then, the doorbell sang. (Most doorbells chime rather than sing, obviously, but that would have been too ordinary for the Crims—their doorbell featured Big Nana singing "Willkommen" in an extremely threatening, incredibly unwelcoming, minor key.) Imogen felt the hairs on her arms stand on end—she hadn't heard Big Nana's voice for over two years. It was almost as though her grandmother was back in the house with them.

"Are you expecting anyone?" Imogen asked when the doorbell had stopped singing (about ten minutes later—it was quite a long song).

"No."

"So who would turn up out of the blue at this time of night?"

"Search me!" said Freddie, holding his arms out so Imogen could frisk him.

She didn't. "You definitely didn't invite anyone over?" she asked instead.

Freddie looked at his phone. "Oh! Yes I did! Remember how you said we should hire a babysitter?"

"I do remember, yes," said Imogen.

"Well, I asked Delia to post an ad on blandthings.com."

Blandthings.com was a local website that people used to advertise jobs and secondhand furniture. Most things on there were pretty boring—there were sale notices for gray sofas and meditation courses, and solicitations for people to watch paint dry. Imogen had a feeling that Delia's ad would have stood out a bit.

"What does the post have to do with the doorbell?" Imogen asked as Big Nana broke into song again.

"Well, I've had quite a few replies to the advert, and I've set up some interviews for this evening. Sorry—forgot to mention it sooner."

"A *few* interviews?"

"Seven." Freddie picked at the duck with his chopsticks without looking up.

"SEVEN?"

"The first one is right now. I guess we'd better get started!"

"WE?"

"You don't mind helping me, do you?" said Freddie. "It's just that I might forget to ask them something important."

Imogen groaned. "But I have to write that letter to my headmistress! And I'm exhausted! And anyway, anyone who would reply to an advert written by Delia is probably quite mad and extremely dangerous."

"That might not be the worst thing in the world. . . . They'll have to control the Horrible Children, after all."

Imogen had to admit he had a point.

"Actually, some of the applicants are very interesting and don't sound *that* dangerous," said Freddie. "*Please* help?" He looked at her the way Delia had when she'd begged Imogen to take the blame for the ice cream van theft. Imogen suddenly saw the family resemblance between them, and she felt an unfamiliar, sad sort of feeling deep inside her. At first she thought it was indigestion, but then she realized it was sympathy.

I must be going soft, she thought. But she said, "Fine."

Freddie hugged her, which was a little bit painful, as he was still holding his chopsticks.

"We'd better answer the door," Imogen said. "Whoever it is has been standing out there for quite a while now, and it probably won't be long before the snakes get them."

The next three hours passed in a blur of shaved heads and prison tattoos and disturbing facial expressions.

The first candidate was Nigel, who had just been released from prison after serving time for twenty different crimes and was trying to start a new life in a quiet town. When Imogen asked him how he'd go about breaking up a fight between the twins, he scratched his armpit and said, "I'd bang their heads together till they made up.

That's my signature move, see?"

Then there was Mary, who had just been released from prison for serving kitten burgers at her fast-food restaurant and wanted to make a new start somewhere peaceful. When Freddie asked whether she'd be happy to cook for the kids, she said, "Oh yes. I'm very resourceful when it comes to ingredients, too. It's amazing what you can pick up on the street or at the pet shop."

And then there was Jamila, who had just been released from prison for dangerous driving and wanted to start over in a nice, safe neighborhood. (Imogen was sensing a theme among the candidates.) When Imogen asked why she had applied for the babysitting job, she said, "I like to challenge myself. I do one thing every day that scares me and other people." And then she smiled, and Imogen noticed that her front tooth was carved into the shape of a skull.

When Imogen had slammed the door on the seventh and final candidate (Leon, who wasn't a criminal, amazingly enough, but who asked whether Freddie and Imogen would be okay with him performing a few scientific experiments on the children), she sighed. "I guess our cousins have a bit of a reputation," she said. "Also, is it me, or has Blandington become a retirement village for ex-prisoners?"

"I know," said Freddie. "And they all want to work with *us*! It's quite flattering, really."

"It's not flattering!" said Imogen, slumping on the sofa. "It's a disaster! Clearly everyone else has rejected them, but they think we'll employ them because we're criminals too."

"But we *will* employ one of them, won't we?" said Freddie. "What did you think of Jade? She likes to make bombs, sure, but she could probably help the kids with their chemistry homework."

"No!" said Imogen. "We can't put a criminal in charge of the Horrible Children."

"You're right," Freddie said sadly. "The children would be a very bad influence on them." He flopped down on the sofa next to Imogen, defeated. "I guess *I'll* just have to carry on looking after them."

"That's a terrible idea," said Imogen. But she didn't have a better one. She looked at her watch. It was almost midnight.

"It's okay. I'll do it properly this time," said Freddie. "I'll buy *at least* three new DVDs for them to watch—they have a two-for-one offer on wrestling videos down the road—and I'll get some hammers and drills and wood for them to play with when they get bored. If we're lucky, we might get a nice bookshelf out of it."

Imogen sat perfectly still, trying to stop herself from responding. She knew what she had to do. Somehow, in between figuring out who had carried out The Heist, clearing her family's name, winning back her place at Lilyworth, writing the perfect speech to put Bridget Sweetwine in her place, and choreographing some kind of comeback walk to use when she reentered school, she was going to have to find time to look after the Horrible Children. She didn't want to do it—she didn't even *like* her cousins most of the time—but the last thing she needed was for more of her relatives to end up in jail or for her family home to burn down or for one of her cousins to drown while trying to steal a goldfish.

"Freddie," she said reluctantly. "I suppose *I* could—"

But that's when the doorbell went again.

Imogen looked at Freddie.

Freddie looked at his phone. "Oh!" he said. "Silly me—I'd forgotten, I actually scheduled *eight* interviews."

"Eight?"

"That's right!"

Freddie bounced up off the sofa and rushed to open the front door. Imogen followed behind, looking at the figure silhouetted behind the cracked glass of the front door. *Who would even come to a babysitting interview at midnight?* The mystery candidate was tiny and seemed to be wearing a strange little hat. Was it some sort of . . . elf?

Freddie opened the front door.

The person on the doorstep was not an elf, luckily, though that would have been fun for a while.

The person on the doorstep was the most perfect babysitter anyone could have dreamed up, even if they'd eaten a lot of cheese the night before.

She was just old enough to be grandmotherly but spry enough to run after children who had just committed a bank robbery. Her eyes were a lovely shade of brown—the color of cocoa or a really friendly dog. She seemed warm and loving, but she had an air of mischief about her—good, wholesome mischief, Imogen thought, as though she might make you a midnight feast or let you stay up late to watch TV or let you name your teddy bear "Fartypants." And the little velvet hat perched on her perfect graying curls made her seem like someone from a different, more innocent time, when everyone was polite to one another and no one framed anyone for a crime they hadn't committed.

Imogen loved her at once. She wanted the babysitter to run her a hot bath and plait her hair and then maybe adopt her. But instead, she held out her hand and said, "Pleased to meet you. I'm Imogen Crim."

"The pleasure's all mine!" said the babysitter, with a wonderful, crinkly smile. "I'm Henny Teakettle. Would you like me to take off my shoes before I come in?"

Imogen had never heard a more comforting name or a more comforting voice or more comforting words. "Definitely don't take your shoes off," she said. "You might step on a toy car or brass knuckles or something."

Imogen and Freddie led Mrs. Teakettle through to the living room, where she sat down in an armchair with a satisfied "Oof!"

"So," said Freddie, looking at his list of questions. "Tell us a bit about yourself."

"Well," said Mrs. Teakettle, folding her hands on her lap. "Where to begin? I've looked after children all my life. I used to be a teacher, and then when I retired, I looked after my own grandchildren—they were ever so naughty at first, but I straightened them out. Now they're all grown up, and I just miss having young people around. I love children." She laughed a lovely laugh, like the sound an apple crumble would make if it could.

"Have you heard anything about these *particular* children?" Imogen asked.

"Ooh, no," said Mrs. Teakettle. "I'm new in Blandington—I decided it was time for me to sell my house and move into a nice little flat. My husband died, you see."

"Oh," Imogen and Freddie said sympathetically.

"But I've just bought a puppy!"

"Ah!"

"But I do still get very lonely."

"Oh."

"But you can't be lonely around children, can you?"

"No," said Imogen. She braced herself. "You know you said your grandchildren were naughty? How naughty are we talking—won't-keep-quiet-during-math sort of naughty? Or . . . can't-be-trusted-around-knives sort of naughty?"

"Oh, they were little tearaways," said Mrs. Teakettle, smiling fondly. "But I like challenging children best of all—they're the most rewarding. What they really need is a mix of love and boundaries—"

That was enough for Freddie. "You're hired," he said, picking up the other CVs from the pile of papers next to his chair and throwing them into the wastepaper basket.

"Thank you very much!" said Mrs. Teakettle. She heaved herself out of the armchair and shook hands with Imogen and Freddie. "Would you like me to start on Monday?"

"Tomorrow, if you can," said Imogen as Freddie led the way to the front door and opened it.

But then Imogen looked over Mrs. Teakettle's shoulder into the front garden—and saw something moving.

"Freddie," she said, grabbing his arm. "What's that?"

"A fox?" said Freddie.

Whatever was in the front garden tripped over something and swore.

"Foxes don't use four-letter words," said Imogen.

"Allow me," said Mrs. Teakettle, whipping a flashlight out of her handbag and shining it into the garden.

There, frozen in the beam of light, were the Horrible Children, all dressed in black, staggering under the weight of a pinball machine. They were all wearing the balaclavas Aunt Bets had knitted for them, but it was still easy to tell who was who—Delia's curly hair was escaping from beneath hers, Henry's balaclava was riddled with burn holes, Sam's Adam's apple was visible beneath his, and the twins' eyes reflected the flashlight identically.

"So *these* are the little darlings," said Mrs. Teakettle.

Imogen scowled at Freddie. "I thought you said they were in bed," she hissed.

"They must have gotten up," said Freddie.

"Wait," said Imogen, looking around. "Where's Isabella?"

"Is she this speedy little lady?" asked Mrs. Teakettle, dropping her handbag and scooping up Isabella, who was crawling toward the piranha pond. Mrs. Teakettle turned toward the other Horrible Children, with Isabella tucked under her arm, and shone her flashlight at each of them in turn. "I think you've got some explaining to do," she said. Her voice was still comforting, but there was something worrying about it now, like a delicious-looking cream cake that's two weeks past its sell-by date.

"Who are you?" squeaked Sam.

"*I'm* asking the questions today, young man," said Mrs. Teakettle.

The Horrible Children stared at Mrs. Teakettle, mouths open.

"I want answers, and I want them now," said Mrs. Teakettle, shining her flashlight into Delia's eyes. "Where did you get this pinball machine?"

"It was a gift," said Delia, shielding her eyes.

"*True* answers, please," said Mrs. Teakettle.

"We bought it," said one of the twins. "There's nothing fun to do in the house, and Freddie and Imogen won't let us go to the skate park or *anything*."

"There isn't a skate park anymore," Imogen told Mrs. Teakettle. "Sam got banned for letting his pet rats loose on the ramps, so he called the council pretending to be the mayor and got them to shut it down."

Mrs. Teakettle shone her flashlight into Sam's eyes. "Good at impressions, are you, young man?"

"Not so much anymore," said Sam, sounding like a miserable donkey.

"I see," said Mrs. Teakettle.

She moved the flashlight's beam away from Sam and shone it at Henry, who had been trying to scrape his name into the pinball machine. "That's quite enough of that," she said. Henry abruptly dropped the pen he'd been using.

Mrs. Teakettle sighed. "My dear children," she said. "You all look very tired. Are you tired?"

The Horrible Children nodded.

"Would you like to go inside now?"

The Horrible Children nodded again.

"Would you like me to stop shining this light into your eyes?"

The Horrible Children nodded for the third time.

"Then you'd better own up to stealing this pinball machine from the Primrose."

Sam gasped. "How did you know we got it from the pub?"

Mrs. Teakettle shone her flashlight on the side of the pinball machine.

"I can't see anything," said Sam.

Nor could Imogen. But when she stepped toward the pinball to take a closer look, she saw that there, stamped on the side, was a tiny yellow flower with the words "The Primrose Pub" in the middle.

Imogen and Freddie looked at each other and grinned. Mrs. Teakettle was *good.*

The Horrible Children slumped. Mrs. Teakettle had won.

"Here's what's going to happen," said Mrs. Teakettle, smiling a little too sweetly. "We're all going to the pub to return the pinball machine, and you'll promise never to steal from them again. Okay?"

"Okay," chanted the Horrible Children.

Mrs. Teakettle looked at Isabella. "Do you need to do a wee before we go to the pub?" she asked.

"Pub!" said Isabella. "Drink!"

"Not for you!" said Mrs. Teakettle, shaking her head happily. "Underage drinking is a terrible idea, unless you're on a cruise ship. Anything goes on a cruise ship. Right—follow me!" And she waddled up the front path, stepping over a straitjacket and several bottles marked "Poison."

"Wait!" said Freddie, hurrying after Mrs. Teakettle. "Let me pay you for your time!"

"Don't worry," said Mrs. Teakettle, smiling again. "I don't mind going to the Primrose. I could do with a pint, anyway! See you tomorrow!"

Imogen and Freddie stood on the doorstep and watched the Horrible Children snake down the hill after Mrs. Teakettle, like rats following the Pied Piper.

"Isn't she wonderful?" said Freddie. "Sometimes things really do work out for the best."

"She's probably a serial killer," said Imogen.

"Well, if one or two of the cousins went missing, it might not be the *worst* thing in the world," said Freddie. "There are an awful lot of them."

"That's a bit harsh, Freddie," said Imogen.

"Sorry," said Freddie, yawning. "I'm getting grumpy—I think it's time for bed."

Imogen woke up the next morning after her first good night's sleep in days. Mrs. Teakettle would be taking care of the kids today, so they were *officially* not her problem anymore. She could get on with clearing her family's name and getting out of this cursed town. As soon as she was dressed, she walked to the Blandington Bakery to buy a box of doughnuts to take to the police station.

PC Phillips was the only officer on duty that day. He was fiddling with something on his desk as Imogen entered the station, but he slipped whatever it was into his desk drawer before she could get a proper look at it. She had a feeling it was a My Little Pony.

"Doughnuts, eh?" he said as she held the box out to him. "You're learning." He took one and put it into his mouth. Then he took two more and slipped them onto his wrist, like bracelets. "In case I get hungry later," he said. "Come on, then. Seeing as you've been so generous, I'll let you *inside* the cell today."

PC Phillips let Imogen into her family's cell and clanged the door shut after her.

Imogen's stomach went cold. "You're not going to lock me in here, are you?"

"Just shout when you want me to let you out again," said PC Phillips, turning the key in the lock. He walked off down the corridor, swinging the keys in his nasty hand and whistling a worrying tune.

Imogen took a deep breath. She had a recurring nightmare in which she was trapped in a tiny space with her relatives—although in the dream everyone was dressed as clowns, for some reason, and she was always late for her history exam. "Hello, everyone," she said.

Her family was asleep.

"Wake up," Imogen said a little louder.

But they didn't.

"What? All these gold bars are for me? And the diamonds, too?" she tried.

All of the Crims' eyes snapped open.

"Gold? Diamonds? Where?" asked Josephine.

"There isn't any gold," said Imogen. "I was just trying to get your attention."

"OI! IMOGEN!" shouted Uncle Knuckles. "DID YOU TELL ANYONE WE DIDN'T STEAL THE LUNCH BOX?"

"No—" said Imogen, backing away from him.

"THAT'S ALL RIGHT, THEN," he said. "WOULD YOU LIKE A GLUTEN-FREE BROWNIE?" He pulled something gooey and brown out of his pocket. "THERE ARE A FEW PIGEON FEATHERS STUCK TO IT SO IT MIGHT TASTE A BIT BIRDY."

"No one wants your disgusting brownie, Knuckles, you dumb yeti," said Uncle Clyde, shaking his head.

"OI! DON'T SPEAK TO ME LIKE THAT! IT HURTS MY FEELINGS!" said Uncle Knuckles.

Imogen decided to ignore her arguing uncles. She

walked over to her mother, who reached out to give her a hug.

"Darling," said Josephine. "Promise me you won't breathe a *word* about us not doing The Heist. PC Phillips said that the police have had several calls from chat shows wanting to interview us. Apparently, a lovely woman called Nancy Grace wants to fly us over so we can appear on her show in America!"

"I don't think the police are going to let you out so you can appear on TV, Mum," Imogen said. "And I *really* don't think they're going to let you leave the country. Unless you tell them you're innocent." She took a notebook out of her pocket and casually sat down on the bench next to Uncle Clyde, looking over his shoulder. He was drawing what looked like a bird drowning in a toilet.

"That's a nice picture," she said.

"It's not just a picture," said Uncle Clyde. "It's a plan for the jailbreak. I think I can bust out of here if I can tame a flock of geese and get them to swim through the sewers and up the toilet into the cell."

"And then what?"

"I haven't got that far yet," said Uncle Clyde, coloring the inside of the toilet a very unpleasant shade of yellow.

"Well . . . it's a very original idea," said Imogen,

resorting to flattery. "All of your ideas are original. The Heist was brilliant."

Uncle Clyde looked up. "Thank you," he said. "I never thought my work would be appreciated in my lifetime. You really think The Heist was brilliant? You're not just saying that?"

"Of course not!" said Imogen. "It was . . . inspired. That's why someone stole it, clearly. . . . Maybe someone overheard you talking about The Heist?"

"Not possible!" said Uncle Clyde, running his fingers through his hair. "I only ever talked about The Heist at home, and strangers never came to the house! Except the postman, obviously."

"The postman," Imogen said thoughtfully, writing that down.

"I always asked him in for a cup of tea. And he did seem very interested in The Heist whenever I mentioned it."

"Right," said Imogen, underlining the postman's name.

"The dishwasher repairman too. He thought The Heist was a great idea."

"I see," said Imogen, making a note.

"And Chuck, of course."

Imogen frowned. "Chuck?"

"He's the homeless man who usually hangs around

outside the train station. We tell each other everything."

"Okay," said Imogen, putting her pen down. "So a lot of people knew about The Heist."

"You could say that," said Uncle Clyde.

"Everyone in Blandington."

"Probably."

Imogen sighed. "So pretty much anyone in town could have framed you."

"Or someone from out of town," said Clyde. "I emailed a few old prison friends about it. One of them lives in Australia now!"

Josephine, who was applying her lipstick, looked up from her hand mirror. "But it's *obvious* who framed us," she said.

"Is it?" said Imogen.

"Of course," said Josephine, snapping the mirror shut. "Think about it. Who are our main rivals?"

Imogen stared at her mother blankly. The Crims didn't have rivals—they were too rubbish to have rivals.

"Come on, darling," said Josephine. "Didn't I teach you anything? It must be the Kruks!"

Imogen blinked.

The Kruks were a crime family too, but unlike the Crims, they were actually capable of pulling off crimes successfully without maiming, bankrupting, or humiliating themselves in the process. The Kruks operated out of

London, and rumor had it that they had built themselves a full-scale replica of Buckingham Palace (known as Krukingham Palace; what else for criminal royalty?) in their vast network of tunnels beneath the city. Accusing the Kruks of being behind The Heist was like getting a parking ticket and taking it up with the queen. Imogen was pretty sure the Kruks had never even heard of the Crims—or of Blandington, for that matter (although it was so boring that even if they had heard of it, they'd probably have forgotten about it straightaway). The Kruks had more important things to think about, like counting their piles of gold and being terrifying.

"It *has* to be the Kruks," said Josephine, nodding at the other Crims, who all looked pretty doubtful.

"I really, really don't think it was them," Imogen said. "Don't they operate out of London? Besides, why would they want to steal that lunch box? They don't need the money."

"The girl has a point," said Uncle Clyde. "I heard that little Violet Kruk takes her lunch to school in a bag made of unicorn skin."

"Don't be silly, Clyde," said Josephine. "Unicorns don't exist."

"I heard that the Kruks killed the last one," muttered Uncle Clyde.

"That wouldn't surprise me," said Imogen. "Apparently,

they have a waxworks exhibition but all the 'waxworks' are real dead celebrities."

"I heard their accounts are in a terrible state," said Al.

"I heard that they eat baby zebras for lunch," Aunt Bets said wistfully. "I've always wanted to eat a zebra. Is the meat stripy? Maybe I'll never know."

"DON'T WORRY, BETSIBOO," said Uncle Knuckles, squeezing Aunt Bets's shoulder. "AS SOON AS WE GET OUT OF HERE, I'LL GO TO THE ZOO AND STEAL YOU ONE. A REALLY RARE ONE. THEN WE'LL BARBECUE IT UP ON THE GRILL!"

Imogen suddenly felt very tired—and strangely hungry, considering all the talk of zebra eating. She looked at her watch: nearly time for lunch. She called for PC Phillips and tried to say good-bye to her family, but they barely noticed. They were far too busy swapping Kruk stories.

"Did you hear about their trampoline? It's made of stolen paintings, stitched together. The ones they're bored of, like the Monets and the Rembrandts," said Josephine. She smiled at PC Phillips, who had arrived to open the cell door.

"I HEARD THAT THEY HAVE TINY PET HORSES THAT THEY WALK ON LEASHES," said Uncle Knuckles.

PC Phillips paused with the key in the lock. "What was that?" he said.

"Nothing," Imogen said. "Can you let me out, please?"

PC Phillips unlocked the door, and Imogen stepped out of the cell. "I'll be back tomorrow, okay?" she said to her family. "Don't do anything stupid in the meantime."

Outside the police station, Imogen took a deep breath and inhaled the fresh air of freedom. Unfortunately, a garbage truck had just driven by, so the air didn't smell so much of freedom as rotten fish and rancid milk and whatever other boring food the people of Blandington had been eating that week.

Her mind was whirring. Could it be the Kruks who had performed The Heist? It felt terribly unlikely, but as it was the only lead she had, she guessed she needed to pursue it. . . .

She was so deep in thought that she almost crashed straight into PC Donnelly, who rounded the corner at that very moment carrying two steaming cups of coffee.

"Morning, Imogen," he said, smiling at her. "Just been on an emergency supply run. We have to keep our energy up now we've got so many crimes to investigate!"

"*One* crime to investigate," Imogen pointed out.

PC Donnelly turned pink. "I'm sorry," he said. "I didn't mean to be insensitive. How are you holding up?"

Imogen looked at him. He looked sincere—maybe she could trust him. He was family, after all. "I'm okay," she said. "But listen—I think you've made a mistake. I don't actually think the Crims are guilty this time."

"Oh, they're guilty," said PC Donnelly, laughing to himself again. "Who else would try to distract the victim with a greased pig? Classic Uncle Clyde! He loves using farm animals for the element of surprise."

"But that's just it—what if someone *else* stole the lunch box, but they followed Uncle Clyde's Heist plans to the letter, to make it look like it was the Crims?"

"Who'd be able to pull off a stunt like that?" asked PC Donnelly.

"Well . . . the Kruks, maybe?" suggested Imogen, watching him for a response.

"The *Kruks*?" Donnelly started laughing. He laughed so hard that he dropped the tray of coffees all over his feet, but that just made him laugh harder. He laughed so hard that a man walking past thought, *I wish I could laugh like that. I'll never laugh that hard while I live in Blandington*, and he went home and packed his bags and moved to Scotland to become a stand-up comedian. He laughed so hard that the birds in the trees, who weren't used to that sort of thing, took off into the sky, sparking a hurricane in Indonesia (but he wasn't to know that). Eventually, he wiped his eyes (and his shoes) and let out the sort of "aaaaah" noise you make when you've been laughing uncontrollably and have accidentally caused a natural disaster on the other side of the world. "No disrespect to our family," he said, "but come on—the Kruks operate on a completely different level from the Crims. The Crims sell counterfeit gift cards on the internet for the Second-Best Steak House. The Kruks sell stolen art to the mafia. Good art—not stuff like that painting of a clown on black velvet that Aunt Bets tried to unload a few months ago."

"I know," said Imogen, reddening, "but—"

"The Crims steal candy bars from delivery trucks. The Kruks *stole a man's foot* once."

"You've made your point—"

"You know I was stationed in London when I first joined the police? I worked on a case the Kruks were involved in. They disposed of one of their enemies by covering him in honey and lowering him into a pit of grizzly bears. Then they killed the grizzly bears by rubbing them with dog food and dumping them into a pool of sharks. Then they killed the sharks by coating them in—"

"Okay!" cried Imogen. She felt foolish, and there was nothing she hated more than feeling foolish. Except for feeling completely and utterly hopeless—and she felt that, too. "I get it! Maybe it wasn't the Kruks! But what if someone *else* set up the Crims?"

"Listen to me, Imogen," said PC Donnelly. "No one set up our family. I'm sorry. If you want to solve a crime, you have to look for motive, opportunity, and knowledge. Who had the motive to steal the lunch box? Who lives right down the road from Wooster Mansion? Who knew how much the lunch box was worth?"

"Uncle Clyde," Imogen said reluctantly.

"So if you really, really think someone set up our family—which I really, really don't think they did—you should start by thinking who would want to."

"You're right," said Imogen, sighing. "Thank you. Look—shall I get you some more coffee?"

"Don't worry about it," said PC Donnelly. "You gave me a good laugh. The Kruks! Setting up the Crims! As *if*!" He waved good-bye and walked back to the police station, still laughing to himself.

Imogen walked home, scuffing her feet miserably on the pavement. She thought about what PC Donnelly had said: Who would want to set up the Crims? It was a tricky question to answer, because nearly everyone who knew the Crims had a grudge against them, ranging from "They stole my Winnebago" to "They turned my cat to a life of crime." But then she realized: There was one person in particular who would love to see Uncle Clyde humiliated. Someone who'd had a grudge against him for years.

The supposed victim of The Heist: Jack Wooster.

And then she remembered something Big Nana used

to say: "Don't feel sorry for the victim until you're sure they didn't commit the crime themselves. Except murder victims. They're usually innocent."

Maybe it was time to pay Jack Wooster a little visit.

JACK WOOSTER LIVED in a huge gated mansion on a high hill above Blandington. He had made his fortune founding WoosterLoos, a company that made surprisingly comfortable portable toilets, and there was no escaping this fact if one visited his home. His crest, which was plastered all over the building, showed a lion and a unicorn fighting over a huge golden portaloo, and his gardens featured a waterfall designed to look like a roll of toilet paper spilling down the hill.

Imogen *had* actually visited Wooster Mansion—once, during a supposed truce between Jack and Uncle Clyde. Jack had invited the Crims to a (very posh) barbecue.

Halfway through lunch, Uncle Clyde had excused himself to go to the bathroom. He was gone for quite a while, but everyone just assumed he was trying out all the special features on Jack's personal, customized WoosterLoo—it was made of titanium, and when you sat down, it assessed your mood (based on your body temperature) and played you an appropriate piece of classical music. Then it sprayed you with perfume. Then it suggested new hairstyles you might like to try. And then (if you hadn't yet run away screaming) it tried to interest you in a one-toilet play it was writing called *Lavatories Get Lonely, Too.* Anyway, when Uncle Clyde stumbled back out to the gardens, it was clear that he hadn't been to the bathroom at all. Because if he had, he'd have looked in the mirror, and he'd have seen that his hands and his face were covered in bright-blue dye.

The other Crims gasped when they saw him—they'd taken part in enough failed bank robberies over the years to know what the blue dye meant. It was the sort of dye that banks plant in stolen money to stain the thief's hand and mark them out as a crook. Jack Wooster had obviously decided to use the same dye to protect his precious lunch box.

Uncle Clyde denied trying to steal the lunch box, of course. He claimed he was blue because he had dressed up as a Smurf as a special treat for Big Nana. But Jack

Wooster wasn't having any of it. He stood up and made the most unpleasant speech anyone has ever made while holding a champagne flute. He talked about how the Crims could never be trusted and how they were all as bad as one another and how Uncle Clyde had just proved that no one should ever be given a second chance. When he'd finished speaking, the family was forced out of the house by security guards in black jackets with golden toilets embroidered on the back.

The whole thing had been horrible and humiliating. Imogen twitched a little bit whenever she thought about it. She'd never been able to bring herself to use a WoosterLoo again, which made going to outdoor events a bit tricky.

Thinking back to the barbecue now, Imogen felt embarrassed. She realized she empathized with Jack Wooster. He was a respectable businessman who respected law and order. He was a self-made billionaire who wasn't ashamed of the way he'd earned his money (quite the opposite, in fact, judging by his toilet-themed mansion). He was a generous, forgiving person who had tried to make peace with Uncle Clyde—and Uncle Clyde hadn't been able to put aside his petty jealousies and mad lunch box–obsession for two hours to enjoy a barbecue. She imagined that Jack Wooster's annoyance with her family was similar to what she felt, sitting in the jail cell, trying to convince them not to take credit for a crime they didn't commit.

Maybe we understand each other, Jack Wooster and I.

Now Imogen stood outside the gates of Wooster Mansion. She was wearing a scarf and sunglasses to make herself look older and richer and generally more like the sort of person who might be welcome there. She pulled herself up to her full height and put out her hand to buzz on the intercom—but then she hesitated. Her heart was thudding. It had been two years since she'd last worn a disguise and sneaked into someone else's house. She didn't know if she still had it in her. *Come on, Imogen,* she told herself. *You can do this. You're not really committing a crime; you're trying to prove that someone* else *has committed a crime.* She pressed the button on the intercom.

"Wooster residence, how may I help you?" crackled a deep voice.

Imogen opened her mouth to speak, but no sound came out.

"Hello?" said the deep voice again.

"Hello there," said Imogen. She tried to speak with purpose, like a Future World Leader, but her voice was wavering. "Imogen Collins here, reporter from the *Blandington Times*. I've come for my three o'clock interview with Mr. Wooster."

"There's no record of an interview scheduled for today," said the crackling voice.

"Are you sure?" said Imogen, playing for time. Why

hadn't she thought about what she'd say next?

"I'm sure," crackled the voice. "If that's all—"

"Wait!" said Imogen. "I—I *do* hope Mr. Wooster hasn't forgotten. The interview is going to be a lead feature in next Saturday's edition."

"You arranged the interview with Mr. Wooster directly?" said the voice.

"That's right," said Imogen, beginning to get in her stride. "He wanted to talk about the theft of his lunch box and see if the public had any leads on its whereabouts. So will you let me in, please? You know how Mr. Wooster hates to be kept waiting."

There was a silence.

Imogen held her breath.

Finally, the voice said, "All right, then," and the golden gates began to open, glinting expensively in the sunlight.

Imogen walked up the path to the mansion itself, past sculptures of cupids spraying air freshener and Greek gods drying their hands on premium WoosterLoos hand towels. The path was unnecessarily long, and Imogen had broken into a sweat by the time she got to the front door, which swung open before she could knock. On the doorstep stood a butler in a black tuxedo. He bowed to Imogen. "Through here, Miss Collins," he said, leading the way to a book-lined study.

Jack Wooster was seated at a desk with his back to

Imogen. He waved her inside. "Sit on the comfortable armchair," he said.

Imogen tried to work out which armchair he meant. There were two of them—a squishy-looking purple one and a stiff-looking red velvet one. Imogen chose the purple one. As soon as she sat down, she realized she'd chosen the wrong one. The seat seemed to be full of pins.

Jack swiveled his chair around to face her. He was wearing a wine-colored dressing gown and monogrammed slippers, and he was smoking a pipe, like rich men do. He looked older and more tired than when Imogen had last seen him.

He wasn't smiling.

"I didn't have an interview scheduled for today," he said.

"Perhaps you forgot," Imogen said, shifting on the uncomfortable chair.

"I don't forget things," said Jack, studying Imogen. "Particularly not faces."

Imogen's heart began to thud again, and she pulled her scarf closer around her face. "I promise this won't take up much of your time," she said, pulling a Dictaphone from her pocket and pressing record. She hoped Jack Wooster couldn't hear the nervousness in her voice. "I'm here to talk to you about the theft of your lunch box. It must be very traumatic to have someone break into your house and steal such a prized personal possession."

"Very," said Jack, puffing on his pipe.

"Do you remember when you first realized that the lunch box was gone?"

Jack leaned forward to look at Imogen more closely. "Aren't you a little young to be a reporter?" he asked.

"No," she said, drawing away from him. "I used to work on the beauty pages, and I got a lot of free samples of very powerful anti-aging cream."

"I see," said Jack, leaning back in his chair and crossing his legs. "You look familiar, that's all."

"Maybe you've read my column—Blandington Bridge Watch? I watch all the bridges in Blandington and write about the things that happen on them."

"No," said Jack. "That's not it. I've definitely met you before. What's your surname again?"

"Collins," said Imogen, more squeakily than she'd meant to.

Jack Wooster put down his pipe and leaned toward her again.

"Are you sure?" asked Jack, studying her face. "Are you sure your name isn't . . . *Crim*?"

Imogen felt as though she'd been punched. She was out of practice, clearly, but still: No one had ever seen through one of her disguises before. Once, she had convinced an entire retirement luncheon's worth of knife salesmen that she was Margaret Thatcher. When she was *seven*.

But what if she'd lost her gift? What if, after two full years on the straight and narrow, she was as useless, criminally speaking, as Aunt Bets's knitted handguns?

Her heart sank at the thought. If she couldn't even pull off a simple disguise, how was she ever going to prove that her family was innocent?

She took off her glasses and scarf, completely defeated. "Fine," she said. "You win. I'm Imogen Crim."

"I *knew* it," Jack said triumphantly.

"Look," Imogen pleaded, hoping that Jack would understand the strange kinship they shared in annoyance levels with her family. "I just have a few questions to ask you about The Heist—"

But Jack laughed at her. "What—Clyde didn't tell you what he did with the lunch box? You want to know where it is so you can get *your* filthy hands on it?"

"My hands aren't filthy," said Imogen, stung. "I washed them just before I came out."

"With WoosterLoos antibacterial hand wash?"

"No. With soap."

"My point exactly," said Jack, looking her up and down. "Do you really think I'm going to help you? I'd sooner travel by *public transport* than help a Crim! I'd sooner go to a pop concert! I'd sooner buy clothes from a thrift store! I'd sooner lick a rat!"

"Please," said Imogen, willing herself not to cry. She

could feel Lilyworth moving farther and farther away. "I'm not asking for much—just yes or no answers. I *know* you wouldn't really rather lick a rat—"

"Yes I would!" shouted Jack Wooster, standing up and towering over his desk toward her. "At least rats have some integrity! At least they are who they say they are! At least they aren't lying, cheating, thieving pond scum!"

"That's very harsh," said Imogen, feeling a bit wounded in spite of herself. She'd known that Jack Wooster hated the Crims, of course, but she was a bit surprised by the ferocity of his hatred.

"You're right," said Jack, standing up. "It's not fair to pond scum. You're all worse than pond scum! Clyde is getting exactly what he deserves. And so will you when I call the police and tell them that you're TRESPASSING ON MY PROPERTY!" He pointed to the door. "GET OUT!" he spat (literally—Imogen had to wipe her face with her scarf).

Imogen was desperate—she couldn't leave without answers. This was her best chance to find out whether Jack had faked The Heist to get revenge on Uncle Clyde—or whether someone else had set her family up. "Please let me explain—" she said, standing up.

But then Jack started marching toward her, and she had to stagger backward to get out of his way.

"OUT!" said Jack, pushing her toward the door.

Jack Wooster chased Imogen out of his office and through the hall, and kicked her out of the front door—so hard that she flew through the air like a bird (a flightless one) and landed with a *thud* on the lawn.

She stumbled to her feet, outraged. Well, she thought. *I may have tricked my way into his house, but he didn't need to treat me like* that. Clearly she had been wrong to imagine that she and Wooster were anything alike. He was a snobbish, cantankerous rich person—and she was a Crim. She realized in that moment that she always would be, to some people—despite her best efforts to forget it.

She rubbed herself where Jack had kicked her and smoothed down her hair, which felt frizzy and out of control, like everything else in her life. She started to limp down the long path that led out of the mansion, hot with humiliation. *That could have gone worse,* she said to herself. *Jack could have killed me or set his dogs on me or something. Except that only happens in movies.*

Which is when she heard the barking.

Imogen turned around to see five of the biggest, muscliest, angriest-looking dogs she'd ever seen running toward her, licking their pointy teeth and dribbling aggressively.

Imogen ignored her limp and began to run, harder than she'd ever run before and then a little harder than that, forcing her legs to take huge strides. . . .

But the barking and snarling and dribbling was getting

closer and closer. . . .

She didn't dare look behind her. Instead, she focused on the huge golden gates in front of her. Just a few more steps and she'd be safe.

But one of the dogs was at her ankles. . . . She could almost feel its slippery, sharp teeth on her skin.

In the split second before the dog could sink its teeth into her leg, Imogen threw herself at the gate and forced it open. She slipped through and slammed it shut, so that when the dogs hurled themselves at her, they hit the gates with a *thunk* instead and slid to the ground, dazed.

Imogen collapsed to the ground on the other side, gasping for air. She'd had many low points in recent days, but this—sitting on the ground, her clothes a mess, dog drool on her leg, humiliated by her family's archenemy—might just be the worst moment of her life. *And I didn't even get any information out of him!*

Imogen stumbled home, so humiliated she could barely lift her eyes from the pavement. She kept replaying the scene with Jack Wooster, thinking of clever comebacks she could have said, trying to work out when he'd first realized who she was, thinking of what she'd do differently next time. But there wouldn't be a next time. She'd blown her chance. Now she didn't have much time left to solve the mystery of The Heist and get back to Lilyworth.

Thinking about school gave her a pang. Nobody would

ever speak to her there the way Wooster had just spoken to her in his study. She had friends and good test scores and a tasteful array of twinsets and a real *future* ahead of her—everybody said so.

In Blandington, she was just one more failure in a family of failures. Jack Wooster's words went around in her head like a horribly catchy Kitty Penguin song: "You're all worse than pond scum!"

But as she replayed his words, an unfamiliar feeling washed over her—something she rarely felt at Lilyworth. Her humiliation hardened into something more satisfying: cold, steely, righteous anger.

Wooster was the pond scum! She reminded herself why she'd gone there in the first place: She suspected *he* was the one who had stolen *his own* priceless lunch box to set up his unfortunate, defenseless former best friend, just to settle a grudge!

No, she didn't feel sorry for Jack anymore. They were nothing alike. She felt sorry for Uncle Clyde instead. No *wonder* he hated Jack so much. Jack Wooster was a pretentious, velvet-wearing, toilet-loving *monster.* How *dare* he treat her like that?

Because he could, Imogen realized. Because the police would always take his side over hers. And because technically, she *had* been trespassing on his property.

He deserves *to have his lunch box stolen,* Imogen thought, her pulse quickening. She took in a deep breath and turned toward home, invigorated by her anger. She'd figure out a way to get to him. *I just need more time . . . and perhaps a farm animal.*

For the first time in a long time, she felt like a Crim.

Crim House was eerily silent as Imogen opened the front door. Usually, when she came home, she was greeted by the sound of a brick (or a cat or a child) being hurled from a top-floor window, but that afternoon she couldn't hear anything except a bird in a nearby tree halfheartedly whistling its usual, boring tune. But as she hung up her coat, she heard a strange sound coming from the living room—something tuneful, something gentle, something completely and utterly un-Crim-like. She pushed open the door, and there, huddled on the sofa, were the Crim children, holding mugs of cocoa and . . . *singing.*

Imogen couldn't quite believe her eyes, so she closed them, but when she opened them the children were still there, smiling and sitting upright and watching Mrs. Teakettle, who Imogen now noticed in the middle of the room. She appeared to be conducting the children, who were singing in tune.

"There's a strange kind of clanging from the chains on our legs
And the bells in the jailhouse, too.

And up in the court, a nasty judge with a grudge
Has sentenced us to one to two (years)."

Mrs. Teakettle, still conducting the children, turned to Imogen and whispered, "The rhyme scheme needs a little work."

Imogen nodded, dazed, and then watched as Delia stood up to sing a solo:

"Good night, my friends, it's time to say good-bye,
I'll probably be in prison till I die."

"That's right," said Mrs. Teakettle, smiling. "That's what'll happen if you don't stop stealing motor vehicles!"

The twins stood up next, looking disturbingly angelic, like something out of a horror film.

"We're sleepy now. We bid you all good night,
We're off to jail for getting into fights."

"Very good, my dears," said Mrs. Teakettle. "Now, you, Sam."

Sam stood up, and at the top of his lungs, screeched, *"Good-BYYYYYYYYE!"* so loudly that everyone else had to cover their ears, and Isabella, who had been calmly rif-fling through Mrs. Teakettle's handbag, began to cry and bang her fists on the floor. Imogen didn't blame her.

"That's enough for today, I think," said Mrs. Teakettle. She turned to Imogen, who was still staring, openmouthed, at the scene before her.

"Now, Imogen, dear, I need to be off—I have a church function this evening. And I can't find Freddie anywhere. Would you mind looking after the children till he turns up?"

Typical, thought Imogen. Even without the children to watch, Freddie couldn't seem to stay in one place for more than five minutes. Where did he keep disappearing? "Of course," she said, and showed Mrs. Teakettle to the door.

The Horrible Children lined up on the doorstep, smiling, and waved neatly to their babysitter as she departed. Imogen shivered. She almost preferred it when they were hitting one another and swearing.

Imogen collapsed into an armchair and closed her eyes, trying to get just a few seconds of peace and quiet to process what had happened that day—but that was impossible, of course. Because in no time at all, the Horrible Children started to do their usual horrible things. Sam picked up his voice distorter and tried to make himself sound less squeaky, Henry grabbed his lighter and held it to the bottom of Nick's and Nate's feet to see which of them had the higher pain threshold, and Delia laid her head on the ironing board and started straightening her hair with the iron.

"So how was your day?" Delia asked.

Imogen hesitated. Should she tell Delia what she'd done and how badly wrong it had gone? "Not great," she said finally. "I tricked my way into Jack Wooster's mansion pretending to be a reporter and ended up getting chased out of the house by his very nasty dogs."

"Whoa!" said Henry, holding out his hand to give Imogen a high five. Imogen's heart lifted a little. It hadn't occurred to her that her cousins would actually think what she'd done was *cool.* She high-fived him and noticed that he'd tried to tattoo "HATE" on his knuckles, but he'd spelled it wrong, so it read "HEAT."

Even Delia was impressed with her. "Seriously?" she said. "You lied to get into his house? You do know that's illegal, right?"

"I do," Imogen said as casually as she could.

"I didn't know you still had it in you," Delia said.

"Thank you," said Imogen, looking at her cousin in surprise. There had been a time when she and Delia had been inseparable in their criminal activities. They wrote in their journals together, and each would offer suggestions to improve the other's plan. When Imogen was eight and Delia ten, they'd successfully stolen a huge balloon in the shape of an octopus that had (inexplicably) sat atop a local ice cream shop. That morning, Imogen was sure she'd spotted a deflated tentacle still poking out of the back of Delia's closet.

Now she glanced down at her lap. It felt strange to remember her pre-Lilyworth life. It felt particularly strange to remember that the good times weren't all connected to Big Nana.

"Sorry if this is an obvious question," said the twin who wasn't in the middle of having his feet scorched, "but why did you want to get into Wooster Mansion?"

Imogen sat up. "Because I think Jack Wooster is the one who framed our family. He's the one who *really* pulled off The Heist."

"WHAT?" said Sam, dropping his voice distorter.

"What are you talking about?" said Delia, straightening up. "Are you trying to say we didn't steal the lunch box? Because we totally did. *Didn't* we?" She made eyes at Henry.

"Oh . . . yeah," Henry said when he'd cottoned on. "We totally pulled off The Heist. I rode a unicycle into Jack Wooster's garden, carrying brownies—"

"That was me, you idiot," hissed Delia. "And I was carrying cupcakes. Ugh. Whatever." She turned back to Imogen. "Are you calling us liars?"

"Yes. Yes, I am," said Imogen, which was quite a brave thing to say, because Delia was still brandishing the iron. "Delia, we both know The Heist would never have worked. If we'd written it up in our crime journals, Big

Nana would have torn it apart. That's why Clyde never attempted it when she was alive." Delia frowned and looked away. "Anyway, the adults have already admitted they didn't do it," Imogen said quickly. "You might as well come clean."

Nick and Nate looked at each other and shrugged. "Yeah, you're right," they said. "It's true. We had nothing to do with it."

"Fine," said Delia, slamming the iron onto the ironing board. "But Big Nana or no—we *could* have done it if we'd really wanted to."

"Of course you could," said Imogen, in her most soothingly insincere voice.

"Whatever," said Delia, throwing herself into an armchair in a huff.

But Delia's bad moods never lasted long. It was one of the things Imogen had always admired about her cousin. Midway through the Octopus Balloon Heist, she'd gotten furious at Imogen for insulting the Jonas Brothers and climbed down off the roof, stranding Imogen with a half-deflated octopus balloon about the size of two large SUVs. Just as Imogen had started to despair, she'd heard footsteps on the ladder, and then her cousin was next to her again. "I suppose their last album wasn't their *best*."

And only a few minutes after her huff, Delia was sitting on the arm of Imogen's chair, saying, "So, do you *really* think Jack Wooster stole his own lunch box?"

"I do. Who else could it have been?" asked Imogen. "He's always had it in for Uncle Clyde. Trouble is, he figured out who I was before I could get any information out of him."

Delia shook her head, disappointed. "I did wonder who would bother to re-create Uncle Clyde's heist—the bouncy castle rental by itself must have been a pain, not to mention finding the pig." She sighed. "Wooster seems like a good bet. But you played it too straight," she said. "You should have tricked him into leaving the house somehow, so you could look around."

Imogen's lips twitched. It was irritating to hear lessons from Delia on how to be a criminal when she'd always been the more accomplished one. Except . . . she had the sinking sensation Delia was right, just as she'd always been when she found a flaw in Imogen's journal. "How should I have tricked him into leaving the house?" she asked.

"By using the Ratcatcher Swindle!" said Sam.

Imogen looked at her cousins thoughtfully. She had no idea what a Ratcatcher Swindle was—some kind of swindle involving rats, she assumed. Anyway, Imogen wasn't sure she wanted her cousins' help; it could backfire in roughly a thousand different ways. But then, Jack Wooster did *deserve* to be swindled, didn't he? And Imogen was out of ideas.

Also, she realized, the idea of pulling off a crime with her cousins after all this time was sort of . . . *exciting.*

"Okay," said Imogen. "So if I wanted to pull off the Ratcatcher Swindle, how would that work, exactly?"

The next day, after Imogen sent Mrs. Teakettle away with the news that the entire Crim family had contracted norovirus, she and the Horrible Children arrived at the gates to Wooster Mansion. Freddie was AWOL, but Imogen suspected he wouldn't be of much help, anyway. They were all wearing blue overalls and carrying buckets (except Isabella, who was in Henry's bucket, disguised as a sponge). Imogen buzzed the intercom, and the same deep, crackly voice from the other day said, "Wooster residence. How may I help you?"

Imogen felt more confident this time around. Having the Horrible Children there with her made her feel safer. Which was mad, really, when she thought about it, so she didn't. She took a deep breath, and in her best Scottish accent, she said, "Hello therrrre!"

"Hello," said the crackly voice on the other end.

"We're frrrrrrom A-1 Creaturrrrre Management," continued Imogen. "We'rrrrre herrrrre to take carrrrrre of your wee rrrrrat problem." Imogen looked at Delia, who gave her a thumbs-up. Imogen nodded, pleased.

"THANK GOD," said the voice, buzzing them in. By

the time they reached the front door, the butler was on the doorstep waiting for them. He ushered them inside, practically bowing with gratitude. "I assume Mr. Wooster contacted you?"

"That is corrrrrect," said Imogen.

Delia gave her a look. Maybe she was overdoing the accent a bit now.

"Not a moment too soon," said the butler. "I have no idea what happened, but it seems as though an entire family of rats moved in overnight! It's no reflection on the cleanliness of this house, of course."

"Of course not," said Sam, smiling. "Rat colonies can be very fast-moving—and they are actually much pickier than people give them credit for. Who can blame them for wanting to live in such a spotless house as this?" He ran his finger along a mahogany side table and held it up. "See? Clean as a whistle!"

"Well," said the butler, blushing, "thank you." Then he looked at the Horrible Children properly for the first time and did a double take. "My! You're very small for exterminators," he said.

Oh no, thought Imogen. *I am not being caught* again.

"Yes," Delia said quickly—before Imogen could think of a lie. "It's very sad, really—the rat poison stunted our growth."

Imogen felt a wave of relief wash over her.

"That's right," said Sam. "I was six foot tall when I was a boy—on the basketball team and everything. Now that I'm forty-five, I have to get other people to get things down from high shelves for me."

"But we love our work!" said Delia. "A-1 Creature Management is a family business. Rat poison runs in our veins!"

The butler took a step backward, clearly a little alarmed.

"Not literally," Delia said. "Anyway, you mustn't worry—we'll get rid of the rats in no time. We just need everyone to leave the mansion while we're working."

"Very well," said the butler, giving a slight bow. "It's just me and Mrs. Pigmore here today; she's the cook. Mr. Wooster is away on business. I'll go and tell her to collect her things." With that, he walked away, nose in the air, to fetch the cook.

Imogen grinned at Delia. He'd bought it!

Ten minutes later, the butler and Mrs. Pigmore left the house. Imogen locked the door behind them. She couldn't believe that Sam's ridiculous plan had actually worked! Maybe her relatives weren't completely hopeless after all. Her heart was thumping, but in a good way. She felt really alive for the first time in ages.

"Right," said Sam. "I'll collect my rats." He put two fingers to his lips and whistled to them. "Where are you, Cyanide? Anthrax, come to daddy!"

As Sam wandered off, calling to his terrifyingly named pets, Imogen gathered the other Horrible Children around her. She pulled the detailed blueprints of Wooster Mansion that Uncle Clyde had given them out of her pocket. "Right," she said. "The rest of us need to split up and search the mansion for clues. Delia, you start in the servants' kitchen. Nick and Nate, you go to the present-wrapping room and the cuff links display room. Henry and Isabella, have a look around the golf-wear wardrobe. I'll start in the guest living room."

Imogen took her time walking through the mansion. She'd brought a copy of the illustrated abridged version of Uncle Clyde's Heist plan for reference. As she wandered through the rooms, she felt a grudging respect for whoever had actually stolen the lunch box. The real criminal had staged the entire Wooster Mansion to make it look as though the Crims had pulled off The Heist. *Whoever did this,* Imogen thought, *they're good.*

But not perfect. Whoever had staged the mansion *had* made a few little mistakes. The real criminals had cut the glass on the window to break in without making a noise. The Crims didn't do clever things like that; they always carried a brick with them for window-breaking purposes. And the real criminal had messed up the Crims' "signature": the crudely stenciled picture of Captain Crook that they left behind at each of their crime scenes. The mystery criminals had sprayed Captain Crook in green, whereas the Crims' signature spray-paint color was an embarrassing shade of pink that they'd bought on sale, thinking it was red, but were too proud to take back to the shop.

Imogen didn't find anything particularly interesting in the guest living room or the indoor swimming pool. The library, which was mostly full of books about toilets, seemed to be a dead end too—at first. She picked up a few of the books and flicked through them, just in case someone had hidden any evidence inside. But when she tried to pick up one of the books from the shelf nearest the fireplace, it wouldn't come out. It seemed to be glued down. Imogen tried another book, and another, but they were all stuck firmly in place. She took a few steps back and looked at the bookshelf properly and saw that there was a telltale gap around the edge of the shelves and down the wall. It wasn't a bookshelf at all: it was a door.

So, thought Imogen, *Jack Wooster is more like Uncle Clyde than he cares to admit.* Uncle Clyde had built five hidden doors in Crim House over the years. None of them led anywhere particularly interesting, but they drove the other Crims crazy. You'd be in the kitchen, trying to cook some pasta, when you'd press the wrong button on the cooker, and suddenly, the whole thing would swing around and you'd be standing outside in the garden in your bare feet.

But when Imogen pressed on a book called *Open If you Dare*, she discovered that Jack Wooster's door *did* lead somewhere useful—Jack's study.

Imogen stood there, her hands on the back of the uncomfortable armchair, looking around the study. Jack's desk filled half the room, and a trophy cabinet took up most of the other half. Jack appeared to have won Tuxedo Wearer of the Month, Blandington Wrestler of the Year, and the Amateur Dangerous Dog Breeder Prize. Shuddering slightly, Imogen moved over to the desk. She opened one of the drawers and gasped.

How very odd! There, among the paper clips and pen caps and gold-toilet-embossed stationery, was a letter addressed to Jack from Charm Ltd.: the creators of Captain Crook.

Why would Charm Ltd. be writing to Jack? Imogen supposed it could have something to do with the Captain Crook website Jack ran. But since Charm Ltd. had essentially dropped Captain Crook after parents complained that he promoted crime, it didn't seem likely.

Imogen sat down on Jack's (toilet-shaped) desk chair and began to read:

Dear Mr. Wooster,

I am writing to you with a proposal that I believe will benefit us both. Charm Ltd. would like to buy your

Captain Crook lunch box for £1,000,000 (one million pounds sterling).

Imogen's mouth dropped open. *That explains why the valuation of the lunch box suddenly tripled,* she thought. *But why would Charm Ltd. pay that much money for a ratty old lunch box?* She carried on reading:

If you accept this sum, you will, in return, hand the lunch box over to a representative of Charm Ltd. under cover of night, in a secure location; you will take down your Captain Crook fan website immediately; and you will deny any knowledge of the lunch box or the Captain Crook character forthwith.

Imogen was even more confused. Why did Charm Ltd. want Jack to deny he'd ever heard of Captain Crook? And *why* did they care about Jack Wooster's incredibly unpopular fan site? Only about three people used it, mainly because Jack moderated the forums ruthlessly, throwing out anyone who used "LOL." He had always refused to give Uncle Clyde a username for the message boards, forcing him to comment as "guest." Imogen had the sense that Jack enjoyed the sense of power that moderating a terribly unpopular message board gave him. Would he be willing to give it up in return for a million pounds?

Imogen was struck by a sudden memory: When PC Phillips had tried to show her the value of the lunch box on a website, the site had been mysteriously down. *Coincidence?* Or had Charm Ltd. offered that site's owner money to take it down too?

She frowned and read the letter again. If Jack Wooster *had* refused to sell the lunch box to Charm Ltd., maybe *they* were the ones who stole it and set up the robbery to frame her uncle?

But something still didn't add up. Even if Charm Ltd. did steal the lunch box, how would they have known about The Heist?

"Imogen?"

Imogen was shaken out of her thoughts by Delia's voice, coming from somewhere downstairs. She looked at her watch—they'd been in the house for half an hour already. "Coming!" she called. She walked back through the hidden door to the library and ran down the portrait gallery (which only contained portraits of Jack Wooster) to the staff kitchens, where she found the Horrible Children playing with Sam's pet rats. "So," she said, trying to catch her breath, "what did you find?"

"Nothing good," Delia said morosely.

"I found something good," said Henry, holding up a tiepin. "Apparently, you use this to clip your tie to your shirt, so you always look professional!"

"You don't own a shirt or a tie," Imogen pointed out. "And you *never* look professional."

"Until now!" said Henry.

Imogen opened her mouth to reply—but then she froze. She had heard a very unwelcome sound: the sound of a key turning in the front door.

"It must be the butler," whispered Delia.

But then the unmistakable voice of Jack Wooster came floating toward them, like an ominous balloon. "Hello? Mrs. Pigmore? Mr. Waits?"

And then they heard his tread on the stairs. Luckily, he'd decided to go upstairs first.

"Quick!" whispered Imogen. "Let's get out before he sees us!"

"I'll have a cup of tea, Mrs. Pigmore," Jack said from upstairs. "But instead of tea, I'll have champagne, and instead of milk, I'll have . . . a little more champagne." And then he laughed his wealthy laugh.

"Let's go! Before he comes down again!" hissed Imogen, picking up Isabella, who was trying to grab one of the rats from Sam's pockets, and ushering the Horrible Children out of the kitchen ahead of her.

They tiptoed down the hall. Delia got to the front door first. She turned the handle silently and held the door open for the others. The twins left first, followed by Henry, followed by Sam—but just as Sam stepped outside,

Isabella lurched forward and grabbed one of his rats by the tail, and the rat, which didn't seem to like having its tail grabbed, turned and bit her, and Isabella shrieked, "BAD RAT!" at the top of her surprisingly powerful and piercing voice, and all the rats jumped out of Sam's pockets, and Sam swore and scrabbled to pick them up, and the whole thing was generally a bit of an extremely loud disaster.

The silence from upstairs was, by contrast, deafening. After several excruciating seconds, it was broken by Jack Wooster saying in a dangerously calm voice, "There's a bad rat in my house, is there? Sounds like *several* bad rats to me!"

Imogen heard his feet walking slowly and deliberately down the stairs. Sam had managed to catch all the rats, but one escaped again, and Imogen was just able to grab it by its horrible, gristly tail. Before she could reflect on what the girls at Lilyworth would say if they could see her now, Jack Wooster reached the bottom of the staircase and saw her. "YOU!" he said, pointing at her.

"YOU!" she said back, just for something to say, and she ran out of Wooster Mansion for the second time in as many days.

"QUICK!" she shouted to the Horrible Children as they stumbled across the lawn. "SPOILER: THERE ARE GOING TO BE DOGS!"

And that's when the dogs appeared, snarling and

gnashing and looking extremely hungry. Imogen pounded across the grass but tripped over a clump of mud and fell. She sprawled face-first on the ground, with the sound of angry dogs getting closer and closer.

Delia stopped and reached out her hand to help Imogen up.

"Thanks," Imogen said breathlessly as she got back on her feet.

They made one final push and raced for the gates, and just in time—they forced them open and slammed them shut before the dogs could get them.

"STUPID DOGS!" shouted Jack Wooster, panting past his toilet roll–shaped waterfall as the animals ran back to him, their tails between their strangely short legs.

The dogs *were* pretty stupid, Imogen realized as she and the Horrible Children collapsed in a heap on the pavement. She'd managed to outrun them twice, and she'd always come in last in the one-hundred-meter race on sports day. Maybe Jack wasn't such a great Amateur Dangerous Dog Breeder after all.

Imogen looked around at her cousins. They were all grinning at her, as if they were really seeing her for the first time.

Delia reached out and hugged her. "So you haven't forgotten how to be a Crim after all," she said.

"Of course I haven't," said Imogen, though honestly,

she was a bit relieved.

"Good to have you back," smiled Sam, holding out his arms so that Assassin, his smallest rat, could run across them.

Imogen blushed. She didn't really go in for emotional declarations. "Yes," she said. "And we'll soon have all the other Crims back too. Because I think I finally have some proof that they didn't steal the lunch box. Plus, now I know who wanted it, apart from Uncle Clyde." She pulled the letter from Charm Ltd. out of her pocket and held it up to show her cousins.

"Wait," said Delia, taking the letter, her eyes wide with what Imogen could have sworn was admiration. "Did you *steal* this?"

"No!" said Imogen, grinning. "I just *borrowed* it."

THE NEXT DAY, Imogen met Mrs. Teakettle at the door as she arrived to look after the Horrible Children. "I'm so sorry," she said before Mrs. Teakettle could take off her coat, "I should have called you before you came all the way out here—Isabella is still a bit pukey, so it's probably best if I look after the kids again today."

"She's still sick?" said Mrs. Teakettle, looking actually disappointed. *She really does like the Horrible Children,* Imogen realized, impressed. "How about the others? Are they eating again? How are their bowel movements?"

"Uh, terrible," Imogen replied, not looking in Mrs. Teakettle's eyes. "I don't think any of us are quite over it, honestly. The loo is getting quite a workout! Ha . . ."

Mrs. Teakettle's eyes narrowed. "Have you cleaned with bleach? Norovirus is notoriously hard to get out of a toilet."

"I keep cleaning and cleaning, but then someone uses the loo again and, well—I'm afraid we're still probably terribly contagious. You really don't want to come in here." *Stop talking,* she told herself. "The fewer the details, the more believable the lie"; that was one of the very first things Big Nana had taught her. Imogen smiled at Mrs. Teakettle apologetically. "I'm so sorry for wasting your time."

"That sounds like a lot of work," said Mrs. Teakettle, patting Imogen's hand. "Why don't you let me come in to help? You're probably still recovering yourself."

"Recovering?" said Imogen. "No, no—I'll look after the kids today. I don't want you to put yourself in danger."

"I have immunity." Mrs. Teakettle tried to enter the house, but Imogen barred her way. Mrs. Teakettle looked at her with surprise.

"I think this is a particularly rare strain . . . ," said Imogen, getting desperate.

"I have immunity to almost everything," said Mrs. Teakettle, with a steely smile. "I was a very unlucky child, illness-wise."

Imogen looked at the babysitter. Was she imagining

things, or was Mrs. Teakettle challenging her to come up with a better excuse? "Look," said Imogen. "I haven't been entirely honest with you. The truth is, I've missed my cousins terribly. I've been away at school, you see. But now I'm back and . . . and I want to look after them by myself today."

Mrs. Teakettle raised her eyebrows. "Why didn't you say so?" she said. "I don't blame you—they're such a delight! Just give me a call when you want me to come back."

Imogen breathed a sigh of relief. That had been more difficult than she'd anticipated. As she watched the babysitter drive away in her tiny car, she called out to the Horrible Children, "The pigeon has flown the nest!"

"Finally," Delia called back. "That bird was always pooping on my bike."

"Not an actual pigeon—Mrs. Teakettle! Operation Charm Offensive has commenced!"

Imogen felt nervous. *Good* nervous. Operation Charm Offensive wasn't just an idea scribbled in her notebook anymore—it was real. She hadn't come up with such a complicated plan since she and Delia had plotted to fly to New York on the back of an American eagle and steal the top of the Chrysler Building to use as a playhouse. But they'd never actually put that plan into action due to inclement weather. Would they really be able to pull this plan off? They would *have* to pull it off if Imogen ever wanted to get back to school.

And she did.

Even if this was the first time she'd thought of Lilyworth since they'd left for the Ratcatcher Swindle.

"Imogen? Ready?" called Delia from upstairs.

"Yes," said Imogen, nodding to herself. "Let's do this."

The Horrible Children started trooping downstairs one by one, dressed in what they imagined ordinary people wore on their summer holidays. Delia was dressed as a pineapple, "because it's a summery fruit"; Henry had given himself a new fake tattoo on his forehead that read "Sunburn Kills"; and Sam was wearing a tuxedo, for no apparent reason. "Remember what Big Nana used to tell us?" he said when he saw Imogen's puzzled face. "You always blend in in a tuxedo. Unless you forget to put on your trousers."

"Which is why Freddie always gets arrested at cocktail parties," said Imogen.

"What's that?" asked Freddie, emerging from the kitchen with a piece of thoroughly burned toast. He glanced at each of the Horrible Children and frowned. "Where are you all off to?" he asked. "I thought I told you, if they ever threw another formal party at the Produce Mart, I want to come too!"

Imogen felt a bit guilty, but her stomach tightened at Freddie's unexpected appearance. *The last thing we need is him coming along and screwing it up somehow!*

"No such luck, Freddie," Delia said, touching his shoulder and pouting slightly. "We're off to something really *boring*, really." She shot Imogen a look.

"Yes," agreed Imogen. "We're—uh—"

"Off to a formal ballroom dancing lesson," Sam said squeakily.

"With monkeys," added Henry. When Delia glared at him, he added, "*Boring* monkeys."

Freddie laughed. "That sounds terrible! Who signed you up for that?"

"Imogen," Delia replied quickly. "You know what a stick-in-the-mud she is!"

"That's her idea of *fun*!" added Henry.

Imogen cleared her throat. "I just thought it would be fun to spend some time with my cousins while I'm home," she said. "I gave Mrs. Teakettle the day off. Would you like to come?"

Freddie shook his head. "Oh, thanks, but no," he said. He picked up his toast and took a bite. It crumbled into a thousand shiny black crumbs. "Got a big exam tomorrow," he added through a mouthful of charcoal. "I've got to study all day."

Ironic, thought Imogen, *since he can never remember to*

show up for the exam. "All right . . . well, happy studying." When he wandered back off into the kitchen, Imogen turned back to her other cousins and asked, "And the twins?"

"Still getting ready," said Delia. "But it'll be worth it when you see their outfits."

Imogen checked her notebook. "Right. While we're waiting, let's go over what we know about Charm Ltd. so far."

"They're the company who created Captain Crook," said Sam.

"Correct," said Imogen, feeling a little more confident. The Horrible Children had actually done their crimework for once. (Crimework is like homework, but with no grades and more potential for death if you get it wrong.)

"Actually, after you went to bed last night, I found a tip on a toy merchandising website," said Delia, pulling a banana-shaped pen from her watermelon-shaped handbag. "Turns out, Charm Ltd. is about to launch a new character called Captain Caring."

"Hmmmm," said Imogen, struggling to take in two new bits of information. One, Charm Ltd.'s sudden possible motive. Two, that Delia had actually worked harder to find answers than she had. She looked at her cousin with new admiration.

"He sounds rubbish," said Henry.

"He is," said Delia. "It says on their marketing materials 'Captain Caring is a police officer with a heart of gold and a complete dedication to law and order.'"

"What kind of role model is *that* for the children of today?" said Sam, shaking his head.

"I know!" said Delia. "And it gets worse: They're launching the character by giving away free action figures with every Fatty Meal at PigMonster restaurants."

"They're dragging hamburgers into this?" said Sam. "Is nothing sacred?"

"Apparently not," Imogen said grimly. "If this is all true, then Charm Ltd. is pouring billions into making Captain Caring a success." She paused, tapping her chin. "So . . . it would be very embarrassing for them if someone dug up anything about Captain Crook."

"Exactly," said Delia. "Captain Crook was evil and fun and encouraged preschoolers to break the law, and these days Charm Ltd. is all about family values and following the rules and being boring. Like Imogen." But she smiled.

Imogen stifled her own smile and rolled her eyes instead. "The point is," she said, "it's obvious from the letter I found in Jack's desk that Charm Ltd. is trying to track down all the Captain Crook products that are still out there. They seem to want to destroy them, so that they can pretend he never existed at all. Charm Ltd. is probably the one who put our family in jail. So what are we going to do?"

"Go to jail as well?" Henry said hopefully.

"No," said Imogen. "We're going to prove Charm Ltd. is the real criminal and save the day! What are we waiting for?"

"Us!" called one of the twins from the top of the stairs. Imogen looked up and saw Nick or Nate, whoever it was, wobbling unsteadily downstairs in a trench coat. He seemed to have grown to about twice his normal height. Almost *exactly* twice, in fact. When he reached the bottom of the stairs, he towered above Imogen, which was strange, because the twins were the shortest of the Crims (except Isabella), and they never towered above anything, except very small things, obviously, like fleas and cutlery made for dolls' houses.

Imogen nodded approvingly. She pulled open the trench coat and saw the other twin grinning back at her, holding his brother's feet on his shoulders. Imogen shut the coat again.

"Very nice," Imogen said. "Let's hear your concerned-dad voice."

Nick (or Nate) coughed and lowered his voice several octaves. "I've never seen such low-quality cotton candy!" he said. "It's like trying to chew on plastic netting!"

"Perfect!" said Imogen. "That means we're ready." Her heart was hammering. "Aren't we?" She looked at the extremely detailed notes she'd written. "Do we have everything?"

"Relax," said Delia, touching her arm. Imogen nodded, eyes still on her notebook.

"Look at me," said Delia.

Imogen looked into her cousin's eyes.

"We can do this," said Delia. Her eyes were warm, and she wore just the hint of a smile.

"We can do this," repeated Imogen, closing her notebook and straightening her spine. This time, she let herself mimic Delia's smile.

"We've got one another's backs," said Delia. "Right?"

"Right," said Imogen, nodding, her heart still racing, but in a good way. *This isn't fear,* she realized, *it's excitement!* It had been so long that it had taken a while for her to recognize it.

Sam insisted that they take a really long and complicated route, just in case they were being tailed. They took a train to London and then a coach to Liverpool, then a bus to Skegness, where they stopped for some ice cream. Then they took a donkey to another part of Skegness, then a fishing boat to Land's End, and then a very empty to train to their final destination: Charmtopia.

Charmtopia was a theme park featuring all the famous Charm Ltd. characters (except Captain Crook, of course). It was also the headquarters of Charm Ltd., which was, of course, the reason Imogen and the Horrible Children were on a train pulling into Charmtopia station. If they were going to find evidence linking Charm Ltd. to The Heist anywhere, it would be here.

As the train stopped, Imogen realized why it was so empty: Charmtopia was not charming at all anymore. When she'd been here with Big Nana as a child, she had loved the place. Everything had been shiny and clean and full of hope and possibility, like really nice new gym shoes before you realize you're not very good at running. But now, the name Charmtopia seemed ironic, like whoever had chosen it had a dark sense of humor—the sort of person who would give you a piece of chocolate cake, wait until you'd eaten half of it, and then tell you it was actually made of rat vomit. Imogen looked out of the train window and shuddered slightly as she saw the huge face of the Friendly Clown looking down at her. The Friendly Clown was one of Charm Ltd.'s oldest characters. She had loved the smiling clown when she was younger, but Charmtopia hadn't bothered changing the lightbulbs that made up his face, so now, instead of smiling, the clown was frowning. Isabella pointed to him and started to cry. Imogen felt amazed that Charmtopia was still open at all. Charm Ltd.

hadn't had a big hit since Imogen's parents were young. Rumors were always swirling that they were about to close the place down, but here it was.

Anyway, they weren't here to have fun. "Come on, then!" she said, standing up and clapping her hands. "Who wants to go on a ride?"

None of her cousins moved.

"Come on," she said. "Charmtopia's great!"

"You obviously haven't been here for a while," said Sam.

"Well, no," she said. She tried to think back to the last time she'd been. She and Delia had had an amazing time on the Princess Kindness water ride. (Princess Kindness rode dolphins and taught children how important it was not to waste water, so the ride was pretty ironic when you thought about it.) The twins had been toddlers at the time, and they'd had a great time on the Helpful Baby merry-go-round. (The Helpful Baby was a baby who helped other babies. No one really knew how, exactly.) Considering the strength of Charm Ltd.'s other characters, it wasn't that surprising they were pinning all their hopes on Captain Caring.

"Last time I came here, it was with Big Nana," said Delia as the Horrible Children began to file off the train. "She managed to lock us into the Happy Monster roller coaster so we couldn't get out, and I had to pretend to be terrified, and she persuaded the management to give us a skip-the-queues pass for the rest of the day!"

Delia smiled at the memory. Imogen smiled too. She wondered what Big Nana would think of the plan they were about to carry out.

Charmtopia was actually surprisingly fun considering how completely creepy and broken-down the whole place was. As soon as they walked in, they were accosted by unnaturally cheerful people dressed as Charm Ltd. characters. Imogen was impressed with the employees' commitment—they didn't break character, no matter how hard Delia tried to make them. First, Delia asked Princess Kindness how she'd ended up working in such a dump. But Princess Kindness just smiled and told her that she loved making the people of Charmtopia happy and sprinkling glitter on their boring everyday lives. Then Delia told her she'd seen a sad-looking kitten stuck up a tree at the other end of the park, and the princess ran off to try to cheer it up. Then Delia turned to the person dressed as the Helpful Baby. She asked her a series of questions: "Could you tie my shoes?" "How would you get to New York from here?" and "Can you do an impression of a dachshund?" The Helpful Baby was very helpful in each instance (though her dachshund impression was really more of a cocker spaniel).

Imogen and the Horrible Children explored all three

sections of Charmtopia, which spiraled out from a huge blue castle in the center of the park. First, they visited Imagineland, which featured unimaginably terrible rides full of giant, animatronic teddy bears and dolls and puppets. Then they went to Yesterland, a medieval village of monarchs, peasants, and serfs (who did not take kindly to Delia's suggestion of an uprising). And finally, Futureland, which was actually the least futuristic thing Imogen had ever seen, including her father's collection of vintage calculators. It featured an underground bunker called "the Home of Tomorrow" and was full of robots in 1950s clothing that were listening to the wireless and getting very excited about elastic waistbands. When Henry started tagging his name on the future robots' faces, Imogen decided it was time to get back to business.

"Right," she said. "That's enough fun for one day."

"That's what's going to be on your gravestone," said Delia. "When you die. Of being *boring*."

"Fine," said Imogen. "You stay here and talk to the weird old robots. I'm going to *infiltrate Charm Ltd. headquarters*. Anyone who thinks that sounds boring is welcome to stay here. Everyone else: Let's go to customer services!"

She started walking. After a few seconds, the others followed her. Including Delia.

When they got to customer services, Nick and Nate, still in their trench coat–dad disguise, walked up to the booth and drew themselves up to their full, wobbly, combined height.

"Can I help you?" said the customer services representative, whose badge said her name was Annie Broccoli.

"I certainly hope so," said Nick (or Nate) in as deep a voice as he could manage. "What do you call this?" he demanded, holding out an ice cream cone they'd purchased on the walk over.

"An ice cream cone?" said Annie Broccoli, clearly wondering if this was a trick question.

"And what's this?" said Nick (or Nate), holding out a razor blade.

"That's a razor blade."

"And do you think razor blades and ice cream mix?"

"No," said Annie, frowning. "Unless maybe you ran out of shaving foam and decided to use ice cream instead?"

"WHICH WOULD BE A VERY STUPID THING TO DO!" boomed Nick (or Nate).

"Oh, I'm sure," said Annie. "I don't have a beard, so I wouldn't really know. But . . . why are we having this conversation, exactly?"

"YOU TELL ME!" cried Nick (or Nate). "Why did my son here," he said, patting Sam's head, "find this razor blade IN HIS ICE CREAM CONE?"

"Oh my goodness!" said Annie, her eyes suddenly wide. "I'm so sorry!"

"I SHOULD THINK SO!" shouted Nick (or Nate), glancing down at Imogen, who gave him a subtle thumbs-up.

"Please allow me to make this up to you," said Annie, smiling anxiously. "I can offer you this coupon. It allows you to skip lines for the rest of the day."

Nick (or Nate)'s eyes widened. Imogen had tried to prepare him for this possibility, telling him to reject everything offered. As a reminder, Imogen elbowed him very hard in the stomach, which turned out not to be his stomach at all, but his twin's face. For a horrible moment, it seemed as though the top twin was about to come crashing to the ground, bringing Imogen's brilliant plan with him, but he righted himself just in time.

"Are you okay?" asked Annie.

"NOT REALLY," said Nick (or Nate). "I just almost collapsed with disbelief because you have the NERVE to offer me nothing more than a COUPON when my ONLY SON NEARLY DIED OF INTERNAL BLEEDING!"

"Your only son?" said Annie, looking pointedly at Henry.

"That one doesn't count," said Nick (or Nate). "He wants to be a tattoo artist when he grows up."

"Oh dear!" said Annie.

"I know," said Nick (or Nate). "But back to the matter at hand. I want to speak to THE MAN IN CHARGE!"

He slid a fake business card across the desk, which Delia had carefully designed and printed up on their computer the night before. It identified him as Rick Roberts, publisher of *Rich Parent* magazine.

Annie's eyes widened even farther as she looked at the card. "Oh, of course, Mr. Roberts!" she said, jumping up. "Let me just speak to my manager." Bowing awkwardly, as if Nick (or Nate) was some kind of royal, she disappeared into the back office.

The Horrible Children heard muffled voices, and a moment later, a small toad-like man in a brown suit entered the booth. He had a nasty way of rubbing his hands together, and a nasty, smarmy voice. "Mr. Roberts," he said, holding out his slimy-looking hand. "I'm Geoff Biscuit. What can I do you for? Ha! Ha!"

"I want to see the man in charge," said Nick (or Nate).

"I *am* the man in charge."

"Of what?"

"Of the food outlets at Charmtopia."

"NO!" boomed Nick (or Nate), slamming his hands on the booth. "I want to see the man in charge . . . of EVERYTHING!"

"All right, all right," said Geoff Biscuit, backing away. "I'll go and fetch the general manager."

After a little more muttering, a woman in a smart-looking navy dress walked into the booth. "Dolores

Cheese," she said. "General manager." She held out her hand for Nick (or Nate) to shake, but he didn't.

"I asked to see the man in charge," he said. "AND YOU ARE NOT EVEN A MAN!"

"That is very sexist," said Dolores Cheese. "I am in charge of this entire theme park!"

"But you are not in charge of THE WHOLE OF CHARM LTD., are you?"

"Not yet," said Dolores Cheese (who was very ambitious).

"And why does everyone who works here SEEM TO BE NAMED AFTER A KIND OF *FOOD*?" asked Nick (or Nate).

"I'll take you to see Mr. Hornbutton," Dolores Cheese said sniffily. "I think you'll find his job title, his name, and his gender to your satisfaction."

As Dolores Cheese turned away, Imogen flashed Delia an excited grin. The plan was actually working!

Dolores Cheese led them back into the middle of the park, to the huge blue castle that loomed above everything else. The castle didn't look like it belonged in Charmtopia—it looked too new and well looked after. "This way," said Dolores Cheese as the huge steel gate to the castle swung open automatically. Their footsteps echoed as they walked down the shiny hallway to the steel lifts in the middle of the building. Dolores Cheese pressed the button for the

193rd floor. *Amazing,* Imogen thought. *The castle doesn't look that tall from the outside!* "Mr. Hornbutton has the corner office," Dolores Cheese said.

Nick (or Nate) nodded, satisfied.

When the lift doors dinged open on the 193rd floor, Dolores Cheese tapped her way down another extremely shiny hallway to a huge office that bore what appeared to be a solid-gold nameplate reading "Derek Hornbutton."

Derek Hornbutton's office was almost as shiny as Uncle Knuckles's bald head, only with less stubble and more vases full of artificial flowers. He had a sign that said "Millions of Bucks Stop Here!" on his desk, next to a framed photograph of himself with his arms around two smiling, well-groomed children, who Imogen guessed were his kids. Derek Hornbutton himself was seated at a gigantic desk, leaning back in his desk chair and waggling what looked like a solid-gold pen in his fingers. He had a thin mustache. Imogen was immediately suspicious. Big Nana had taught her "Men with mustaches usually have secrets. Even Charlie Chaplin. He had an eleventh toe."

Derek Hornbutton didn't look very pleased to see them. "Mrs. Cheese?" he said. "Surely these people are looking for some sort of budget fast-food restaurant and not my personal office?"

"Actually, sir," said Dolores Cheese, "they have already been to a fast-food outlet—the Scoopadoopa Ice Cream stall. But they got an unexpected surprise in one of their cones."

"A voucher for a Captain Caring pajama set?"

"No."

"A Princess Kindness key ring?"

"No."

"A Helpful Baby dummy that doubles as a bath plug—now, those really do come in handy."

"No, sir," said Dolores Cheese. "Please stop guessing."

"Then spit it out!" said Derek Hornbutton.

"That's exactly what my son had to do . . . BECAUSE OF THIS RAZOR BLADE!" Nick (or Nate) said sternly, holding out the slightly rusty blade.

Imogen tried not to smile. She'd forgotten what good actors the twins were.

"This is Rick Roberts," Dolores Cheese said hastily. "Publisher of *Rich Parent* magazine."

"Well, why didn't you say so?" cried Derek Hornbutton, all smiles suddenly. "Rick! Please! Come and sit down! Would you like a cigar? Some whiskey? A surprisingly expensive pair of socks? Please! I have so many of them! My secretary keeps buying them for me!"

"I'll take the socks," said Nick (or Nate) as he and Imogen and the other Horrible Children walked into the office. Derek Hornbutton waved a finger at Dolores Cheese, and she picked up a tray full of socks from the sideboard and offered them to Nick (or Nate). He selected a red-and-yellow polka-dot pair and put them in his jacket pocket.

"Thanks," he said.

"That'll be all, Mrs. Cheese," Derek Hornbutton said, waving her away.

Dolores Cheese winced a bit, then turned, straightened herself up, and walked out. Imogen listened to her *tap-tap-tap* down the hallway. A small part of her hoped that Captain Caring really caught on with kids, so that there would still be a Charm Ltd. for Dolores Cheese to manage someday.

"So," said Derek Hornbutton. "Can I get you anything else?"

"I WOULD LIKE THE DELICIOUS ICE CREAM FOR MY SON, WHICH I PAID FOR!" boomed Nate (or Nick), just as Imogen had told him to.

"Coming right up," said Mr. Hornbutton, buzzing his receptionist. "Hi, Jonathan," he said. "Could you fetch an ice cream cone for this fine young gentleman?" He winked at Sam. "Was it vanilla? One scoop or two?"

"Two scoops—" squeaked Sam, slapping his hand over his mouth. "Please," he finished, in a much deeper voice.

Derek Hornbutton chuckled and shook his head. "Don't worry, boy," he said. "I know how awful it is when your voice is breaking."

"His voice wasn't broken until this morning, when it was cut to pieces by a razor blade . . . *IN YOUR THEME PARK*!" cried Nick (or Nate).

"I really am so sorry," said Mr. Hornbutton.

"And as you can imagine," said Nick (or Nate), "I won't be comfortable giving the ice cream to my son unless you have fetched it for me personally. Considering recent events, you'll understand why I can't trust anyone else."

"Well," said Mr. Hornbutton, chuckling again, "I don't know about that. It isn't really typical for the president of a major company to go on an ice cream run."

"Oh. That's fine," said Nick (or Nate).

"Thank you for being so understanding," said Mr. Hornbutton.

"Not at all. I'm sure *you'll* understand that *Rich Parent* magazine will have to revise our review of Charmtopia in light of today's events. Which is a real shame. Because you'll remember that last year, we named Charmtopia as the Number-One Place to Conspicuously Spend Your Fortune."

"No! That won't be necessary! Of course I'll get the ice cream!" said Derek Hornbutton, leaping to his feet like an overpaid gazelle. "I won't be long. Make yourselves at home."

As soon as Hornbutton had left his office, they made themselves *right* at home.

And as we know, Crim House wasn't exactly the tidiest of homes. . . .

Imogen and the Horrible Children started ransacking the drawers and bookshelves and secret compartments under the desk, looking for anything that could tie Charm Ltd. to the missing lunch box. They found a few odd things—something that looked like a rhino's horn, a bottle of pills labeled "Overexcited Child Suppression Tablets," and the manuscript of an unfinished autobiography called *Lonely at the Top: Derek Hornbutton's Story*, which seemed to be written entirely in rhyme. But just as Imogen was beginning to think they'd looked everywhere, Delia let out a yelp.

"What?" said Imogen, rushing over.

Delia held up a piece of paper bearing a family crest: a stocky man and a stocky woman, each holding a machine gun, standing triumphantly over a dead grizzly bear.

Written on the bear's stomach was a single word: "KRUK."

"Wait, what?" said Imogen.

This didn't make any sense at all. What would Charm Ltd. have to do with the Kruks, an *actually successful* criminal family, which put them on an entirely different level from the Crims? She took the letter from Delia, but she only managed to skim the first line, which said something about "moving forward with our lawsuit," before she heard the *ding* of the lift and Derek Hornbutton's footsteps walking back toward the office. And all too quickly, there he was, framed in the doorway like a furious painting. His jaw dropped open. The ice cream fell to the floor. "WHAT IN CHARMTOPIA IS GOING ON?" he cried.

Imogen looked around. Things *had* gotten a little out of hand while they'd been searching the office, she realized. Nick and Nate had taken off the trench coat and were jumping wildly on the expensive white leather couch for no apparent reason—possibly they were just overjoyed not to be standing on each other's shoulders. Isabella, Imogen could see now, had taken a Cross-Eyed Cat doll from Derek Hornbutton's vintage toy shelf and pulled it to pieces.

"Let me explain—" Imogen started, but Derek Hornbutton was in no mood for explanations.

"Who *are* you?" he cried. "NO ONE IS ALLOWED UP HERE BUT RICH PEOPLE!" He pressed a button on his desk, and big red lights started flashing and an alarm blared out: "Unidentified commoners in the office! Evacuate the building immediately."

Imogen didn't need to be asked twice. She'd had enough of being forcibly removed from buildings by rich old men. She and the Horrible Children ran down the corridor and pressed the lift button.

"First floor. Going up," said the lift.

"We don't have time to wait!" yelled Imogen as the

Horrible Children skidded to a halt next to her. "Quick! Down the stairs!"

They raced to the spiral staircase that stretched all the way down the castle. Imogen stared down and thought she might be sick—she could barely see the bottom.

"Come on," said Delia, setting off down the stairs, closely followed by Henry (clutching Isabella) and Sam.

"Come on," said Nick (and Nate) as they sat on the banister and began to slide down. "It's quicker this way!"

So Imogen closed her eyes, sat on the banister, and pushed herself off. What was the worst that could happen? Apart from falling to a very undignified death in a very bad theme park. She decided not to think about that.

But then they were at the bottom of the staircase, and Derek Hornbutton didn't seem to have caught up with them. They burst out of the blue castle. "Which way is the exit?" asked Delia.

"This way!" said Imogen, running toward the terrifying Friendly Clown face. She looked back toward the castle—and was stunned to see Derek Hornbutton careening toward them, dodging around the other families in the theme park, as if he was worried he might catch ordinariness from them. *How did he catch up to us so fast?* "Quick!" she yelled.

"Stop those children!" shrieked Derek Hornbutton, blowing the rhino horn from his office.

Several costumed characters forgot what they were doing and started running toward them, arms outstretched, faces blank and smiling. Imogen felt a shiver of panic. *This is worse than being chased by giant dogs!* At least you knew what giant dogs would do when they caught you; they would eat you. Which would be terrible, clearly—but Imogen had a feeling being caught by the Friendly Clown or Princess Kindness might turn out to be a lot scarier.

"I'll catch 'em, Mr. Hornbutton!" lisped the Helpful Baby, too helpful by half, as it started lumbering in their direction surprisingly quickly. When the baby reached them, it tried to grab Delia in its big, squishy arms.

Delia slipped out of the way just in time. She stuck her tongue out at the Helpful Baby and kept running toward the exit, grabbing a bag of Gobstoppers from the sweets stall as she ran.

Nick and Nate dodged past all the characters and overtook the rest of the Horrible Children. Imogen watched them race through the exit gates toward the train station. Sam and Henry and Isabella and Delia made it through too, and Imogen wasn't far behind. She just had a few more steps to go. . . .

"Come on, Imogen," called Delia, hanging back to wait for her.

Imogen willed her legs to go just a bit faster. . . .

But then she heard a voice calling "LEAVE IT TO ME, MR. HORNBUTTON!" in a terrifying voice. A very *friendly* but terrifying voice. She turned around and saw the Friendly Clown himself, running toward her in slow motion.

Imogen kept running at her usual speed, and she made it out of the exit before the clown had even taken his fourth step.

"NOOOOO!" he screamed (in slow motion again) as Delia grabbed Imogen's hand.

"Thanks for waiting," said Imogen.

"That was close," said Delia.

"It wasn't really," said Imogen.

"No, it wasn't," admitted Delia. "It just sounds better if you say that sort of thing sometimes, doesn't it?"

They made it on to the train just in time, and they bought hot chocolate and cookies from the refreshment cart to celebrate making it out of Charmtopia alive.

"Wow," said Sam, looking at his cookie respectfully. "I've never eaten anything I've paid for myself before."

"It tastes so much better," said Henry. "This is, like, blowing my mind." He dipped his finger in his hot chocolate and wrote his name on the train window. "Got to mark the moment," he said.

Imogen pulled out the letter she'd taken from Derek

Hornbutton's office from her pocket. "Want to hear what it says?"

"YES!" the Horrible Children yelled in unison.

"Right," said Imogen, unfolding the letter and clearing her throat, impressively. "Here goes:

To The Man in Charge:

As you and your associates at Charm Ltd. have not addressed our complaints about the Captain Crook character to our satisfaction, and continue to suppress evidence of the character's existence, we are left with no choice but to find another way of attracting your attention. I understand that you are very attached to your two pet poodles, Dollar and Bill. . . . If you want to see them alive again, I suggest you try a little harder to deal with our concerns. Otherwise, they'll be turned into very expensive cat food and fed to a very expensive cat.

Yours sincerely,

The Kruks and Patrick the tiger."

"The Kruks?" said Sam.

"The Kruks," said Imogen, nodding. She put the letter down. She noticed that her hands were trembling.

"I can't believe it!" said Delia, shaking her head. "Poodles should never be fed to tigers! Tigers much prefer Jack Russell terriers. And why do the Kruks care so much about

Charm Inc. trying to hide Captain Crook?"

"I don't know," Imogen said grimly. "Mum said she thought it was the Kruks when I visited them at the police station. At the time, I thought she was crazy, but . . ." She paused and shook her head. "Based on this letter, I think they actually might have stolen the lunch box."

BY FOUR O'CLOCK the next day, Imogen was behind bars. Not because she'd been arrested—though she had tossed and turned all night, worrying that Derek Hornbutton would figure out who she was and send the police after her—but because she wanted to update her family on her progress. Her family was on the edge of their seats as Imogen told them about the trip to Charmtopia. Uncle Knuckles actually fell *off* his seat and had to be helped back up by Uncle Clyde, all while rubbing his back and telling everyone he hadn't been doing enough yoga since he'd been arrested.

"Anyway," Imogen said when her uncles were back in

their seats. "Nick and Nate managed to pull off the trench coat–man disguise—"

"Me and Jack Wooster invented that, you know," said Uncle Clyde.

"And then we tricked our way into the big blue castle by pretending to be rich!"

"That's my girl!" said Josephine, stroking her fake diamond necklace.

"And then . . . ," said Imogen, building up the tension. "You're going to love this. . . ."

"What?" chorused the Crims.

"We tricked Derek Hornbutton into leaving his office, and when we were going through his files, Delia found . . . this." She held up the letter from the Kruks.

Aunt Bets snatched the letter from Imogen's hands. "The Kruks?" she said, her eyes wide.

Josephine grabbed the letter from Aunt Bets and read it, growing pale. "Oh. Oh *no*! If the Kruks really are caught up in this, then . . . then . . . we are in the most terrible danger!" She shuddered, as though she couldn't bear to look at the letter anymore, and handed it to Al.

"This is definitely from them." Al nodded grimly. "I did an MA in letter forgery, and this is genuine Kruk stationery."

Al passed the letter to Uncle Clyde, who seemed almost reluctant to read it. When he did, his shoulders slumped.

His face fell. Even his hair, which usually stuck straight up, seemed like it couldn't be bothered to look messy and sat limply on his head. "The Kruks are . . . very dangerous," he muttered. "They're not like us at all. If they have my lunch box, I'll never get it back."

Josephine started to cry. She pulled a handkerchief with a *P* embroidered on it from her pocket—she'd probably stolen it from someone named Peggy or Polly or Petunia—and dabbed her eyes. "You *can't* go after the Kruks, Imogen, darling!" she said. "You'll get yourself killed!"

Imogen scowled, feeling frustrated. She'd done such a lovely job of pulling off the Charmtopia plan! She thought they'd be proud of her, but instead they were . . . *worried*? She had never seen her family worried before, even when they really *should* have been worried, like when they were locked up for a crime they didn't commit. The Kruks must be *really* terrible if her family didn't want her to go after them. "But, Mum," said Imogen, "you're the one who told me the Kruks were behind this in the first place. Don't you remember?"

"Well," said Josephine, looking a bit sheepish, "I didn't really believe it—I just got caught up in the drama of it all. Wouldn't it be glamorous if the Kruks *did* want to fight us for our territory? But they don't, of course. Who would want Blandington?" Uncle Clyde frowned at Josephine. Aunt Bets raised her knitting needle and shuffled toward

Josephine's direction, but Uncle Knuckles grabbed it from her and shook his head. "They just want Clyde's lunch box for some unrelated reason. Anyway," said Josephine, "it'll be fine. We don't need to prove our innocence. We'll just go to prison for The Heist. That's what we've been aiming for all along, anyway!"

"Actually," said Al, raising his hand, like a shy kid in the back of history class, "strictly speaking, what we've been trying to do is get *away* with crimes. Not get caught. It's a technicality, I know—"

"Oh, hush, Al," said Josephine, crossing her arms. "I was just trying to look on the bright side." She started weeping again.

Al stood up and beckoned Imogen over. He gave her an awkward hug.

"My dear," he said quietly, motioning for her to sit down next to him. "I'm proud of you for getting this far in your investigation. And I don't say this sort of thing very often, but your mother is right." He smiled at her sadly. "You're a sensible girl. I've always let you make your own decisions, haven't I?"

"Yes," said Imogen. She remembered the hurt in her father's voice when she'd told him she wanted to stay at Lilyworth for another year. But he hadn't tried to change her mind.

"So you know I wouldn't ask this of you unless I

thought you were in very real danger," he said. "Please—I'm begging you—promise me you won't go after the Kruks. Will you do that for me?"

Imogen's stomach twisted. Her father had never asked anything of her, and she wanted so badly to make him happy, but she shook her head. "I can't, Dad. If I don't go after the Kruks, you might never get out of here," she said. "You'll lose your bookkeeping business—"

"I could cope with that if I knew you were safe," Al said stoically, pushing his glasses up his nose. "Anyway, PC Donnelly lets me do the officers' petty cash accounts to stay in practice. *Please,*" he said again. "Just go back to school and forget all about this. Once you graduate from Lilyworth, the world is your oyster!"

Imogen winced. She wasn't sure what about her father voicing her exact beliefs made her so uncomfortable. "I *can't* go back until I've proven you're innocent," she pointed out.

"You're clever. You can argue your way back in somehow," he said.

Could I? The fact that her father believed she could made her wonder. But no—Imogen shook her head again. "Sorry, Dad," she said.

But her father wasn't giving in. "Look," he said. "I don't know if you heard about what the Kruks did to those grizzly bears . . ."

"I heard," said Imogen, trying not to think about it.

"The bears asked for it, really, Al," said Uncle Clyde, overhearing. "They tried to bite the Kruks. Remember what Big Nana used to say?"

"'Never bite a Kruk if you want to keep your internal organs,'" the other Crims chanted in unison.

Uncle Knuckles started to shake.

Aunt Bets hit him over the head with her handbag to calm him down.

"THANK YOU, MY PET," he said after he had recovered. "I DON'T KNOW WHAT I'D DO IF THE KRUKS GOT TO YOU."

"Look," said Imogen, turning back to her father. "I'm not even sure the Kruks were actually involved in The Heist. But I have to find out! Don't worry, all right? I won't do anything unless I'm absolutely certain I'm safe."

Her father smiled at her sadly again. "I know you won't," he said.

Uncle Clyde pushed Al aside so he could give Imogen a hug too. "Take care of yourself, now," he said. "You know, the way you've thrown yourself into getting us out of here . . . It's just the sort of thing Big Nana would do."

"Oh," said Imogen, flustered. She wasn't entirely sure what she thought about that comparison. She wasn't really sure what she thought of a lot of things lately.

But she left the police station surer than ever about one

thing: She *had* to get her family released from custody.

And if she could get herself back to Lilyworth in the process . . . that would be good, too.

A couple of hours later, Imogen was walking home from Blandington Library. She had planned to spend the rest of the afternoon in the true crimes section, researching the Kruks, but the more she read about the murders they'd committed, and the millions of priceless works of art they'd stolen, and the number of wild animals they'd pushed a little closer to extinction, the more impossible it seemed that she'd be able to get close to them without being killed, painfully and humiliatingly, along with an unfortunate panda.

She flipped through *Kidnapped by the Kruks and Forced to Wear a Tutu: A Victim's Story* in the hope that she'd get some tips on how to escape from them if it came to that, but the author had only been saved when a freak tornado destroyed the dungeon they were holding him in. Imogen wasn't sure she could rely on extreme weather events to save her. *Heists, Guns, and Badly Stuffed Animals: Life with the World's Strangest Crime Family* was even more chilling. She hadn't known you could use kitchen utensils to commit so many terrible crimes. Eventually, Imogen couldn't bring herself to read anymore. She needed to get home to think.

As Imogen walked through the streets of Blandington, she was grateful, for once, for the predictable, gray, non-Kruk-filled town she lived in—and she was even grateful for her family. At least they had never stolen the contents of the British Museum and murdered the guards with an ancient Egyptian spoon. Despite their . . . eccentricities, they all really cared about one another. And they really cared about her, too, she realized now—she'd seen that in the way they'd reacted to the idea of her going after the Kruks.

She was beginning to feel ashamed that she'd felt ashamed of them for so long.

Crim House was eerily quiet when Imogen got home. Clean, too—Mrs. Teakettle must have been there. She walked through to the kitchen and found a note stuck to the fridge with a "Crime Pays" magnet:

> *Hello, Imogen dear,*
>
> *I've taken the little darlings to a local production of* Mary Poppins. *They've promised to be practically perfect in every way! I'll bring them home in time for tea. Spit-spot!*
>
> *Mrs. Teakettle*

Mrs. Teakettle was another thing that Imogen was grateful for. She decided to make a cup of tea in her honor, but as she was boiling the kettle, she heard voices coming through the vent in the kitchen wall. Were there people in the house?

She stood on her tiptoes and put her ear close to the grate. One of the voices was slightly mumbling and very, very familiar—she could have sworn it was Freddie. But he was out at his bookkeeping class.

Wasn't he?

Imogen abandoned her cup of tea and picked up a kitchen knife. She wandered around the house, trying to work out where the sounds were coming from, but all the rooms seemed to be empty.

Imogen remembered Uncle Clyde's hidden doors. She checked the one behind the bookshelf in the library, but she only found a stash of stolen comic books. She looked under the trapdoor beneath the toilet and discovered a tank full of surprisingly healthy-looking tropical fish. She knew there were other secret doors somewhere in the house, but she'd never come across them. Well, there was no time like the present.

Imogen started in the dining room, prodding at paneling and pulling vases in case they were levers. Imogen hadn't spent much time in here as a child—the adults held very argumentative dinner parties in the dining room on Friday nights, and Imogen had been only too glad to stay up in her room, updating her crime journal. Which is why she had never looked properly at the portrait that hung on the wall: the portrait of Sir Henry Joseph Crim, the Crims' most illustrious ancestor, who was rumored to have started the Great Fire of London while trying to burgle a bakery. Now that she looked at it properly, she noticed that the wall below the portrait was a slightly different color from the rest of the room.

Imogen put her ear against the wall below the painting. Yes, this was definitely where the voices were coming from. And one of the voices was definitely Freddie's. But why was he hiding in his own house? Surely he couldn't be *that* desperate to get away from the Horrible Children? They weren't even home.

She felt the wall until she found the lock for the hidden door under a loose piece of wallpaper. She jimmied it open with the kitchen knife—she hadn't lost her touch—and pushed the door open.

Imogen had to bend over slightly to peer through the small doorway. On the other side was a dark, smoke-filled room—so dark and smoky that it took her a while to see anything except shadowy silhouettes at first. When her eyes got used to the lack of light, she could make out a round table in the middle of the room, with a single dim lightbulb hanging over it. Six men were sitting around the table, playing some kind of card game—poker, maybe. Imogen took a step forward, being careful to stay in the shadows, so that she could see the men more clearly.

One of the men was Freddie.

No one noticed Imogen at first. The strangers were too busy staring at Freddie, and Freddie was too busy threatening one of them in a low, steely voice.

"You've got to pay up, Pete," said Freddie, leaning toward him. "You owe me for last week, too, remember? That's seven hundred pounds in total. Do you know how many monogrammed shirts I could buy with that much money?"

Wait, thought Imogen. *Freddie doesn't wear monogrammed shirts. This is very weird.*

But things were about to get even weirder.

"When are you going to get me the money?" Freddie said in his quiet but extremely threatening voice.

"I don't know!" said Pete, holding his hands up in surrender. "I don't have a penny, I thwear! I have nothing left—I gave you my vinthage denture collection lath month!"

"Some of those teeth weren't even that old," Freddie said coldly. "I only got 240 pounds for them on eBay."

"What?" said Pete, horrified. "That wath my life'th work! Thothe teeth were worth at leath 260 pounth!"

"Shouldn't have got into debt, then, should you?" said Freddie. He crossed his arms. "So, Pete. What are we going to do about our little problem? You know I can't allow players to get away with not paying what they owe."

"I know," said Pete, hanging his head.

"And most men would turn to violence in a situation like this. But I'm not most men. I'm just one, quite young, extremely peace-loving man," said Freddie.

"I know," said Pete again.

"So what are you going to do?" Freddie asked, his voice dripping with malice.

"I'm going to punch mythelf in the fathe," Pete said, miserably raising a fist.

"That's right," said Freddie. "Not as hard as you did last time, though; I'm still picking up your teeth from the floor! I've saved them for you, actually, in case you want to start a new denture collection."

Pete looked even more miserable. "Thothe were my real teeth!" he lisped. "They're worthleth on the denture market. You've taken everything from me, Crim!"

Freddie, unmoved, nodded toward Pete's fist. "Not quite everything," he said. "Maybe the pain of punching yourself in the face *again* will remind you of where you can find that seven hundred pounds, eh?"

Pete shook his head, letting out a pitiful sound somewhere between a growl and a whimper. He screwed up his eyes and raised his fist. . . .

Imogen couldn't take it anymore. She walked into the light and screamed, "Stop this madness!"

"It's all right, Imogen," Freddie said absently. Then he realized what he'd just said, and did a double take. "Wait—*Imogen*?" he said. "What are you doing here?"

The men all turned to look at her.

"What are *you* doing here, more like!" she said.

"Well," said Freddie, going a little red, "these kind fellows were just doing some role-playing with me to help me prepare for my bookkeeping exam. . . ."

"You're gambling," said Imogen. "Actually, are you *running a gambling ring*?"

Freddie held up his hands. "Fine. You've got me. But it's just a little lighthearted bingo, isn't it, chaps?"

But Freddie's fellow "bingo" players were tripping over themselves to get out of the room, none faster than unfortunate Pete. Freddie shrugged at Imogen.

Her heart was racing. This man looked just like the Freddie she had always known—toothpaste on his collar, a large hole bitten out of his sweater, mismatched shoes—but she realized now she hadn't known Freddie at all. "Is this where you've been disappearing to?" she said, trying not to let her nerves show. "I just figured you were getting lost coming from your bedroom to the living room or searching for clean underwear!"

"I'm so sorry," said Freddie. "It must be my turn to do the washing up." He stood up and tried to leave the room.

Imogen blocked his path, her hands on her hips, hoping

she looked a lot braver than she felt. She could still hear Freddie's new, cold voice threatening poor Pete. "You're not getting out of here till you admit what you're doing. And until you tell me exactly how it works," she said.

Freddie sighed. He straightened up, ran his hand through his hair, and wiped the toothpaste from his collar. He seemed to notice the hole in his sweater for the first time, frowned, and adjusted it so it wasn't quite as noticeable. "All right," he said, not sounding like the Freddie she knew; his voice was smoother and deeper and more confident. "I run Blandington's most popular illegal gambling ring, that's all."

"*Most popular* gambling ring?" said Imogen. That was the most surprising thing of all.

"It's quite profitable, actually," said Freddie.

"So . . . is that how you've been paying Mrs. Teakettle?" She'd been wondering. She thought maybe he'd been selling items from the Loot Cellar on eBay.

Freddie nodded. "See? I'm using my money for the good of the family."

Imogen didn't know what to say.

"The police are always trying to figure out who's running the poker ring, but they don't suspect me at all," continued Freddie. "I've perfected the being-hopeless-at-everything routine."

Imogen's head was spinning. She sat down on one of

the chairs around the table to try to gather her thoughts. "You mean forgetting to put your trousers on in the morning is an act? And you *do* know what day it is and what your name is and how to spell the word 'butter'?"

Freddie sat down on the chair next to her. He nodded. "Friday, Freddie, and B-U-T-T-E-R. I'd have to be really stupid not to know how to spell *that*," he said.

"I know!" said Imogen. Freddie was a far better liar than she had ever been, she realized—and she had pegged him as the most hopeless Crim of all. She felt a little bit nervous around him now, and slightly betrayed.

"It takes a lot of brains to act this dumb," Freddie said sadly, pointing to the hole in his sweater, and his mismatched shoes—one hiking boot, one bed slipper. "All I want to do is get up on time, shave, and get dressed in one of my many nice monogrammed shirts. But if I did that, the police would know something was up. So I suffer for my art."

Imogen shook her head. She still couldn't get her head around what she was hearing.

Freddie sat down beside her. "I hope you're not offended that I didn't tell you the truth," he said. "I haven't told anyone in the family about the gambling ring. I know they'd just steal all my money."

This was true. "But I'm not like the others," said Imogen.

"Well, there's that, too," said Freddie. "You were at that posh school for such a long time, and every time you wrote a letter home, you talked about how well you'd done on your math test without cheating."

"I got ninety-eight percent on my last one," Imogen said sadly.

"Exactly," said Freddie. "No *real* Crim could get ninety-eight percent on an exam without stealing the questions in advance. So I wasn't sure I could trust you. But I've been watching you, and I've seen how hard you've been trying to get to the bottom of The Heist . . . and I want to apologize. You were a real Crim all along." He put his arm around Imogen. "I hope you're not angry with me," he said.

"I'm not *angry*, Freddie," said Imogen. "I'm a bit shocked, maybe. And annoyed, possibly. And definitely quite creeped out. But also . . . *impressed*."

Freddie looked at her. "Impressed?"

"Yes!" said Imogen. "You do realize you're the only Crim who makes any money off crime?"

"I know." He nodded bashfully.

"You're the most successful Crim since Big Nana."

"I don't know about that," Freddie said.

"*I* do," Imogen said seriously, scooting around to face him. "And I know something else, too. The Horrible Children are very sweet in their own way"—she ignored

Freddie's skeptical frown—"but they can only get me so far. If we're going to get our family out of jail, I'll need someone really cunning and devious. A really talented criminal." She took a deep breath and said something she never thought she'd say to her eldest cousin: "I need *you*."

"STUPID TOURISTS!"

Imogen scowled at the rude, important-looking man who had just insulted her. He was the tenth person to have elbowed her out of the way in as many minutes. She and Freddie were standing on the pavement outside Big Ben, trying to get to the middle of Parliament Square, the grassy area across the street—but there were no traffic lights and no crosswalks, and apparently, the only way to get to the square would be to leap in front of the traffic like an extremely depressed lemming, which Imogen wasn't. Maybe it shouldn't have been that surprising that there was no easy way of getting to the square. Most people probably didn't want to spend their time in one of the world's greatest cities on a square surrounded by four lanes of traffic.

"I thought you said we could get there from here," Imogen said.

"That's what the directions said!" Freddie pulled a printout of an email from his pocket and studied it again.

The email was a reply to the letter that Imogen and Freddie had sent the Kruks, posing as the law firm representing Charm Ltd. Imogen had persuaded Freddie to put his illegal (but successful) gambling ring on the back burner for a few days to help her solve The Heist, and he'd turned out to be a genius at fake letter writing. He had watched so many terrible crime shows on TV while he was pretending to be useless that he knew a lot of useful legal phrases, like "without prejudice" and "our clients" and "suing for damages," and he wrote to the Kruks saying that Charm Ltd. wanted to hold talks with them about an "appropriate settlement."

The email had arrived from an anonymous account just a day later, telling Freddie (or Nigel Greystone, as he'd called himself) to come to Kruk headquarters that Tuesday at three p.m. *Proceed to the middle of the large square outside Big Ben, and you will be instructed where to go next,* the email had said.

It was now Tuesday.

It was three p.m. exactly.

But Imogen and Freddie were still standing on the pavement, staring across the roaring traffic at the square.

"We're just going to have to run for it," Freddie said.

"We'll die!" Imogen said, leaning out of the way as a forklift sped past.

"We *might* die," Freddie said, "but the statistical likelihood of dying in a road traffic accident in London in any given year is one in twenty thousand, and the statistical likelihood of our family getting out of prison if we don't find the lunch box is one in two million, roughly, so—"

"All right, Freddie!" said Imogen, who was still getting used to Freddie's newfound fondness for quoting facts, which was probably to make up for all the time he'd pretended not to know what a pencil sharpener was. "Let's do it. Together, on the count of three?"

Freddie nodded.

Before she could change her mind, Imogen reached out for his hand.

The traffic blurred past in front of them.

Imogen took a breath and began to count. "One, two . . . three!"

Freddie burst into the middle of the road first. Imogen darted after him, dodging cars that screeched to a halt just in time, blaring their horns.

But they made it. They slumped to the ground in the middle of the square and sat there, chests heaving, as they tried to catch their breaths.

Imogen looked around for the person who would tell them were to go next. But the square was empty, apart from the two of them, a couple of bushes, and some old drink cans. "Do you think this is a trap?" she asked Freddie. "Do you think the Kruks were assuming we'd die before we got this far?" She'd read too much of *Making It Look Like a Very Weird Accident: Killing People Kruk Style* not to at least consider the possibility.

But then one of the bushes at the edge of the square waddled up to them and whispered, "Nigel Greystone?"

Imogen would have thought she was hallucinating, except that "Nigel Greystone" isn't the sort of name you would hallucinate.

"That's me," said Freddie, trying to sound gruffer than he really was.

Imogen stared at the bush, which she could see now had a man inside it—she could just make out the outline of his body, but there were too many twigs and leaves in the way for her to see his face. His disguise was so good that a sparrow was roosting on one of his branches.

"Who's this, then?" said the bush, either talking about Imogen or a pigeon that happened to be strutting past them.

Freddie assumed he meant Imogen. "This is Ginny," he said. "She's doing work experience at my law firm. I said she could come to a settlement meeting to see how it works."

The bush was not happy about this at all. "No way," he said. "No kids allowed in meetings with the Kruks. She can come inside, but she'll have to wait in another room."

"Fine," said Freddie. "But how do we actually *get* to this meeting?"

The bush pointed one of his twigs toward a much taller bush at the edge of the square. "You've got to get inside that bush over there," he said.

"Is there a tiny person in that bush too?" asked Freddie.

"I'm not a tiny person," said the bush. "I'm almost six feet tall when I'm standing up straight."

"I'm sure you are," said Imogen.

"And no. There isn't a person in the bush. Stop asking so many questions and do as I say."

Imogen and Freddie walked over to the taller bush and pushed their way through the twigs and leaves to the very center. From inside the bush, the traffic sounded quite far away, and the light was dappled and green. Imogen felt strangely at peace for a moment.

But only for a moment, because then a steel trapdoor opened in the ground next to them, revealing steep metal stairs leading down into blackness. Imogen gasped and took a step back, so she wouldn't fall in.

"Proceed," hissed the first bush, who had apparently followed them into the second bush without them noticing.

Imogen's mouth felt dry. She and Freddie looked at each other. They didn't really have much choice.

"After you," said Freddie, gesturing down the stairs.

"After *you*," said Imogen.

"No, I insist," said Freddie.

"If one of you doesn't walk down those stairs soon, I'll kick you down," said the bush.

So Imogen held tight to the banister and reached her foot out for the first step.

The staircase was long and steep and very, very dark. *This is fine,* Imogen told herself. *This is just like Alice in Wonderland, but with a trapdoor instead of a rabbit hole. And we probably won't find a talking rabbit at the bottom. Except we've already met some talking shrubbery, so anything is possible. . . .*

When she and Freddie reached the end of the stairs, a door opened in front of them. A stiff-looking butler bowed to them slightly and said, "Welcome to Kruking-ham Palace."

He stood aside, and Imogen and Freddie walked into a huge, ornate entrance hall. Imogen felt like she'd been there before, which was strange, as she didn't spend a lot of time in ornate entrance halls, or indeed, crime family headquarters located in underground bunkers. And then she realized: This hall looked exactly like the entrance hall at Buckingham Palace.

Big Nana had taken Imogen and Delia on a trip to Buckingham Palace the summer before she'd died. They'd watched the Changing of the Guard and stared at the priceless paintings and porcelain vases (while Big Nana examined the security systems), and then Delia had sat on one of the thrones to take a selfie, and they'd been chucked out. But Imogen had never forgotten the feel of the thick red carpets beneath her feet or the way the gold leaf on the walls had gleamed in the sunlight or how lovely the gardens looked when they were full of flowers instead of broken-down cars and failed Halloween costumes.

She'd never forgotten the sweeping golden staircase at the end of the palace entrance hall, either—and there it was now, in front of her. In fact, she realized as the butler led them up the stairs, Krukingham Palace *was* an exact, full-size replica of Buckingham Palace, just like the rumors said. She had no idea how the Kruks had managed it. Clearly they really *were* on a different level from the Crims, crime-wise and cleverness-wise and generally-being-successful-wise.

"This way, please," said the butler, leading Imogen and Freddie down a corridor lined with marble busts. Imogen remembered walking down a similar corridor in the real Buckingham Palace; there, the busts had been of kings and queens and dukes. Here, the marble heads were of men with stubbly faces and gold teeth. Imogen guessed that they were Kruks. She also guessed she wouldn't have enjoyed running into any of them on a dark night.

The butler stopped abruptly and opened one of the doors that led off the hall. "Your meeting will be in here, sir," he said to Freddie, and ushered him in. Imogen could see four men with side parts and dark suits and fountain pens sitting at a long table. The oldest-looking man, who had a neat gray beard and a smile that looked uncomfortable, as though he didn't use it very often, stood up and offered Freddie his hand. "I'm Luka Kruk," he said in a thick German accent. "Niklas's son."

"Nigel Greystone," Freddie said gruffly.

Imogen was sure she had seen Luka somewhere before too—probably in one of the books about the Kruks she'd read in the library. She held out her hand to him, too, but he just stared back at her, and then the butler cleared his throat.

"If you'd like to accompany me to the sitting room, miss?" he said.

Reluctantly, Imogen followed the butler down the hall to a luxurious sitting room. She sat on a velvet sofa and looked around, admiring the grand piano and the slightly less grand piano and the actually quite ordinary-looking piano.

"Why don't you do some coloring while you're

waiting?" said the butler, handing her a book and some crayons. "I love it myself. They say it's very good for relaxation."

The book he had handed her, however, was the least relaxing coloring book in the history of coloring books. On the front was the Kruk crest and the family motto: *"Wir werden Sie zu töten und nehmen Sie Ihr Geld."* Imogen had studied German at school (and she'd been top of the class, of course), so unfortunately, she knew what that meant: "We will kill you and take your money." Inside the book were black-and-white pictures of the Kruks committing their most impressive crimes.

"That brown crayon's really good for dried blood," the butler said helpfully.

"Thanks," said Imogen, picking it up and reluctantly starting work on the picture of the grizzly bear–shark incident.

"Would you like something to drink?" asked the butler.

"Yes, please," said Imogen. "What do you have?"

The butler handed her an impressive menu.

It contained every drink that Imogen had ever heard of and lots that she hadn't heard of before and never wanted to hear of again, including "shark juice" and "small-child cordial." The last thing on the menu was "Chef's special smoothie using any ingredients of your choice."

Imogen had a cunning idea. Her heart started to beat

faster—in a good way.

"I'd like a smoothie, please," she said to the butler.

"No problem, miss," he said, picking up a notepad to write down her order. "Strawberry and banana?"

"Yes," said Imogen. "But also kiwi fruit and seven grapes, half a grapefruit, a grating of lime zest, the white flesh of three cucumbers, a teaspoon of honey, five ice cubes, three tablespoons of oats, and a splash of coconut milk. And some sapphire dust."

"Of course, miss," said the butler, scribbling it all down. "Blue sapphires or yellow?"

"Which are rarer?"

"Yellow."

"Yellow, then, please," she said.

"Very well, miss. I'll be back as soon as I can. But it might take a little while."

"Take as long as you need," said Imogen.

As soon as the butler shut the door behind him, Imogen leaped up, her body tingling with a mixture of terror and excitement. She reckoned she'd bought herself about fifteen minutes of snooping time. She walked down the hallway; past a cage of live tigers; a room labeled "Sensory Deprivation Chamber"; and John Travolta, who seemed to be polishing silver cutlery with a toothbrush. The paintings on the walls were very stolen and very valuable. In fact, the real *The Storm on the Sea of Galilee* was hanging on the wall of the guest toilet. Imogen felt the hairs on her arms stand on end when she saw it. For the first time since she'd been thrown into the swimming pool without armbands when she was five, she felt out of her depth.

You can do this, she told herself. *You have to figure out if the Kruks set up your family. Otherwise, how are you going to get your place at Lilyworth back?* But somehow that didn't motivate her as much as she thought it would. Still, she had come this far, and she wasn't going to give up now.

She walked into a study and found a pile of invitations waiting to be mailed—invitations to Gustav Kruk's sixty-fifth birthday party, which was apparently being held in the Krukingham Palace ballroom that Friday. Oddly, Friday would have been Big Nana's sixty-fifth birthday too. Imogen tried to ignore the pang in her stomach.

She put one of the invitations into her pocket, left the study, and walked farther down the hall, eyes darting around to make sure she wasn't being followed, until she reached a large drawing room. Photos and paintings of Kruks long dead and recently dead covered the walls. She read the labels beneath the paintings: "Augustus Kruk Committing His First Criminal Act: Escaping from a Set of Wooden Stocks and Then Stealing Them, 1532"; "Sibylle Kruk Steering the *Titanic* Into an Iceberg, 1912"; "Jan Kruk Stealing the *Mona Lisa* and Replacing It with a Very Good Fake, 2013." Imogen shook her head. It was hard not to be impressed with the Kruks crime-committing abilities.

She turned around to look at the pictures on the other wall, and gasped. There, on the wall in front of her, was a painting of a Kruk who looked just like Captain Crook. The same small eyes, the same neat beard, the same toothy, slightly evil smile. She looked at the label: *Niklas Kruk, 1897–1992.* That must be why Luka Kruk looked so familiar, she realized—he looked a lot like Niklas Kruk, who looked a lot like Captain Crook. Imogen was slightly unnerved. This couldn't just be a coincidence. Was that why the Kruks were angry about the Captain Crook character?

Imogen looked at her watch and realized that she'd been gone for twenty minutes. She ran back to the sitting room where the butler was waiting for her, holding her (quite revolting-looking) smoothie on a tray.

"Where have you been?" the butler asked coldly. "Visitors are *not* allowed to wander the halls unescorted."

"I'm sorry," said Imogen, trying to look as meek and innocent as she could. "I had to use the loo."

"What did you see?" demanded the butler.

"Well, I saw the toilet, and the toilet paper, and the sink—"

The butler narrowed his eyes and held out her smoothie.

Imogen sniffed it. It stank of cyanide—the oldest poison in the book. She was almost disappointed. Obviously the butler had been ordered to kill any guest who left the sitting room—but really, she expected better from the Kruks. She faked a sip. "Delicious!" she said.

The butler narrowed his eyes even farther—they were basically shut by this point—and said, "Perhaps you'd like a tour of the building. The, ah, children's playground is just over here. . . ." He led her out of the room, clearly headed toward the tiger cage.

Imogen's stomach went cold. "I don't really feel like playing right now," she said, desperately looking around for an escape.

And then, just in time, there was Freddie, walking down the hall, followed by another butler. Imogen had never been so glad to see anyone in her life. "Meeting's over!" he said. "Time to go!"

Imogen's butler walked up to the second butler and whispered something to him.

The second butler shook his head.

Imogen didn't really want to wait around to find out what would happen next.

She grabbed Freddie's arm and hissed, "We need to go." Then she ran as fast as she could down the golden staircase and up the beautiful entrance hall to the front door.

Luckily, the butlers weren't very good at running. "Come back here!" they shouted as Imogen and Freddie dashed up the stairs to the trapdoor and slammed it shut behind them. They were outside again, in the middle of the grassy square. Barely thinking about the traffic now, they ran across the four lanes to the pavement outside Big Ben and kept going, losing themselves in the crowds.

Imogen felt a bit claustrophobic after her time in the underground, tiger-filled, cyanide-flavored palace, so she suggested that they walk to a slightly farther away tube station. "That was a bit of a stressful afternoon," she said as they strolled along by the banks of the river Thames.

"But worth it!" said Freddie. "They completely believed that I was a lawyer from Charm Ltd. My research told me that eighty-nine percent of lawyers wear white shirts and blue ties to client meetings, so I think that helped."

"I'm not sure the butler believed I was a work experience student," said Imogen. "He did give me a coloring book—but then he tried to poison me."

"Oh! Well, at least he didn't *succeed* in poisoning you. That's the main thing!" said Freddie, who was surprisingly optimistic these days. "So. Here's what I found out: The Kruks are suing Charm Ltd. because they think Captain Crook was inspired by a Kruk," said Freddie.

"I think they're right," said Imogen. "I saw a painting of him—Niklas Kruk."

"Toothy, evil smile? Very small eyes?"

"Exactly!" said Imogen.

Freddie nodded grimly. "So that gives the Kruks a motive to steal the lunch box—they're trying to prove that Captain Crook looks just like a Kruk, and Charm Ltd. is trying to destroy all evidence that Captain Crook ever existed."

"But if we're going to prove to the police that it *was* the Kruks who stole the lunch box, we have to actually *find* the lunch box," said Imogen.

"And the odds of surviving another trip to Krukingham Palace are somewhere around one in three million," said Freddie. "Which is about the same odds as getting a royal flush in poker. It does happen, but you're much more likely to get eaten alive by tigers."

"But we have to give it a go, don't we?" Imogen pulled the invitation out of her pocket. "Do you fancy going to a birthday party?"

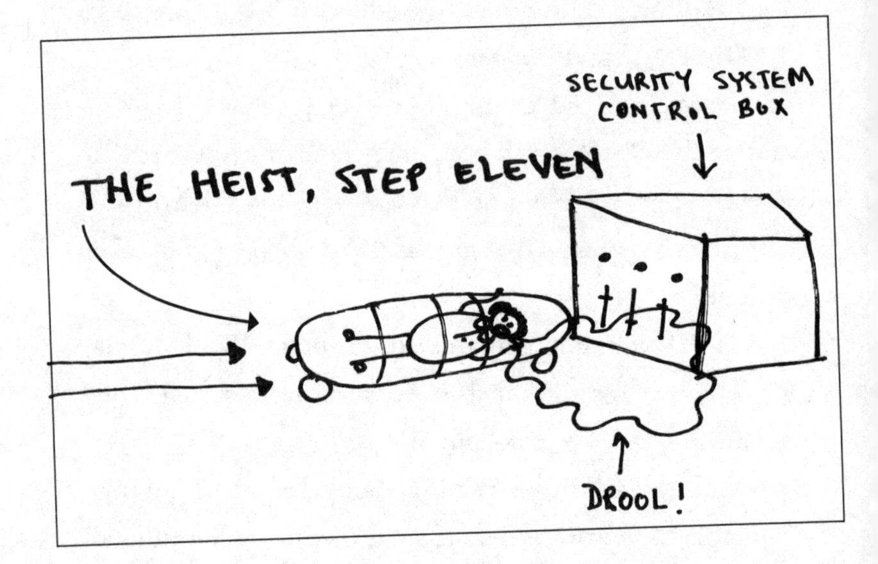

THE NEXT MORNING, Imogen went back to the police station to visit her family. She had practiced her relaxed, no-big-deal smile in the mirror before she went out. If she presented her visit to Krukingham Palace as a fun little caper, maybe they wouldn't be so worried about her. And if she forced herself to think about it like that too, maybe she wouldn't be so worried about herself.

The Crims were all sitting bolt upright in their cell, looking as dressed up as people who have been wearing the same clothes for over a week can look. They also looked as upset as people in a prison cell can look, which is very upset indeed. Al explained that they had just been interviewed via satellite by Nancy Grace from the United States, and it hadn't gone well.

"She was very unpleasant!" Josephine told Imogen. "She called us all sorts of names, and she didn't compliment my hair *once*!"

"Well, I have some good news," said Imogen, smiling.

"You've found my lunch box?" asked Uncle Clyde.

"No," said Imogen. "But I think I know where it is: at Krukingham Palace! And I think I know how to get it back."

"You don't mean—" said Uncle Clyde, turning as white as a terrified sheet.

"I do," said Imogen. "We're going to gate-crash Gustav Kruk's sixty-fifth birthday party and find it!"

"No!" cried Josephine, bursting into melodramatic tears. "You *can't* go sneaking around Kruk headquarters! The Kruks are *monsters*, darling! They fed someone to *tigers* last week!"

Imogen laughed uncomfortably. "Those are just silly rumors," she said. "The Kruks are no more dangerous than we are."

"Tell her, Al," said Josephine, whacking her husband's knee.

But Al just smiled up at Imogen sadly. "Imogen knows I don't want her to go. But we have to respect her decision. And if anyone can get out of there alive, she can." He nodded, as though he was convincing himself. "I'm sure she has a brilliant plan."

Imogen looked at her father gratefully. "I have the *beginning* of a plan," she said. "The Horrible Children will distract the guests while I search the palace for the lunch box. But I *will* need some help finishing the plan. . . ." She looked sideways at Uncle Clyde, who had perked up at the word "plan." "Do you think you could help me?" she asked. "You're such an expert when it comes to complicated plans like this."

"Of course!" said Uncle Clyde, smiling his mad smile. "Sit down." He handed Imogen his notebook and a pen. "Right. First, you need to sketch a blueprint of Krukingham Palace. . . ."

That Friday, Imogen, Freddie, and the Horrible Children dressed up as the sort of people who might be invited to a sixty-five-year-old master criminal's birthday party. Imogen was a wealthy widow, with a black veil over her head; Freddie put on a pair of glasses and a gold necklace and told everyone he was a crooked lawyer; and the Horrible Children put on party dresses and wigs and pretended to be spoiled, criminal children, which wasn't too much of a push for them, really. Imogen felt almost relaxed as they set off for London. She was on top of her criminal game again. And she couldn't wait to get inside the palace.

They arrived at Big Ben at eight thirty p.m. and dashed across the traffic to the square, carrying a huge bunch of balloons. Almost immediately, the talking bush waddled up to them. "What are you doing here?" it said.

"We're here for the party," Freddie said casually.

"You're supposed to go through the Westminster tube station entrance," said the bush. "It says so on the invitation."

Imogen looked at her invitation. "So it does!" she said, chuckling. "It's just that we're such good friends with Luka Kruk that we use this entrance all the time. I just assumed . . ."

The bush looked wary (as wary as shrubbery can look). There was an uncomfortable pause. But then the bush led them to the trapdoor and opened it. "Have a good time," said the bush, as though it wished it could come to the party with them.

When they reached the ballroom, the party was already in full swing. Acrobatic waiters were swooping through the air, serving tiny, expensive canapés to the well-dressed partygoers who were standing around, laughing at one another's jokes. Imogen recognized several of the guests—a famous singer, a guy who had once played a corpse on her favorite TV medical drama, a billionaire who owned a major internet company, and a couple of North American river otters who had been the breakout stars of a recent nature documentary.

The Crims mingled for a while, eating as many mushroom vol-au-vents as they could cram into their mouths, but when Nick and Nate started to make "polite" conversation with a Hollywood starlet (they asked her whether she'd had a nose job), Imogen decided it was time to put Uncle Clyde's Party Distraction Plan in motion.

Her heart pounding, she gave the Horrible Children the signal (she pretended to make a cheese sandwich—which is quite a tricky thing to mime, actually). Like a not particularly well-oiled machine, everyone split up, and chaos soon ensued.

Henry walked up to the buffet table and turned the knob on the chocolate fountain into high gear. He ducked out of the way as the fountain spewed hot brown liquid over the guests' fancy outfits.

"Rats," said the internet billionaire, wiping down his suit.

"*Actual* rats!" shouted the starlet, pointing to the birthday cake. Sam's pet rats were crawling out of it, nibbling on the icing and running across the table.

Everyone started screaming and standing on chairs—but a second later, they were all laughing uncontrollably. Because Delia had popped the nitrous oxide–filled balloons they had brought to the party, spreading laughing gas throughout the ballroom.

This was Imogen's chance.

She slipped out of the room just as Nick and Nate released their secret weapon: a greased pig inexplicably wearing a clown's hat. As she hurried down the corridor she could hear crashes and bangs and squeals—the pig was clearly charging through the ballroom as planned, knocking over tables.

Imogen padded silently downstairs to the basement to start her search for the Kruks' Loot Room. She was starting to feel nervous now, but then she heard someone shout, "Stop that pig!" and she felt a little better—the greased pig was still causing chaos. Everyone would be focused on trying to catch the pig (which would be tricky, because it was slippery), and no one would have noticed she was missing.

The Loot Room wasn't in the basement, it turned out—that's where the shark tank and the weasel dollhouse were (the weasels actually looked very sweet dressed up in Victorian clothes, but they could probably kill you in seconds). Imogen was growing more and more anxious. Every second she didn't find the Loot Room, she was a second closer to getting caught and killed in a very unpleasant way.

She climbed the stairs back to the ground floor, and she was about to keep going to the first floor when Luka Kruk, covered in chocolate and grease, stormed out of the ball-room and walked down the corridor, muttering to himself in German. Imogen crouched down on the staircase so he wouldn't see her. She couldn't understand everything he was saying, but she caught the words "humiliate" and "culprit" and "slow and painful death." She swallowed hard. She had to find the lunch box and get her cousins out of there before he realized they were behind the mayhem!

Imogen searched the first floor as quickly and silently as she could. There was a cuckoo clock on the landing that seemed to be mocking her by ticking particularly quickly. Time was slipping away, and she had nothing to show for it. She looked at her watch—they had been in Kruking-ham Palace for almost two hours. Even if she didn't find the lunch box, she would have to get her cousins out of there soon.

She moved on to the second floor, and then the third floor, feeling increasingly hopeless and desperate. She couldn't find the Loot Room anywhere.

She sat down for a while on the third-floor landing, her head in her hands. There was nowhere else to look. *I tried my best,* she told herself. *No one can hold that against me.* But she felt heavy and hopeless, the way she did when she got an A- on a test at school or thought about Big Nana dying.

Big Nana had once called her the best potential

criminal the family had seen in generations.

And now she couldn't find a Loot Room?

Maybe I am out of practice, Imogen thought. *Maybe I'm just a Future CEO now, thanks to Lilyworth.* She thought of Derek Hornbutton. Surely *he'd* be completely useless in this endeavor.

Or maybe Big Nana was just wrong about me.

But there was no point sitting there feeling sorry for herself. She stood up to make her way back down to the ballroom.

Then she noticed the door.

It was small and set back from the hallway, which is why she hadn't seen it at first. A small silver plaque read: "Broom Cupboard." And beneath the plaque was a combination lock.

Why would a broom cupboard, of all boring cupboards, have a combination lock?

Imogen felt a rush of pure happiness—she'd done it! She'd found the Loot Room! Any minute now, the lunch box would be in her hands.

She just had to figure out the code before anyone found her.

Hands shaking, she started keying in combinations.

She tried the names of all the famous criminals she could think of.

She tried every name of every Kruk, and their

birthdays—and their death days—and the names of some of their most famous heists.

She tried a few swearwords, too, because you never know.

Nothing worked.

The seconds ticked by.

Come on Imogen. Denke! she told herself, which means "think" in German—the Kruks were German, after all.

And that's when she realized—the combination would probably be in German. And she had a feeling she knew what it would be. . . .

She flexed her fingers and started typing the Kruks' motto into the combination lock: *Wir werden Sie zu töten und nehmen Sie Ihr Geld.*

The door to the broom cupboard slid open.

Yes! She hugged herself with triumph, wishing the other Crims were with her to share the moment.

Imogen held her breath as she stepped inside the Loot Room—and then she gasped. Because the Loot Room wasn't so much a room as a warehouse the size of a large airplane hangar or a small country in South America. It was filled to the rafters with incredible things: a complete T. rex skeleton, the Davidoff-Morini Stradivarius violin that had been stolen in 1995 and never recovered, a golden cup that Imogen was pretty sure was the Holy Grail, and a whole underwater town in a huge fish tank that may or may not have been the mythical city of Atlantis.

How was she ever going to find the lunch box in time?

Panicking, she began her search, glancing at things and tossing them aside carelessly—the actual *Mona Lisa*, suitcases full of cash, a cage full of very unpleasant camels (although she didn't toss those aside—she didn't have that much upper body strength).

There was no sign of the lunch box anywhere.

She stopped in the middle of the room to think, trying to control her breathing. *Calm down,* she told herself. *If you don't relax, you'll miss something.*

But telling yourself (or someone else) to calm down usually has the opposite effect.

She searched on for what felt like hours, growing increasingly desperate, until her eyes started blurring and her back started aching.

She looked in every box and behind every stolen wardrobe and under every gigantic stolen bell (there were a lot of them—Luka Kruk was rumored to be a very talented bell ringer).

She looked at her watch. It had been almost an hour since she'd left the party, and she had no idea how her cousins were faring. She was stupid to have stayed away for so long. She had no choice but to leave.

Tears of frustration filled her eyes—she had come *so close.*

Just a little bit longer, she thought. *You can look for five more minutes, and that's it.*

And then, as she was searching through a pile of Middle Eastern antiquities, something caught her eye from the far corner of the room. Something that made the hairs on the back of her neck stand on end.

It was a toy hippo.

Not just any toy hippo. Imogen had seen it before—in every childhood photo of Big Nana. She was always clutching this very hippo tightly, as though she was worried someone would steal it. She had been right to worry, it seemed.

Imogen picked up the hippo and realized that the head was attached with Velcro. Inside was the My First Lock-Picking Kit that Big Nana had used as a child to break into department stores and steal the toys that her parents refused to buy her for Christmas. Imogen was stunned. How had the Kruks managed to get ahold of this? Imogen had never had reason to believe that the Kruks knew the Crims existed. But if that was the case, why did they have Big Nana's toy? Did they go around stealing toys from random children, just to be mean? Probably, Imogen thought. They *did* go around feeding grizzly bears to sharks. But she still had a very bad feeling about it.

Right, she said to herself. *That's enough. Maybe the lunch box just isn't here.* She looked at the hippo. She felt as though it was looking back at her reproachfully. *I know,* she thought. *I've let Big Nana down.*

Dragging her feet, she went to put the hippo back where she'd found it.

But then, crammed into the corner where the hippo had been, she saw something else—something old, something slightly rusty, something familiar.

Imogen walked over to it, her heart beating out of her chest.

Please don't let me be wrong, she thought.

But she wasn't wrong. IT WAS THE LUNCH BOX!

THE ACTUAL LUNCH BOX!

Imogen couldn't quite believe it. She felt dizzy, and she had to close her eyes for a second. Was this actually happening? Had she *really* found it?

She picked it up to prove to herself that it was real. It was lighter than she thought it would be, and dented, and the paint had yellowed a bit, but there was Captain Crook, smiling out at her merrily from the front, one hand forcefully pushing a kid's head into a rubbish bin, the other hand grabbing the kid's lunch box. She turned it over and saw Uncle Clyde's initials written on the bottom in black marker.

She felt a surge of triumph, so strong that she actually jumped up in the air. She'd gotten it right! The Kruks *had* stolen it! Here it was: the lunch box that her uncle had spent twenty years plotting to steal from Jack Wooster . . . the lunch box that had cost her her place at school and landed her whole family behind bars . . . the lunch box that had brought her back home to Blandington and back to a life of crime. Who would have thought that an inanimate object could be so powerful?

She just had to get it out of Krukingham Palace without being caught and hand it over to the police. Then finally, she'd be able to go back to Lilyworth, where she belonged.

Of course she still belonged there.

Her joy was seeping away now and was being replaced by a cold, creeping dread. She was going to *steal from the Kruks.* If she even managed to make it out of the house alive, the Kruks would find out she had taken it. And then . . . She didn't know what would happen next, but she was sure it would be very, very painful.

Too late to think about that now, she told herself, balling her fists to make herself feel braver. She hid the lunch box in the folds of her big black dress. And then, as an afterthought, she hid the toy hippo under her veil, too. She took a deep breath and marched out of the Loot Room with as much purpose as she could muster.

When Imogen got back to the ballroom, everything was back to normal (as normal as a party at Kruk headquarters can be, that is—in the middle of the room, the president of an Eastern European country was dancing the tango with a very large lizard). The rats had been caught, the laughing gas had dispersed, the chocolate had been cleaned up, and the pig was nowhere to be seen. Imogen found the Horrible Children and Freddie and gave them the signal that she had found the lunch box (she pretended to eat a sandwich). They signaled back that they understood (they pretended to get sandwich crumbs stuck in their throat), and they all began to head for the door.

This was it. Just a few more minutes and they'd be safe—for now, at least.

But before they could leave the ballroom, a woman Imogen assumed was a Kruk—she had the same tiny eyes and large teeth as Luka Kruk and Captain Crook—blocked their way. She turned to the guests and clapped her hands. "It's time for the Kruk children to go to bed," she announced, smiling a surprisingly sweet smile. "But first, they'd like to entertain you all with a little song."

The six Kruk children lined up in the center of the room in height order and began to sing:

"There's a strange kind of jangling from the coins in our purse,
And the diamonds in our pockets too.
And up in the tiger cage, our stripy friends
Have got some human bones to chew."

Imogen felt like she might fall over. Was this real, or was she was in the middle of a terrible nightmare?

The song was almost identical to the one Mrs. Teakettle had taught the Horrible Children, only with more disturbing lyrics. She looked over at her cousins—they were all staring openmouthed at the Kruk children, too.

Nothing about this was exciting anymore. Imogen was terrified. Her former belief that the Kruks didn't even know the Crims existed seemed naive at best, idiotic at worst. Why were their children singing the same song? Why was Big Nana's hippo in their Loot Room? She just wanted to get out of Krukingham Palace and never come back. But was it even safe to go home?

Could the perfect Mrs. Teakettle be . . . a *Kruk*?

The eldest Kruk child stepped forward to sing her solo:

"Good night, my friends. I'm so glad I'm a Kruk.
I have a maid, a nanny, and a cook."

A serious-looking boy with slicked back hair stepped forward next:

"Good-bye, good night! Come wake me if you dare.
But if you do, you'll end up like the bears."

And then the littlest Kruk child smiled a terrifying smile and sang *"Good-BYYYYE!"* in a surprisingly beautiful voice. (The Kruks were rich; they probably all had singing lessons.)

Everyone cried "Bravo!" and clapped, and the Kruk children took bow after bow. Imogen forced herself to clap along. When the children had finally gone upstairs to bed, the Crims glanced at one another in confusion—then Freddie made the signal again, and they all ran out of the room and down the hallway to the front door.

"Where did Mrs. Teakettle get that song from?" Imogen panted to Delia as they climbed the stairs to the trapdoor.

"She said she made it up!" said Delia.

Imogen had a very, very bad feeling about this. Her mind surged with questions as they exited the trapdoor, then ran across the four lanes of traffic and down into the tube station. She had always feared Mrs. Teakettle was a little too good to be true. What were the chances that the perfect babysitter would turn up out of the blue in a tiny town and love spending her time with a family of criminals? What were the chances she'd teach a strange, made-up song to the Horrible Children—and that the Kruk children would just happen to know the same song?

Was it possible that Mrs. Teakettle could have been sent to Blandington to keep an eye on the Crims?

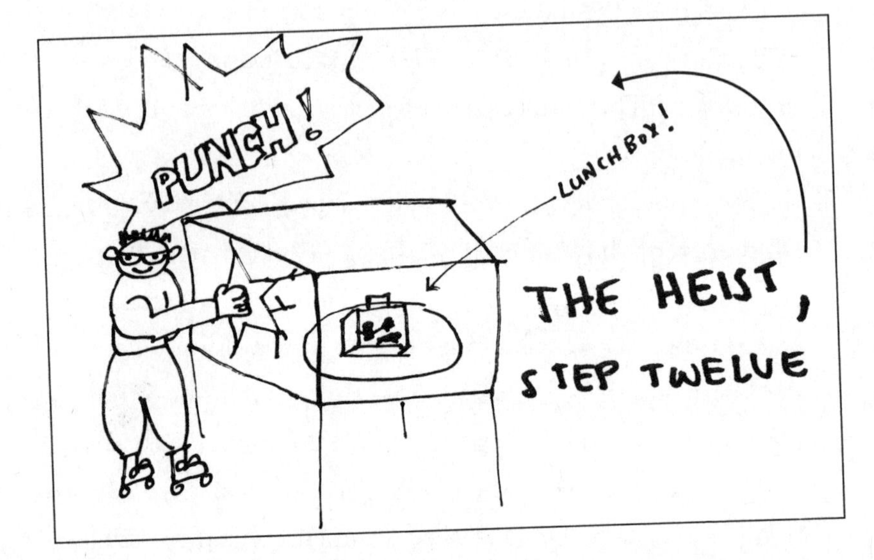

IMOGEN WOKE UP before sunrise the next morning, partly because Sam was practicing voice-lowering exercises in the room above her and partly because there was a deep, nagging dread in the pit of her stomach. She knew she should be happy, and she was, sort of—she'd pulled off her first heist in two years and stolen the lunch box from right under the Kruks' noses. But now that she was sure that Mrs. Teakettle was connected to the Kruks, she couldn't relax. Her family was in danger. She would have to fire Mrs. Teakettle. But, of course, firing someone connected to the Kruks was quite a risky thing to do.

Think positive, Imogen told herself. *You achieved what*

you set out to achieve. You've succeeded! There was nothing Imogen liked more than succeeding—although when people like Bridget Sweetwine *didn't* succeed, that came a close second.

And speaking of Bridget Sweetwine . . . Imogen just had to get down to the police station, give them the lunch box and get her family's name cleared, and write a guilt-inducing email to Headmistress Gruner, and she'd be back at Lilyworth. There was still over a week to go till the head girl elections—plenty of time to polish her campaign speech. Though, something about the thought of going back to Lilyworth made her feel uneasy.

I'm just nervous, Imogen thought, forcing herself to get out of bed. *I just really, really want to go back to school, and I really, really want to become head girl. That's all.* As she got dressed, she focused on all the good things about going back to Lilyworth—the croquet championship, the weekend waffle bar, not spending her time worrying about whether she was going to be murdered in a creative but extremely painful way by a family of master criminals—and by the time Freddie knocked on her door to ask if she was ready to leave for the police station, she felt much better.

She packed the lunch box in a shopping bag, along with the Kruks' coloring book, and set off, arm in arm with her cousin.

"Here's the plan," she said to Freddie as they walked along. "We go straight to the Crims' cell, show everyone the lunch box, let Uncle Clyde say good-bye to it properly, and then we hand it over to the police. Then this whole horrible mess will be over, and the adults will come home, and we can fire Mrs. Teakettle without her knowing we suspect anything about her being a Kruk. Deal?"

"Deal," said Freddie, nodding. "And I can go back to spending my gambling money on beautiful tailored clothes that I can only wear in the privacy of my bedroom. Let's get this over with!"

The police officer on duty was PC Donnelly, and unfortunately for Imogen and Freddie, he seemed to be in the mood for company. "Hang out with me for a bit!" he said, after Imogen and Freddie asked to see the other Crims. "Have you had breakfast yet? I've just put the kettle on! We can have tea and toast!"

Big Nana had always told Imogen, "Always say yes when a police officer offers you food. Unless it's seafood—police officers always buy dodgy oysters." So she and Freddie sipped their tea and watched the time tick by on the gray police-station clock as PC Donnelly told them about the rubbish crimes their ancestors had committed.

"Those were the good old days. . . . I remember my mum telling me about great-granddad Gary Crim committing the Not-So-Great Train Robbery. All he got was a packet of crisps and a roll of very thin toilet paper. . . ."

Imogen and Freddie nodded and smiled, cursing PC Donnelly for choosing this moment of all moments to reminisce about family history.

When he'd run out of interesting ancestors to talk about, PC Donnelly turned to Freddie. "How's the book-keeping course going?" he asked.

"Really well," said Freddie, beaming. "I keep learning things that blow my mind. Did you know there are *negative* numbers?"

PC Donnelly shrugged. "If you say so," he said. "You really take after your uncle Al, Freddie."

"Speaking of Dad," said Imogen, drinking the last of her cup of tea. "Is it okay if we go and visit him and the others now? We have a couple of things to show them."

"Like what?" asked PC Donnelly.

Imogen and Freddie exchanged glances.

"To begin with . . . this," said Imogen. She reached into her shopping bag, pulled out the coloring book she had been given at Krukingham Palace, and pushed it across the desk. "Do you think a court would accept confession by coloring book?"

PC Donnelly opened the coloring book. "Ah, the Kruk family coloring book! These are legendary," he said. "I came across one in London when I was investigating the

Eviscerated Engine Driver Case. Someone pulled out this poor guy's internal organs and then crashed into him with his own engine! Terrible, really. It would have been a lot less painful if they'd crashed his engine into him first. . . ."

Freddie gave Imogen another look.

Imogen gave him one back.

"You've colored in the Kruks' monogrammed pistols purple!" said PC Donnelly, turning the page. "Interesting choice."

"I picked up the wrong crayon by mistake," explained Imogen, glancing up at the clock again. "By the time I realized it wasn't gray, it was too late to switch."

"Of course," said PC Donnelly, nodding. "You wouldn't want the colors to get muddy."

"So . . . can we use the book as proof that the Kruks committed all these crimes?"

PC Donnelly shook his head. "Afraid not," he said. "We can't prove that the Kruks drew the pictures or that they're based on actual events. And going after the Kruks is a dangerous business, anyway. Did you ever hear what they did to poor Inspector Sheldon when he tried to pin the Eviscerated Engine Driver Case on them?"

"I—" Imogen wanted nothing more than to stop PC Donnelly from telling his story, but he seemed absolutely determined to get the words out. Words that were already quite terrible on their own—"moist," "laceration," "overripe," and "plopped"—but that were taken to a whole new level of horrifying when they were combined into this improbable, nightmare-inducing tale.

"I—" Imogen tried to excuse herself politely, but she began vomiting almost immediately upon opening her mouth, so she clamped it shut and bolted for the ladies' toilet, where she surprised herself both in terms of volume and ferocity.

A few moments later, there was a knock at the door, and Imogen heard Freddie's voice saying, "Imogen? Can I come in?"

"Mmmmhgh."

The door inched open, and Freddie's head appeared. "Are you okay?" he asked.

Imogen rested her forehead on the cool toilet seat. She was sure she'd seen at least one small but essential organ go by, like her pancreas. "I don't know," she said.

She was still struggling to come to terms with the implications of PC Donnelly's story. She had planned to hand the lunch box to the police today, to prove that the Crims were innocent and the Kruks were extremely guilty, and to be on a train back to Lilyworth by the weekend. But if *that* was how the Kruks treated whistle-blowers, she wasn't sure she could go through with her plan. What the Kruks did to Inspector Sheldon was worse than death. It *was* death, obviously, but all the stuff they did to him before he was actually killed was . . . inhuman. She liked to think of herself as brave, but no one was *that* brave. And even if she was prepared to put her own life at risk for the sake of justice, she couldn't put the rest of her family in danger. *I love them too much,* she realized.

"That story—" said Freddie.

"Don't say it," said Imogen, closing her eyes.

"Who even knew that a deck of cards could—"

"I know," Imogen said quickly, worrying she might vomit again. "Please, can we never talk about it ever again?"

Freddie sighed. "Good idea," he said. And then he opened his mouth to say something else, but changed his mind and shut it again.

"What is it?" Imogen asked.

"Okay," said Freddie. "I'm all for justice. And I want to get the Crims out of jail, obviously. But—"

"But we can't go after the Kruks," Imogen finished for him. She sighed. "I know. We don't want to end up like Inspector Sheldon."

"We really, really don't," said Freddie. "It's strange, though—the Kruks actually seemed quite nice at the party. Those children, singing that sweet song . . . and Luka, with his nice little beard . . ."

"And that butler who tried to poison me and feed me

to the tigers," said Imogen, resting her head on the toilet seat again.

"Good point," said Freddie, nodding. "And he was just the butler. So . . . what do you say we find a way to clear our family's name without telling the police that the Kruks were the ones who stole the lunch box? Mission aborted?"

"Mission aborted," Imogen replied. She gave Freddie a sad smile. After everything they'd been through, she hated the idea of letting the Kruks get away with what they'd done.

When Imogen had washed her face and smoothed down her hair, and Freddie had ruffled his hair up to disguise the fact that he'd combed it that morning, PC Donnelly showed them to the Crims' cell. At last.

Their family was very pleased to see them, and Imogen found that she was very pleased to see them, too. *It doesn't matter about the Kruks,* she told herself. *What matters is getting my family out of jail, so we can all be together again.* But how would she be able to prove it wasn't them if she couldn't pin the crime on the real culprits?

Josephine hugged Imogen and insisted on helping Freddie put his shirt on the right way around. "You've got it on inside out!" she said fondly. "Honestly, darling. You are hopeless!"

Imogen avoided Freddie's eye and smiled at Uncle Clyde instead, who was walking up to her, rubbing his hands. “So?” he said. “Did the plan work?”

“See for yourself,” said Imogen. She held the shopping bag out to Uncle Clyde.

His eyes lit up. “It’s not . . . ,” he said.

“It is,” said Imogen, laughing.

He snatched the bag from Imogen, reached a hand in, and triumphantly pulled out . . .

“MY LUNCH BOX!”

All the other Crims gasped—except Aunt Bets, who screamed (because Uncle Knuckles had stepped on her toes in all the excitement)—and Freddie and Imogen, obviously, because it wasn’t much of a surprise for them.

Uncle Clyde cradled the lunch box tenderly in his arms (much more tenderly than he cradled his children, if you remember what happened to poor Henry). “It’s really you!” he cooed to it, tears in his eyes. “I never thought I’d see you again! Did you miss me?”

The lunch box didn’t reply.

“I don’t mean to interrupt . . . ,” said Imogen.

“Then don’t,” said Uncle Clyde, holding the lunch box up to his face and stroking it.

“It’s just . . . You do know that you can’t keep it, right?”

Uncle Clyde’s smile dropped. “But it’s MINE!”

“I know it’s yours,” Imogen said carefully. “But technically, it’s not. So we’re going to have to give it to the police.”

"Don't call my lunch box 'it.' It's a 'he,'" said Uncle Clyde, stroking the lunch box one last time and wrapping the towel around it like swaddling.

"So," said Al, blinking nervously, "did the Kruks really steal it, then?"

"Steal *him*," corrected Uncle Clyde.

Imogen nodded. "I found it—sorry, him—in their Loot Room."

Uncle Clyde shook his head. "I can't believe they wasted my genius heist on gathering evidence for a stupid lawsuit about whether or not Captain Crook looks like one of their ancestors," he said.

"But don't you see?" said Josephine, clutching Uncle Clyde's arm. "The Kruks knew about The Heist! Which means they know about *us*! They probably know our names! It's too, too thrilling!"

Imogen winced, remembering that she still had to fire Mrs. Teakettle. "Here's the thing, though," said Imogen. "We're not really sure what to do next. Because"—she braced herself—"we can't go after the Kruks."

The Crims were outraged.

"WHY NOT?" shouted Uncle Knuckles. "WHAT THOSE KRUKS DESERVE IS A NICE FAIR TRIAL."

"I know," said Imogen, sitting down on a bench. She took a deep breath. "But did you hear what happened to Inspector Sheldon after he went after the Kruks for the

Eviscerated Engine Driver Case?"

The Crims shook their heads.

Ten minutes later, everyone had stopped vomiting. Uncle Knuckles hadn't stopped shaking, but Aunt Bets was doing her best to comfort him (by repeatedly hitting him around the head with one of her shoes).

"Fine," Uncle Clyde said weakly. "I get it now. We can't go after the Kruks."

"But how are we going to prove that we didn't do The Heist?" asked Aunt Bets.

Al had his head in his hands. "I really want to get out of here," he said. "I really miss being an accountant. . . . What I wouldn't give to do some long multiplication!"

Imogen felt as though she'd let everyone down. "I haven't given up," she said firmly. "I'm still trying to think of a way to get you out of here." She smiled at everyone as encouragingly as she could, but their eyes all shared the same bleak expression. Imogen felt pretty bleak, too.

"I need to get out ASAP too," said Uncle Clyde. "It's the Obscure Cartoon Character Conference this weekend."

Uncle Clyde went to the Obscure Cartoon Character Conference every year, dressed as Captain Crook. Jack Wooster went every year too, also dressed as Captain Crook, except his costume was better and more expensive.

Jack was always invited to speak on a panel (usually about how Captain Crook had inspired him to do wonderful things with his life), and Uncle Clyde always went to watch and threw rotten tomatoes at Jack.

Imogen suddenly had a thought. "Is Jack definitely going to be there this year?" she asked.

"Yes," said Uncle Clyde. "He'd never miss it! I normally wouldn't either, but of course, I'm in jail."

"So he definitely won't be home this weekend?"

"No," said Uncle Clyde. And then he straightened up. "Wait a minute," he said, drumming his fingers thoughtfully on his chin.

Imogen felt hope begin to bubble up inside her again. "Are you thinking what I'm thinking?" she asked Uncle Clyde, a slow smile spreading across her face.

"I think so," said Uncle Clyde, nodding. "There might be a way to get the lunch box back to the police . . . and humiliate Jack at the same time. . . ."

"SHH! ALL OF you!" hissed Imogen.

This was the moment she had been waiting for.

Any second now, they would pull off the biggest reverse heist in history.

As long as her cousins didn't spoil the whole thing by coughing and giving them away . . .

She closed her eyes and counted to five, the way Big Nana had taught her to do when things (or her family) got too much. She was hiding in a small wardrobe in a large bedroom in an enormous mansion—Wooster Mansion to be exact. She was squashed up against the Horrible

Children, and one of them didn't smell very good. She suspected it was Henry—he'd drawn the blueprint of the mansion on his stomach the previous Thursday, and he'd refused to have a bath since.

And then suddenly, they all froze—the bedroom door had creaked open. The Horrible Children started jostling for the best view out of the crack in the wardrobe door.

"It's Jack Wooster's maid!" hissed Nick (or Nate).

"Shh!" said Imogen again, her heart pounding.

Luckily, the maid hadn't heard them—she was humming the old Captain Crook theme tune to herself as she started to dust.

The maid was an irritatingly thorough duster, it turned out.

She dusted the bedside table and the wardrobes and every tiny china trinket on the mantelpiece. There were a lot of them.

The Horrible Children were starting to get cramps.

Imogen thought her heart might beat out of her chest.

Finally, the maid moved on to the broken, empty glass cabinet where the lunch box had been displayed before it was stolen; she stopped humming at this point, as a mark of respect. And then—

"AAAAAGHGGHGHGGHHGGH!" screamed the maid.

The Horrible Children jumped and swore at one another and generally made quite a lot of noise inside the wardrobe.

But the maid didn't notice. She was at the floor beneath the glass cabinet.

Because there, peeking out from behind an umbrella stand, was . . .

The lunch box!

The maid grabbed a phone. "I'VE FOUND IT!" she yelled.

Then she realized she hadn't dialed a number yet.

She tried again.

As soon as Jack Wooster answered, she shouted, "I'VE FOUND IT! I'VE FOUND THE LUNCH BOX! WHAT DO YOU *MEAN* WHICH LUNCH BOX? THE CAPTAIN CROOK ONE!"

Imogen felt like she might cry or collapse with relief. She grinned at Delia, which was hard, because her head was pressed up against Sam's elbow. Delia grinned back, and she reached out to hold Imogen's hand.

Imogen couldn't quite believe it. She had actually done it. *They* had done it—together. She felt purely happy—like she had really achieved something, something really worthwhile, and that everything was right with the world. This was *real* satisfaction—it was so much more intense than the feeling she got when she came in at the top of the class in a physics test. She hadn't felt this happy, this excited, for over two years. Since before Big Nana died. Since the last time she had pulled off a brilliant, ingenious crime caper with her brilliant, ingenious family.

"So in conclusion," said PC Donnelly, standing behind the podium at the press conference a few days later, "the lunch box wasn't stolen at all. It looks like it was all one big misunderstanding."

The press groaned. The most exciting news story in the history of Blandington had turned out not to be a news story after all.

"What does Jack Wooster have to say about this?" called a grumpy journalist.

"I'll tell you what I have to say," said Jack Wooster, striding up to the podium and pushing PC Donnelly out of the way. "If this is a 'misunderstanding'"—he made air quotes—"then my name is Clyde Crim. WHICH IT CLEARLY IS NOT. BECAUSE I AM A THOUSAND TIMES THE MAN HE WILL EVER BE. There is CLEAR evidence of Clyde's ridiculous 'heist'"—he made air quotes again—"ALL OVER MY MANSION. Would I smash the glass in my own glass display cabinet? Would I dress a greased pig up as a young girl and let it run loose in my own mansion? Would I blow up a bouncy castle in my own back garden? Would I even deign to *own* something as down-market as a bouncy castle? The answer is NO!"

"Be that as it may," said PC Donnelly, elbowing his way back to the podium. "Now that the lunch box has been recovered, the Blandington Police Department has no choice but to release the Crims from custody. Immediately."

The press cheered at this; the Crims being released definitely counted as news. And they cheered even more when the Crims themselves walked into the room. They could always be relied upon to look ridiculous in photographs.

Uncle Clyde walked up to the podium and smiled. "I'll happily take any questions you have about The Heist and how brilliantly I planned it," he said to the journalists. "Except from you," he said, pointing to the grumpy journalist who had spoken earlier. "I don't like your mustache."

Hands went up all over the room.

"Yes?" said Uncle Clyde, pointing to a woman at the back of the room. "You, with the face."

"Do you still plan to carry out The Heist one day?" asked the woman with the face.

"Absolutely!" said Uncle Clyde.

Imogen watched Jack Wooster shoot a look at PC Donnelly. PC Donnelly just shrugged.

"Another question," said Uncle Clyde. "Yes—you, in the middle, with the arms."

The man with the arms asked, "Did you think you'd ever get out?"

Uncle Clyde smiled. "I can honestly say that I thought we'd be in prison for the rest of our lives. And we would have been . . . if it hadn't been for one incredible person."

He winked at Jack Wooster's maid, who was sitting in the audience, blushing.

"She's remarkable—modest, determined, great with a vacuum cleaner . . ."

Jack Wooster's maid sat up a little taller.

"And she's my own flesh and blood."

Jack Wooster's maid looked a little confused.

"We owe this all to my niece, Imogen Crim . . . the sharpest mind in this family since my legendary mother!"

The journalists burst into applause. The maid burst into tears. And Imogen felt so proud she felt like she might *literally* burst, but she didn't, because that would have been messy. Uncle Clyde had *actually compared her to Big Nana*—and this time, she felt she almost deserved it. When she'd been little, all she had ever wanted was to be as good a criminal as Big Nana—and now she was. She had proved that she was every bit as talented as Big Nana thought she could be. She vowed to memorize Uncle Clyde's words and think about them whenever she doubted herself. Except the bit about being good with a vacuum cleaner—she had no idea what that was about.

Imogen smiled as she looked around the room. Her eyes rested on her father, who was sitting quietly on a chair on his own, polishing his glasses and beaming in her general direction (he really was quite blind when he wasn't wearing them). She rushed over to give him a hug.

"Imogen," he said, grasping her hands. "I'm so proud of you. And grateful. Finally, I get to use a calculator again, and it's thanks to you."

"You're welcome, Dad," Imogen said. Everything had been worth it to see the smile on his face.

He nodded, a bit of sadness creeping into his eyes. "And for you . . . It's back to school, isn't it? I'm sure you can't wait to get back to all the great things you were doing there. Will you come home this summer, do you think?"

"I'm not sure," said Imogen. She was having trouble picturing the summer. She was having trouble picturing herself at Lilyworth, too, although surely that was temporary. "I can't wait to go back," she said, trying to sound confident.

She and her father sat in silence for a while, watching the rest of their family hugging one another and the police and random journalists in the audience. Imogen was feeling something she hadn't felt in a long time: a fierce, bitter love for them all. Suddenly, she realized why it was so hard to picture herself at Lilyworth: Her family wouldn't be there.

I'm going to miss them, she admitted to herself. *I'm going to miss them* so much.

IMOGEN SAT IN the kitchen the next morning, sipping a cup of tea, listening to the ticking of the cuckoo clock that Aunt Bets had stolen from an old people's home. She couldn't hear screaming children or illegal gambling or any of the noises she usually heard when the other Crims were awake, because the other Crims were very much asleep. Everyone had stayed up very late the night before—a lot of warm champagne had been drunk, a lot of out-of-tune songs had been sung, a lot of misguided text messages had been sent. Luckily, Josephine had accidentally sent Imogen the text she'd intended for PC Donnelly, confessing to the Jack the Ripper murders of 1888 and claiming to look “very good in a top hat.”

Imogen smiled as she thought about the previous night. She and Delia had stayed up chatting for hours, doing impressions of the other Crims and making fun of each other and generally remembering why they had been such good friends in the first place. She had told Delia all about Lilyworth, and Delia had admitted that it actually sounded like fun—and then Delia had forced Imogen to listen to a Kitty Penguin song over and over again until Imogen actually found herself *liking it*. A bit.

But the best thing had been watching her family together—her mother and father waltzing, gazing into each other’s eyes, Uncle Clyde and Uncle Knuckles doing ill-advised arm wrestles (Uncle Clyde had to lie down on the floor for a while until he had enough energy to stand up), and Henry and the twins teaching Aunt Bets to beatbox. She turned out to be a natural. The evening had reminded Imogen of all the nights she had stayed up late with the grown-ups when she was little, feeling *so proud* to be a Crim. The only trouble was, everyone being together again made her miss Big Nana more than ever. But Imogen shook that thought off. Her family was out of jail, and Jack Wooster had his lunch box back. Everything was all right.

Everything was more than all right, actually, Imogen thought as she opened her laptop and reread the email she’d received from Ms. Gruner that morning:

Dear Miss Crim,

As it appears that your family was wrongly accused, we will be happy to restore your place at Lilyworth Ladies' College, effective immediately—

"Morning, Imogen." Imogen looked up to see Delia standing in the kitchen doorway, wearing her Kitty Penguin pajamas. "Aren't you going to make me a cup of tea?" said Delia—and then she noticed Imogen's luggage piled up neatly in the front hallway. She stared at Imogen, open-mouthed with outrage. "No way. You're not *leaving*, are you? You can't!"

Imogen looked away. She had been dreading this moment. She knew Delia would make fun of her for still caring about Lilyworth, but she *did* care—just like Delia cared about taking selfies in inappropriate places and getting her thefts featured in *Teen Shoplifter* magazine. The election for head girl was only two days away. Imogen had booked a train ticket back to school for that afternoon. It was too late to change her mind now. "I'm sorry, Delia," she said, shaking her head. "I have to go."

Delia crossed her arms. "You don't *have* to go. We've been having fun together, haven't we? It's been just like things used to be before you forgot who you were and got all stuck-up and started caring about obeying the law."

Imogen sighed. "Look—" she started.

But then the doorbell went. Imogen jumped up to answer it, grateful for the distraction.

"Willkommen, bienvenue," sang Big Nana's voice from the doorbell.

Delia followed Imogen into the hallway, arms still crossed. "What would Big Nana think of you abandoning us again?" asked Delia.

Imogen didn't want to think about that right now. She didn't want to think about the hurt in Delia's voice, either. Or how much it hurt *her* to think about leaving her family again. So she ignored Delia and opened the door—and there, on the doorstep, stood Mrs. Teakettle, adjusting her little velvet hat on her curly gray hair.

Imogen smiled at her warily. Mrs. Teakettle looked so innocent and so unlike a Kruk. But as Uncle Knuckles's fondness for tiny kittens and hatred of violence proved, appearances can be deceiving. . . .

"Hello, my dear!" said Mrs. Teakettle. "Are the children dressed yet? We're going on a lovely nature hike today! I'm going to teach them the names of all the different trees in Blandington—the plane tree and the beech tree. That's it. Blandington doesn't have much wildlife diversity, have you noticed?"

"Oh," Imogen said uncomfortably. "You must not

have seen the news. . . ."

"The news? Has something happened? Is everyone okay? I can't bear the news these days—all that terrible crime!"

"Everything's fine," Delia said quickly. "It's just that our family has come home. From their . . . travels."

"Well, how wonderful!" said Mrs. Teakettle. "Remind me where they went?"

Imogen started to say "Thailand" at the same time that Delia said "Cuba."

"Thailand and Cuba? Goodness!" said Mrs. Teakettle, raising her eyebrows.

"Yes . . . they all decided to see the world before they retired," said Imogen, glancing at Delia.

"You have a family business, don't you?" said Mrs. Teakettle. "What is it again?"

"Hat making," said Imogen, at the same time Delia said, "Taxidermy."

"Hat making and taxidermy? How niche!" said Mrs. Teakettle.

"Yes," said Imogen. "We specialize in stuffing people's pets and then making little outfits for them. We're very popular on Etsy."

"Stop talking," Delia hissed in her ear.

Imogen stopped talking. Then she smiled apologetically at Mrs. Teakettle and said, "I'm sorry we didn't let you know sooner. Now that everyone is back, we won't need you to babysit the children anymore."

She braced herself. How would Mrs. Teakettle react? She wished Freddie were here as backup, but he was back in his illegal gambling den.

But Mrs. Teakettle just gave Imogen and Delia a sad little smile and said, "Oh, that's such a shame! They are such darlings, and so well behaved. They loved my reading bedtime stories to them—their favorite was *Hard Times* by Charles Dickens. Such an uplifting book, that one. Isn't it, Delia, dear?"

Delia nodded. "Whenever I've had a bad day, I think, *At least I haven't died falling down a mineshaft like Stephen from* Hard Times. That always cheers me up."

Imogen tried not to let the relief she felt show on her face. "I promise that if we ever *do* need a babysitter, you'll be the first person we'll call," said Imogen.

"Thank you," said Mrs. Teakettle, squeezing her hand.

"Thank *you*," said Delia.

"Well," said Mrs. Teakettle, "if I'm not needed here, I suppose I'd better get home." She nodded to them both and opened the front door.

I must have been wrong about Mrs. Teakettle, Imogen thought as Mrs. Teakettle stepped onto the front path. *She's harmless—she* can't *be a Kruk.* But there was still the matter of the song. . . . "Mrs. Teakettle?" Imogen asked.

"Yes, dear?" said Mrs. Teakettle, turning around.

"You know that song you taught the children? Did you make it up?"

Mrs. Teakettle nodded. "I was quite proud of that one. I've always wanted to write a song that rhymed 'judge' and 'grudge.' Why?"

Imogen hesitated. But Mrs. Teakettle was being so reasonable—surely it couldn't hurt to ask? "Well . . . I was in London the other day, and I heard another family singing another version of the same song."

Imogen studied Mrs. Teakettle's face for a reaction. But Mrs. Teakettle's crinkly smile did not waver for a second.

"Oh—do you mean the Kruk family?" Mrs. Teakettle said airily. "I babysit the Kruk children, too, sometimes."

Imogen and Delia looked at each other. Mrs. Teakettle didn't seem to have a problem admitting this at all. So she *couldn't* have been sent to spy on them. Could she?

"Isn't it annoying having to go all the way to London to look after them?" asked Imogen. "Over an hour on the train, there and back . . ."

"Oh, I don't mind that," said Mrs. Teakettle. "I'm an old friend of the family. Met them when I was a little girl. I hear they have a bit of a reputation in the press, but you shouldn't believe all of that—they're really lovely people when you get to know them, especially the children. Little darlings!" Her smile hardened a little, the way cupcake frosting does if you don't eat it quickly enough. "Why?" she asked. "Is that a problem?"

"No!" said Imogen, her voice slightly too high-pitched. Was it really just a coincidence that Mrs. Teakettle babysat for two families that made their business in crime? Imogen shook the thought away. It didn't matter now, anyway, even if Mrs. Teakettle *was* a Kruk. She wouldn't be looking after the Horrible Children anymore.

"Well, then, my dears," said Mrs. Teakettle. "I suppose this is good-bye."

"We'll really miss you," said Delia.

"Come here, both of you," said Mrs. Teakettle, and she pulled Imogen and Delia into a hug. "I'll miss you, too," she said.

And then she gasped and took a sudden step backward.

She was looking at something behind Imogen and Delia, in the hallway.

Imogen turned around—Mrs. Teakettle was staring at Big Nana's soft toy hippo, which was sitting by her luggage. She had decided to take it back to school with her.

"Where did you get that?" Mrs. Teakettle asked, pointing at the hippo. Her voice was several octaves lower than usual, and gravelly. It sounded . . . familiar.

"I found it in a secondhand shop in London," lied Imogen, watching Mrs. Teakettle's expression.

"It's very nice," said Mrs. Teakettle, her eyes clearing,

her voice returning to normal. "Very unusual. I've been looking for one like that for . . . many years." She had a strange, faraway look in her eye, as though she was remembering something that happened a long time ago.

And then she suddenly snapped back to herself. She blew Imogen and Delia a kiss and scurried off down the path, like an elderly but energetic mouse, waving to them over her shoulder and saying, "Good-bye, my dears! Tell the children: 'Always eat your broccoli, unless you suspect it's been laced with arsenic!'"

Imogen watched her go, suddenly feeling queasy. Was she just imagining it?

The hippo.

The gravelly voice.

The interest in the Kruks.

Delia's eyed widened, and she turned to look at Imogen. "Was that . . . ?" she began.

"It couldn't be," said Imogen. "But . . ."

And then she dashed down the path after Mrs. Teakettle, crying, "WAIT!"

Mrs. Teakettle didn't want to wait. She clutched her hat and hitched up her skirt (revealing surprisingly sturdy legs—legs that looked as though they were used to making a quick getaway) and broke into an all-out run.

"Stop!" called Imogen, pounding down the pavement after her.

Mrs. Teakettle didn't want to stop. She scrambled up a fence into the neighbors' back garden and jumped down onto the lawn.

Imogen climbed the fence after her, ignoring the rose thorns that scratched her ankles. She could see Mrs. Teakettle in the next-door garden, using a rake to vault herself over another fence. Imogen ran across the grass, and climbed up the fence on the other side of the yard, but by the time she was at the top, Mrs. Teakettle was jumping over a fence three doors down. She must have bounced off a trampoline.

Imogen paused at the top of the fence to catch her breath. Mrs. Teakettle was too far ahead, anyway—Imogen would never catch up with her now. She sat there and watched Mrs. Teakettle sprint across another back garden—the last before the main road—apparently not noticing the children's toys strewn in her path.

"Watch out!" shouted Imogen.

But Mrs. Teakettle didn't watch out. She didn't see the tricycle until it was too late. She tripped and fell face-first into an ornamental fish pond. When she had heaved herself out of the pond, she was covered in lily pads, and a small frog was sitting on top of her hat. She stopped to take her shoes off and shake the water out of them.

She shouldn't have stopped.

Because Imogen had jumped down off the fence and

was chasing her again.

"Keep going, Imogen!" shouted Delia, who was somewhere behind Imogen.

So she did. She found the trampoline, bounced over the fence, and made it to the ornamental fish pond just as Mrs. Teakettle got to her feet.

When Mrs. Teakettle saw her, she ran a little bit harder.

But Imogen ran a little bit harder than that.

Her lungs were burning and her legs felt like rubber, but she had almost caught up with her now.

"Grab her, Imogen!" shouted Delia.

So Imogen reached out to grab Mrs. Teakettle's arm. She missed and caught hold of Mrs. Teakettle's little velvet hat instead.

The hat came off in Imogen's hand, the frog bounding off with an irritated "Ribbit!"

Mrs. Teakettle's curly gray hair came off with it.

Mrs. Teakettle shouted some very rare swearwords. Swearwords so rare and unusual that Imogen had only heard them once before, when she was a very young child. Swearwords so exotic and powerful that Imogen had gone temporarily deaf upon first hearing them and had only been cured by listening to jazz for several days (jazz always cures swearing-induced deafness in children). Imogen put her hands over her ears to protect herself.

Mrs. Teakettle turned around to look at Imogen. She

said something, but Imogen couldn't hear what it was, because she still had her hands over her ears.

But it didn't really matter what Mrs. Teakettle said. It mattered what she looked like. It mattered who she *was*. Because now that her wig had come off, Imogen could see the line where her prosthetic nose and chin joined her face. And she could tell that Mrs. Teakettle wasn't Mrs. Teakettle at all. She was—

"BIG NANA!" screamed Imogen.

Big Nana stood there on the lawn like a sweaty, out-of-breath mirage, a familiar crooked smile spreading across her face. She grabbed Imogen and hugged her tightly. "Oh, Imogen," she said, in her deep, gravelly voice. "I'm so proud of you!"

Imogen decided not to catch her train that afternoon. For once, something seemed more important than getting back to Lilyworth and getting her own back on Bridget Sweetwine: Her grandmother had come back from the dead. Except that it turned out Big Nana hadn't actually died during the submarine heist. She'd simply stripped her clothes off and dumped them into the sea, so that people would find them and assumed she'd drowned. Then she'd swam away, never to be seen again.

Until now, that is.

The other Crims were shocked—they had been

stunned into silence for the first time in their very noisy lives for at least half an hour—but they had all been delighted to see Big Nana again, fussing around her, making her tea, offering her some stolen cakes from the bakery. And although on one hand Imogen was delighted that Big Nana was alive—of course she was—she was *so angry* with her that she wasn't sure she could bear to speak to her ever again.

Imogen sat on the sofa as the other Crims clamored to hear Big Nana's stories, silent and shaking with cold white rage. For the last two years, she had believed Big Nana was dead. Her heart had ached every time she thought about her. Remembering Big Nana and the way her life had been hurt *so much* that she'd abandoned her family and her plans for the future and enrolled at boarding school. And now it turned out that Big Nana had been alive all this time, and the last two years had been a lie. She was beginning to feel like her whole life had been a lie.

"I'm surprised you all believed I'd drowned, really," Big Nana said, cradling her fifth cup of tea. "You all know I'm a strong swimmer. I got a distinction in my Advanced Elderly Swimming badge."

"Actually, we assumed you'd been eaten by a shark with a clothes allergy," said Josephine.

"Well, I wasn't."

"SO WHERE DID YOU GO?" shouted Uncle

Knuckles. "IF YOU DON'T MIND ME ASKING."

"A little island off the coast of Scotland," said Big Nana. "Beautiful place, and the people were lovely, but you know what I always say: 'If you're going to burgle your neighbors regularly, make sure there are more than four of them.' I had to move on before they got suspicious. And that's when I came up with the character of Mrs. Teakettle. I miss being her, actually. She was a lovely woman."

"But, Big Nana," asked Henry, "why did you fake your death? Were you sick of us or something? Or did you just think it would be cool?"

"No, my little persimmon tree," said Big Nana, reaching out to rub his head. "I could never get sick of you. I'd never have left you if I hadn't believed it would be in your best interests." She sighed. "You may remember that when I was alive—officially alive, that is—we Crims were actually quite good at committing crimes. And that made a lot of people unhappy. Don't you remember all those threats we used to get? That anonymous letter threatening to dip us all in molten metal and turn us into garden ornaments unless we stopped stealing herbaceous borders?"

"And that other one saying that if we didn't stop committing bank robberies, we'd all be kidnapped and forced to work in a bank," said Al.

"That was the worst threat," said Josephine, shuddering. "Have you *seen* the outfits bank tellers wear?"

"I didn't think it sounded that bad," Al said wistfully.

"Right," Big Nana said grimly. "I think we can all remember the worst threat. None of us would be here now if they had carried out the *worst* threat."

Imogen had never heard about these threats before. She supposed the adults must have kept them to themselves so as not to scare the children. That felt like yet another betrayal. She had believed that she was closer to Big Nana than anyone else, but Big Nana had kept so many secrets from her.

"Who threatened us? Who's 'they'?" Imogen demanded, her voice cold.

"Never mind," Big Nana said quickly.

"It was the Kruks, wasn't it?" said Imogen.

"Perhaps it was, perhaps it wasn't," said Big Nana. "The point is, I knew that they'd never leave us alone while I was alive. So I died."

"*Pretended* to die," said Delia.

"And the threats went away," said Sam, nodding.

"Exactly," said Big Nana. "My plan worked, as my plans always do, unless they involve soufflés—soufflés always let me down. But now things are getting really dangerous for you again."

"Dangerous? How?" asked Uncle Clyde.

Big Nana shook her head. "I can't really tell you any

more than that at the moment—you're just going to have to trust me."

"Why should we do that?" muttered Imogen.

But Big Nana either didn't hear or didn't want to hear. "Over the next few months, you're going to be facing very serious threats from some seriously threatening people. You'll need to be in tip-top criminal shape to survive. So I've come back to help you."

Imogen couldn't keep quiet any longer. "You *didn't* come back, though, did you?" she said, standing up. "You disguised yourself as a babysitter and spied on us!"

"I didn't *spy* on you," Big Nana said gently. "Though I do think you look lovely in those tartan pajamas."

"You'd never have come clean at all if I hadn't figured out who you really were," Imogen said, her fists clenched.

"Hey, I figured it out too," Delia said sulkily.

"I would have told you who I was eventually," said Big Nana, touching Imogen's arm. "You know I would."

Imogen jerked her arm away.

"I just wanted the time to be right, Imogen," continued Big Nana. "But of course, I should have known you'd figure it out—I trained you well. You're just as brilliant as I knew you would be when you were a little girl. You're so much cleverer than the others—"

"Hey!" said Delia again.

Imogen found herself softening toward her grandmother—she still remembered how close they'd been!—but then, a moment later, she felt angrier than ever. "How could you *do* this to me?" she demanded. "Don't you get how hard your 'death' was for us? When I heard you were dead, my whole *world* fell apart. I felt so lonely." Her tears were flowing freely now. Big Nana reached out to comfort her, but Imogen pulled away. "And worst of all, I thought that if you, of all people, could die during a heist, then no one was safe. You made me believe what no Crim has ever believed before: You made me believe that *crime doesn't pay.*"

The other Crims gasped, horrified.

Imogen nodded. "I know. Unbelievable, isn't it? I've spent the last two years at boarding school, trying to forget everything that you ever taught me!"

"And I'm very, very sorry about that," Big Nana said seriously, looking Imogen in the eyes. "It was an unfortunate, unplanned side effect of my 'death.' I can't imagine how hard boarding school must have been for you. Team sports! Eating custard! Wearing a tie in a nonironic way!"

"There is nothing wrong with wearing a tie," snapped Imogen, looking away. "They're smart and comfortable and neat. . . ."

"She's been brainwashed," muttered Josephine, shaking her head.

"Imogen, my ripe kumquat," said Big Nana, taking

Imogen's hand. "I came back to put things right with you. I wanted you to find your inner Crim again."

Imogen allowed herself to look at Big Nana, and as she did, she felt a rush of love for her grandmother despite everything. She really did look very sorry.

"That's why I pulled off The Heist," Big Nana continued quietly. "So that everyone would be arrested and you'd get kicked out of school and come back to us, here, where you belong."

Imogen stopped breathing. She stared at Big Nana, incredulous.

But Big Nana didn't seem to be joking.

Imogen looked at the other Crims to check that they had just heard what she had just heard.

Big Nana had pulled off The Heist?

Everyone was staring at Big Nana blankly.

The ground beneath Imogen's feet felt unstable all of a sudden. She reached out to steady herself against the wall. "Are you saying . . . that . . . that *you* were the one who pulled off The Heist?" she said slowly.

"Of course," Big Nana said matter-of-factly.

"WHAT?" shouted Delia.

"WHAT?" shouted Sam.

"WHAT?" shouted Josephine.

"WHAT?" shouted Nick and Nate at the same time.

"PARDON?" shouted Uncle Knuckles.

"I said, *of course* it was me who pulled off The Heist," said Big Nana, taking a sip of tea. "I made a few deliberate mistakes so that Imogen would know the rest of you weren't guilty—I didn't want you all to end up in prison for the rest of your lives. And also, that plan was ridiculous, Clyde. Everyone knows pigeons and roller skates don't mix."

The room pretty much exploded after that. Al had to hold Uncle Clyde back from throttling Big Nana. Josephine had to hold back Aunt Bets from karate kicking Big Nana. Sam and Henry were taking advantage of the situation to steal everyone's wallets and phones. Freddie was taking bets from Delia, Nick, and Nate about who would end up in the hospital first. Isabella was crawling around on the floor trying to bite everyone's ankles. And Uncle Knuckles was weeping quietly in a corner, muttering about his nerves.

The louder and more upset everyone else got, the calmer Imogen felt. Maybe "numb" would be a better word; she felt as though she were floating above herself, watching what was going on from a great distance. She looked at her watch. She still had time to catch the train to Lilyworth. And now it seemed clear that she had no choice but to go back to her exemplary, law-abiding life at school and try to forget everything that had happened in the last few weeks. She would be elected head girl, then in a year she would graduate . . . then the world would be her oyster, and she would swallow it down in one glorious, slightly mucous-y gulp. She stood up and walked to the hall to collect her luggage.

"Good luck with everything," Imogen called icily as she opened the front door.

There was a momentary pause in the madness.

"Imogen! Don't go," said Big Nana, standing up and rushing to the hall.

"Sorry," said Imogen, forcing her voice to remain steady. "I'm glad you're alive, Big Nana. But I'll never forgive you for ruining my life, then getting me kicked out of school and very nearly ruining my life again."

She slammed the front door behind her.

She could hear Big Nana calling to her, but she didn't want to listen. She started to run down the hill toward the train station, which is a difficult thing to do when you're carrying three bags and a toy hippo. Big Nana and the other Crims chased after her.

What are you doing? a voice inside her said as she ran. *Why are you running away from Big Nana when all you've ever wanted was for her to be alive again?* But she wasn't sure she knew who Big Nana was anymore. She wasn't even sure she knew *herself* anymore. When she had lost Big Nana, she'd given up the only thing she'd ever been good at: crime. She had gone to school, and she'd become good at something else: playing the game. She'd begun to think she might be a good businesswoman, a good politician, a good *police officer*, even—but over the last few weeks, she had begun to rethink the decisions she'd made. She had succeeded in freeing her family. She had proved that she was still a gifted criminal. And she had realized that she still loved crime.

But Big Nana had been manipulating her all along. Had she *ever* had control of her own life? And what was she going to do now?

"Wait!" cried Big Nana.

"Why should I?" Imogen yelled as she ran against a red light, ignoring beeping horns and screeching cars.

"Because the family is in trouble!" shouted Big Nana. "The Kruks—"

Imogen stopped running. She turned and looked at Big Nana, eyes narrowed, hands clenched.

Big Nana and the other Crims stopped running too.

"The Kruks?" said Imogen, her voice full of venom. "The Kruks could have killed me because of you. They could have killed the Horrible Children, too. What kind of grandmother lets her grandchildren infiltrate the headquarters of the world's most dangerous crime family? Oh yeah—the kind of grandmother who *fakes her own death*."

"I'm sorry, Imogen," Big Nana said, her gravelly voice

cracking. "I'm so, so sorry. But don't you see? We need you."

"No," said Imogen, shaking her head. "*I'm* the one who's sorry. I'm sorry I ever believed a word you said."

She turned and sprinted toward the station without another backward glance. She got there just as the train was pulling into the station.

As she jumped onto the train, she heard Big Nana's voice behind her. Big Nana really was a surprisingly fast runner.

"Don't you remember what I always told you?" panted Big Nana as the train doors shut. "It's never too late to change your mind. Until your funeral. And even then . . ."

But the stationmaster blew the whistle, and the train gathered speed. Imogen stood at the train door, watching through the window as Big Nana faded into the distance, growing smaller and more insignificant by the second.

"Good riddance," whispered Imogen, choosing a forward-facing seat. She pulled a book from her bag—*The Seven Habits of Highly Effective Head Girls*—and started to read.

"AND THAT'S WHY you should elect me as your head girl." Imogen stood back from the podium and shielded her eyes against the bright lights of the great hall. She didn't like to brag, not even silently, in her head, but the speech had gone quite well. It was her final speech of the head girl campaign, and she'd ended on a high. At the side of the stage, Mrs. Pythagoras was saying something and giving her a thumbs-up, but she couldn't hear her over the whoops and cheers of the crowd. She walked back to her seat in the front row and took a seat next to her clique.

"You were amazing," Lucy said adoringly.

"We've missed you," Alice said needily.

"We have?" said Catherine. "Why, have you been off sick or something?"

"Never mind, Catherine," Imogen murmured, just as she had a thousand times before. In fact, *nothing* at Lilyworth had changed. Imogen had slipped back into her old life so easily that her time with her family seemed like a lifetime ago. She couldn't quite believe that just one week ago she'd been running through a theme park, chased by giant cartoon characters. Her friends would never believe her if she told them where she'd really been. Luckily, she didn't need to. Ms. Gruner hadn't wanted any of the parents to hear about Imogen's criminal connections, so she had told everyone that Imogen had gone home to care for her sick grandmother. Now that Imogen was back at Lilyworth, though, she felt strange about lying to everyone. More than ever, it seemed that she was living a double life.

Mrs. Pythagoras was back on the stage now, tapping the microphone. "Hello, girls!" she said. "Please welcome to the stage our second candidate for head girl. She's like a prime number—you can't help but love her! It's . . . Bridget Sweetwine!"

Everyone clapped as Bridget Sweetwine skipped onto the stage, her curls bouncing pleasantly. Imogen felt the old, familiar hatred rise up inside her. She was almost grateful for the feeling—it was a change from the numbness that had taken her over since she'd come back to school. As she watched Bridget curtsey to Mrs. Pythagoras and arrange her notes on the podium, she thought, *I could learn a thing or two from Bridget Sweetwine. She's been living a double life for years, but only I've guessed the truth about the evil beneath the sickly sweet surface.*

Bridget Sweetwine smiled out at the audience. "Thank you so much for clapping for me!" she trilled. "Isn't clapping just the loveliest thing? Almost as lovely as a daisy chain. Or a bunch of sunflowers. Or daffodils, dancing in the breeze. Or . . ."

Imogen took a deep breath and zoned out for a moment. She worried that if she listened to Sweetwine much longer, her eardrums might spontaneously explode. When she zoned back in again, Sweetwine was still talking.

"And the nicest thing of all is having Imogen back with us! Everyone give Imogen a round of applause!"

Imogen blinked.

Everyone was looking at her and clapping and smiling.

Imogen tried to smile too, but it just looked as though she was baring her teeth.

What was Sweetwine up to?

"I think it's clear from Imogen's brilliant speech tonight that she's by far the best candidate for head girl," Sweetwine continued. "And that's why I've decided to pull out of the race. So congratulations, Imogen! You're head girl of Lilyworth!"

Everyone got to their feet and cheered, hugging Imogen and congratulating her.

It was over.

She'd *won.*

But Imogen felt nothing at all.

This was typical Sweetwine. Stealing her thunder. Raining on her parade. Being passive-aggressive with all sorts of weather. Imogen watched in a daze as Bridget Sweetwine simpered her way through the crowd and left the great hall through the back door. And then she began to feel angry. Really, really, *really* angry. Her face grew red. Her hands begin to shake. *She's trying to deprive me of winning fair and square! She knows I would have won, so she's pulling out before she can be humiliated!*

She was not letting Bridget Sweetwine get away with this.

Imogen caught up with her nemesis in the corridor outside the dormitories.

"Sweetwine," she said, cornering her. "Just what are you up to?"

"Right now?" asked Sweetwine. "I'm just going back to my dorm to write in my diary. Why? Do you want to have a midnight feast tonight or something?"

"You know what I mean," said Imogen, leaning toward her. "Why did you pull out of the race? What's your endgame?"

"Endgame?" asked Bridget Sweetwine, her blue eyes as wide and round as two incredibly innocent dinner plates. "I don't know what you mean! I'm just so happy you're back!"

"Oh *really*?" asked Imogen, crossing her arms. "If you're so glad I'm back, why did you try to get me kicked out in the first place?"

Bridget Sweetwine looked at her blankly. "Kicked out? Of where?"

"Of school, obviously."

"What?" said Bridget Sweetwine, apparently genuinely shocked. "I would never do that!"

Imogen opened her mouth to argue with her, but she had a horrible, gnawing feeling that Sweetwine might be telling the truth.

A terrifying thought occurred to her.

What if Sweetwine really *was* just incredibly annoying and incredibly nice?

What if she'd never actually *been* Imogen's nemesis?

But then, who got me kicked out of school?

Imogen began to feel sick with rage. But she wasn't angry with Bridget Sweetwine this time. She turned and ran down the corridor to her dorm room.

She slammed the door behind her, heart thudding, and pulled her memory box down from the top shelf of her wardrobe, where it had been hidden since she'd first arrived at Lilyworth.

The memory box was an old shoebox with "Ashes of Millie the Dachshund, 2005–2016" written on it in ball-point pen to put off snoopers (a classic Imogen trick). She wiped the dust off the lid and opened the box. Her breath caught for a moment. The box smelled of Crim House.

Imogen shook herself. She did *not* miss her family. Her family was *awful and mad*. She took a deep breath and started sifting through the things she'd brought with her from home: an old tie of her father's, a lipstick her mother was always trying to get her to wear, the lyrics for a musical she and Delia had written for the Horrible Children to perform, called *Burglar on the Roof*. At the bottom of the box, she found what she was looking for—the "congratulations" card Big Nana had made for her when she'd stolen Freddie's bike, aged seven. The message inside, written in spidery green ink, read:

Dear Imogen,

Congratulations—committing a crime against a fellow criminal isn't easy, but you pulled it off. You remind me a lot of me when I was a little girl: innocent, fond of cats, and very handy with a crowbar. May this bike theft be the first of many.

With love from

Big Nana xxxx

Imogen rooted around in her chest of drawers for the letter that had gotten her thrown out of Lilyworth. She'd kept it in its envelope, hoping that one day she'd be able to prove that Bridget Sweetwine had written it.

But she'd never be able to prove that now.

Because as Imogen compared the handwriting on the envelope with the handwriting in the card she was holding, she began to shake.

The letter that got her kicked out of school had been written by Big Nana.

Imogen slammed the letter and card down on her desk and curled up on her bed. Hot, horrible tears began to soak into her pillow. She had never felt so trapped—not even in Jack Wooster's wardrobe or in the cell in the police station or onstage as Prince Charming, saying "I love you, Cinderella" to Bridget Sweetwine and kissing her on her horrible, smooth cheek. She *hadn't* ever had control of her own life. She'd thought she'd get away from Big Nana by coming back to Lilyworth; she had thought she was safe from her here. But Big Nana had been controlling Imogen like a tiny criminal puppet from the moment she was born.

And she was still controlling her now.

A few hours later, Imogen sat on her bed in her dorm room. Her suitcase was still lying open on the floor next to her, half unpacked. Big Nana's toy hippo stared at her from the top.

"Don't look at me like that," Imogen said to the hippo, walking over to pick it up. She scowled into its reproachful plastic eyes. "Big Nana's the one who should feel guilty. Not me."

Big Nana clearly did feel guilty. She had sent Imogen several emails since Imogen had gotten back to Lilyworth, but Imogen hadn't opened any of them.

Imogen had ignored Delia's emails too, and the fifty missed calls from her dad, and duck-faced selfies from her mum with the message **Come home, Sweetie**. But she *had* opened an email from Freddie that morning by mistake, thinking it was her subscription to *Ex-Cons Monthly*. (Freddie had set up a new email account to trick her.) In the email, Freddie had told her that the Crims were having a big belated sixty-fifth birthday party for Big Nana that weekend, and begged her to come home. *Everyone really misses you,* he'd written. *Isabella keeps naming her teddy bears "Imojim" and then sticking pins in them. It's really sweet.*

Imogen hadn't written back.

She put the hippo back in the suitcase where it couldn't stare at her, and she flipped the lid down on top of it. As she did so, something fell out onto the floor. It was the notebook with "Photographs of My Favorite Verrucae" written on the front—her old criminal plans journal.

Imogen sat back down on her bed and began to flip through the notebook. As she read through her old schemes, she smiled at how clever and creative her younger self had been. Sure, the plan to replace Freddie's cologne with bathroom cleaner so he'd smell like a toilet was a bit immature, but she still liked the idea of hacking into the police's walkie-talkies. What was clear from every page of the notebook was that Imogen had *loved* writing these plans—they were at least as ambitious as Uncle Clyde's Heist, but better thought through. There were little notes from Big Nana in the margins of some of her best ideas—"Brilliantly nasty!" "Wonderfully evil!" "You, my little tangerine, are a genius!" She felt a bittersweet pang as she realized that Big Nana really *did* think she was gifted.

Imogen read a few more pages and paused at a plan to steal the inflatable elephant that sat outside a car dealership near Blandington. It had been a natural progression from the octopus balloon, but she'd never finished this particular scheme for some reason. She studied her notes—the idea had been that she would dress up as a car, hide in the car dealership, wait until everyone had gone home for the night, and then cut the inflatable elephant free and float home on it, as if it were a hot-air balloon or Mary Poppins's umbrella. But in order to do that, she'd need a way of controlling the elephant's direction . . . and she'd never figured out a way. As she looked at the notes now, though, she had an idea. What if she managed to break into a car in the dealership, strip it of its controls, and build some kind of car-elephant hybrid? She sat down at her desk so that she could think properly. She opened one of her physics textbooks—she was sure that she could harness the helium from the inflatable elephant somehow, to power a small car engine. . . .

Two hours later, Imogen looked up. It was dark outside. She'd missed dinner.

But the plan was finished.

She smiled to herself.

She opened her laptop. Maybe she would email Freddie back, after all. As she waited for her emails to load, she scanned the latest news headlines on her homepage—and then she froze. Because a familiar face was staring up at her from her laptop.

Derek Hornbutton.

The headline above his head read: "President of Charm Ltd. Goes Missing."

Imogen remembered the letter they'd stolen from Charmtopia, where the Kruks threatened Hornbutton's poodles. She felt sick. Clearly the Kruks had decided to up the ante. Once they'd realized that Freddie wasn't really a Charm Ltd. lawyer, they'd also have realized that Charm Ltd. hadn't responded to their threats. . . .

Imogen remembered the smiling children in the photo on Derek Hornbutton's desk. Hornbutton had been awful to her and the Horrible Children, but in his defense, they *had* been trying to implicate his company in a complicated and ridiculous crime. And she was sure that, just like the most eccentric members of her own family, Derek Hornbutton had people who dearly loved him.

The Kruks couldn't be allowed to get away with this. Someone had to find Derek Hornbutton fast—before he was turned into tiger food, too, or forced into cutlery-polishing duty or forced to go swimming with unfriendly sharks. . . .

Heart pounding, Imogen opened the most recent message from Big Nana.

> I'm so sorry, Imogen. There's no excuse for what I did. But we need you.

Imogen swallowed. She couldn't quite believe what she was about to do, but then a lot of unbelievable things had happened to her over the last couple of weeks. She unpinned her head girl badge from her blazer and threw it, clanking, into the bin. Then she picked up her suitcase and put it on the bed.

She was going back to Blandington.

AS IMOGEN WALKED down the Blandington Community Center's corridor to the hall that Friday, squeaking past the balloons and ducking under the bunting, she thought back to all the happy times she'd had there as a child: the twins' joint first birthday party (they'd ended up in the hospital after they tried to eat each other); Josephine's fortieth birthday (she'd spent all night sobbing into her stolen handkerchiefs, wailing, "I'm so old!"); and her own tenth birthday, just after Big Nana had died. Everyone had been too shocked to buy her a present, except Henry, who had bought her a T-shirt and then ruined it by writing "Henry Crim Woz Ere" all over it in permanent marker.

Okay, maybe "happy times" was a bit strong.

Imogen took a deep breath and pushed the hall doors open just as everyone started singing "Happy Birthday." The room was packed—she hadn't realized Big Nana had so many friends. And they weren't all petty criminals, either—the curator of the Blandington Art Gallery was there, for some reason, and so, incredibly, was the entire Blandington Police Department. Maybe they were just there for the free cake. Now that the Crims were free, Imogen didn't bring doughnuts to the police station anymore.

And there, in the middle of the room, was Big Nana. Imogen felt her stomach twist as she saw her grandmother again for the first time since the scene at the train station. Despite Big Nana's many, many, *many* flaws, Imogen still loved her, and she had decided to forgive her. After all, nobody was perfect. Big Nana was just slightly less perfect than everyone else.

Imogen hovered by the doors and watched as Big Nana blew out the sixty-five candles on her very large cake. She fluffed up her bright red hair and got to her feet to make a speech.

"Thank you all so much for coming," she said, smiling around at everyone. "It's so good to see all my friends and family and former enemies here together. And it's so good to be alive again—officially! Like I always say, 'It's better to be alive than dead, unless you're a chicken. They don't have very happy lives, so you might as well eat them.'"

Everyone cheered again, and Big Nana bowed—she loved to bow, even when she was in the stand on trial for eating public property or impersonating a spaceship. As she stood up straight again, she noticed Imogen standing at the back of the room. She gave a little cry and ran headlong through the crowd toward Imogen. It was quite scary, actually; like standing in the path of a small, red-haired train.

Before Imogen could say anything (or get out of the way), Big Nana launched herself at her, giving her a very painful hug.

"Happy birthday, Big Nana," Imogen said—or rather tried to say, because her head was wedged in Big Nana's armpit.

"You came!" said Big Nana.

"I did," said Imogen. "And I brought you something." She held out a brown-papered parcel.

Big Nana snatched the present from Imogen's hands and unwrapped it. "My hippo!" she cried, hugging the stuffed animal and then hugging Imogen again. "I wanted it so badly that day, when I was pretending to be Mrs. Teakettle and I saw it in the hallway. Do you remember?"

"Of course I remember," said Imogen, smiling.

"Where did you find it?"

"The Kruks' Loot Room," Imogen said casually.

Big Nana shook her head. "I don't understand how I missed it," she whispered. "I looked all over their Loot Room to find the perfect hiding place for the lunch box—just hidden enough for it to be a challenge, but not so hidden that you'd get murdered by the Kruks before you found it. . . ."

"Is that why you babysat for the Kruk children?" Imogen whispered back. "So you could hide the lunch box in the Kruks' Loot Room?"

"Of course." Big Nana shrugged, as if she did that sort of thing all the time, which she probably did. "I had to make sure you'd think the Kruks had committed The Heist." She went back to gazing at her hippo adoringly.

Now that Imogen thought about it, it was sort of flattering, the insane lengths Big Nana had gone to make Imogen a true Crim again. *Sort* of flattering—and sort of completely mad.

"Were you lonely in that horrible Loot Room, my darling?" Big Nana cooed, stroking her hippo, just as Uncle Clyde had stroked his lunch box. The family resemblance between them had never been stronger.

"How did your hippo get into the Loot Room in the first place?" Imogen asked.

"How does *anything* get into the Kruks' Loot Room?" Big Nana shrugged. "The Kruks are all-seeing and all-powerful! You know the Bermuda Triangle?"

Imogen nodded.

"It's not real! The Kruks have just been stealing aircraft and ships from that patch of sea for years! And you know how socks always go missing down in the washing machine?"

Imogen nodded again.

"They don't, really! It's the Kruks. They have a huge secondhand mismatched sock empire in Norway. If you ever go to Oslo, you might spot someone wearing half of your favorite pair."

"But . . . How do they . . . ," started Imogen.

"Best not to ask," said Big Nana, tapping her nose. "The Kruks move in mysterious ways, just like antelope do."

"Are you sure you want them to know you're alive?" Imogen asked. "You know . . . Throwing a big party like this, word is sure to get back to them."

Big Nana nodded, her expression becoming more troubled. "Oh, Imogen," she said. "With the way things are changing, I want them to know I'm here, still protecting you all."

Imogen shivered. *That sounds ominous.* Which reminded her . . . "Did you hear about Derek Hornbutton's disappearance?" she asked, twitching slightly as she thought about it. "The Kruks must be behind that too."

"Of course they are," said Big Nana. "When a truly impressive crime is committed, it's usually them."

"But they really had nothing to do with the lunch box?"

"Goodness, no," said Big Nana, shaking her head. "The Kruks didn't even know they had the lunch box in their Loot Room. It's such a mess up there, isn't it? John Travolta really needs to do a better job of tidying that place up. Anyway . . . there are big changes going on at Krukingham Palace, and none of them are good. Gustav Kruk has retired as head Kruk, and his daughter Elsa is replacing him."

"We saw her at the party," said Imogen, remembering the woman who had introduced the Kruk children's performance. "She seemed quite sweet. She loved that song you made up—"

Big Nana shook her head, disappointed. "Imogen. What have I always taught you?" she asked.

"'Never trust first impressions,'" chanted Imogen. "'Unless they're first impressions of an alligator, because you probably won't have time to make second impressions.'"

"Exactly," said Big Nana, nodding. "Elsa is the worst of all the Kruks. She's crazy. She's violent. She kills someone for fun, once a day, just to wake up."

Imogen felt her pulse quicken with fear—and a little

excitement, too. "So is that why we're in danger? Because of Elsa?"

"Exactly so, my dear," said Big Nana.

"But why would the Kruks want to hurt us? It's not like we're competition. If they didn't pull off The Heist, maybe they don't know we exist after all."

Big Nana sighed. "It's a little more complicated than that, my tiny, dried apricot," she said, smiling sadly at Imogen.

But before she could say any more, Delia turned and spotted Imogen. "You're back!" she shrieked, running over and hurtling herself at her. "I mean . . . I hope you're back as a *real* Crim and not that Goody Two-Shoes Imogen who drove me crazy," she said, but then she winked.

"Imojim!" gurgled Isabella, crawling up to Imogen and biting her ankles.

"Darling! You came!" cried Josephine, fluttering over to her daughter. "You're looking terribly pale. All that studying and playing by the rules is awfully bad for your health."

"What made you come home?" said Freddie, clapping Imogen on the back. "I thought you wanted to be head girl of Lilyworth?"

"Well remembered," said Imogen, grinning at him. "I suppose I realized that no matter how annoying you all are, and how many crazy capers you drag me into, you're still my family. So I'm leaving Lilyworth—for good."

"That's my girl," said her father, nodding proudly. "And we won't let you get behind on your schoolwork. If you want to keep up your mental arithmetic, you can help me out with my bookkeeping."

"Thank you, Dad," said Imogen.

"Well, this is lovely," said Big Nana, beaming at everyone, with her hands on her hips. "All my chicks back together again! All our eggs in the same rickety basket!"

"Hear! Hear!" said Uncle Clyde, pulling a crumpled piece of paper out of his pocket. "And to celebrate us all being back together again, I've revised The Heist to make sure that it completely goes to plan when we pull it off for real! I was thinking we could give it a go next Monday, after lunch. Now that you're back, Imogen, you can go into Wooster's bedroom and distract him—we won't need to disguise a greased pig in your clothes anymore. Which is just as well, because I've used up my grease."

"Actually, Clyde, we don't need to pull off The Heist anymore," said Big Nana.

"What do you mean?" said Uncle Clyde.

Big Nana gave him a mysterious smile. "Come into the kitchen. I've got something for you. I don't want the other guests to see. . . ."

"But it's not my birthday," said Uncle Clyde.

"Shh," said Big Nana, hustling Uncle Clyde into the kitchen.

The other Crims crowded around the kitchen door as Big Nana reached under the sink and pulled out a plastic bag.

"Here you go," she said, holding it out to him.

He gasped, excited. "It's tea bags, isn't it? You noticed I've run out?"

"I'm afraid not, dear," said Big Nana.

"It's toilet paper, isn't it?" said Uncle Clyde, still excited, as he felt the bag.

"Just open it!" boomed Sam in a surprisingly deep voice. He clapped his hand over his mouth. "I don't believe it! My voice has finally broken!"

But no one was paying attention to Sam. Everyone was staring at Uncle Clyde, who had reached into the plastic bag and pulled out . . .

"MY LUNCH BOX!" cried Uncle Clyde.

Imogen gasped. She couldn't believe what she was seeing. How had Big Nana gotten hold of the lunch box?

"Thank you, Mummy!" said Uncle Clyde, beaming.

"I told you never to call me that again," Big Nana said sternly.

"But . . . how did you . . . ?" said Uncle Clyde. "Imogen and Freddie took the lunch box back to Wooster Mansion!"

Exactly, thought Imogen. Had Big Nana broken in and stolen it again? In which case why hadn't the theft been reported?

"Actually, my boy, they returned a *replica* to Wooster Mansion. This is the real deal!"

Uncle Clyde hugged his lunch box to him and looked around at his family with tears in his eyes. Imogen felt a lump in her throat. Big Nana was really quite thoughtful when she wanted to be. And it was wonderful to see Uncle Clyde reunited with his lunch box after all this time. His ridiculous dream had finally come true.

"Thank you all," said Uncle Clyde. "Each and every one of you. Even you, Knuckles, you big, soppy idiot."

"OI! STOP IT! YOU'LL MAKE ME CRY!" shouted Uncle Knuckles, who was already crying.

"I hope you and your lunch box are happy together for many years to come," said Big Nana. "Just think—now you can take sandwiches with you wherever you go instead of buying junk food."

"I'll save so much money." Uncle Clyde wept happily.

"Although, make sure you always cover it with a paper bag or something," said Imogen.

"Just don't let it make you go soft. Okay?" said Big Nana. "I'm going to need you all on top form over the next few months. You're going to need to be tough, like overcooked meat. Big things are about to happen. Big, scary, dangerous, incredibly criminal things."

The Crims looked at one another, scared but excited.

"But what do I always say?" said Big Nana.

"'No one can defeat us Crims when we work together!'" everyone chanted.

"Except for that kung-fu fighting robot, that one time," Uncle Clyde added. "But I think we can agree that thing was possessed."

"That's right!" said Big Nana, and everyone cheered.

Imogen cheered louder than anyone. Because that kung-fu fighting robot *was* possessed. But more importantly, because even though most things Big Nana did were very, very wrong . . . somehow, she was always right.

ACKNOWLEDGMENTS

THANK YOU TO my amazing writing circle: Sarah Courtauld and Zanna Davidson; to the wonderful members of Write Club: Linas Alsenas, Jack Noel, Annalie Grainger, Amelia Vahtrick, and Molly Maine; and to my wife, Victoria.

Most of all, thanks to the brilliant editors at Working Partners and HarperCollins, particularly Stephanie Lane Elliott, Conrad Mason, Samantha Noonan, Lynn Weingarten, Jocelyn Davies, and Erica Sussman.

Lastly, thank you to puns and the letter *e*, without which this book would never have existed.